About the Author

Award-winning author Heather Peck has enjoyed a varied life. She has been both farmer and agricultural policy adviser, volunteer covid vaccinator and NHS Trust Chair. She bred sheep and alpacas, reared calves, broke ploughs, represented the UK in international negotiations, specialised in emergency response from Chernobyl to bird flu, managed controls over pesticides and GM crops, saw legislation through Parliament and got paid to eat Kit Kats while on secondment to Nestle Rowntree.

She lives in Norfolk with her partner Gary, two dogs, two cats, two hens and a female rabbit named Hero.

Also by Heather Peck

THE DCI GELDARD NORFOLK MYSTERIES
Secret Places
Glass Arrows *
Fires of Hate **
The Temenos Remains **
Dig Two Graves **
Beyond Closed Doors
Death on the Rhine (novella)
Death on the Norwich Express (novella)
Milestones (thriller)***
BOOKS FOR CHILDREN
Tails of Two Spaniels **
The Pixie and the Bear
The Animals of White Cows Farm
*shortlisted for the East Anglian Book Award prize for fiction 2021
**Firebird Book Award Winner
***Page Turner Book Awards 2024 best crime novel

Buried in the Past

DCI GREG GELDARD BOOK 7

Heather Peck

Ormesby Publishing

Published in 2025 by Ormesby Publishing

Ormesby St Margaret

Norfolk

www.ormesbypublishing.co.uk

Text copyright © Heather Peck 2025

Author photograph by John Thompson 2021

This is a work of fiction. Names, characters, places and incidents either are products of the author's imagination. Or are used fictitiously. Any resemblance to actual events or persons, living or dead, is entirely coincidental.

British Library Cataloguing in Publication Data

A CIP catalogue record for this book is available from the British Library.

Page design and typesetting by Ormesby Publishing

Dedication

Most of this book is set in 2020.
At that time the UK, like the rest of the world, was
dealing with the Covid-19 pandemic.
This had a profound impact on how everyone lived: the
old and the young, the good and the bad.
I have tried to reflect those difficult times in this book,
which is dedicated to the memory of all who lost their
lives and all who worked so hard to make things better.

Acknowledgments

My thanks to Gary for everything

and many thanks yet again to my beta readers Geoff Dodgson,
Alison Tayler and Gary Westlake for their constructive
criticism and comments.
This book is all the better for your help.

Thanks also to Sharon Gray at CluedUpEditing for her
meticulous and knowledgeable proof editing.
And to Lizaa for the cover design.

Contents

Key Characters

Norfolk police
Chief Superintendent Margaret Tayler
Main investigative team:
DCI Greg Geldard
DI Jim Henning
DS Jill Hayes
DCs Bill Street, Jenny Warren and Steve Hall
Ned George – crime scene manager
Yvonne Berry – deputy crime scene investigator
Al Thorpe – recruit to forensic science
PD Turbo – springer spaniel
Police in Great Yarmouth:
Sergeant Briscoe
Constable Drake

Suffolk police
CI Pritty
DI Chris Mathews
DI Richards

Legal services
Frank Parker – Crown Prosecution Service
Joseph Streeter and Kenneth Wood – solicitors
Terence Batley-Shaw – magistrate

Medical experts
Dr Paisley – police pathologist

Norfolk Children's Services
Lily North – case coordinator
Helga Ratcliffe – foster mum

Baddies
Joanne Hamilton / Chalmers
Nick Waters
Ade Waters (Nick's brother)
Jacko Green
Mick O'Hanlon

Other participants
Commander Fisher – Norfolk Fire Service silver command
Mr Geldard senior – Greg's father
Bobby – Greg's cat
Tally – Chris's foul-mouthed parrot
Karen and Jake Mirren – children
Tim Simmons – friend of Karen and Jake's mother
Diana Grain – teacher friend of DS Jill Hayes.
Hamish Grey – Leyton Farm's estate manager
Jeff and Jane Wyatt – proprietors of Welsh Farm
Bob Chalmers – ex-partner of Joanne Hamilton

Glossary

ANPR automatic number plate recognition
ATV all-terrain vehicle
CCTV closed circuit television
Chaser bin grain cart with built-in auger, used to collect grain from a combine and transfer it to bulk transport
GPR ground-penetrating radar
ITU intensive therapy unit
'leccy bill' slang for electricity bill
Nightingale courts temporary courts set up in response to the Covid-19 pandemic
TWOC taking without consent (also 'twocking')

1

June 2020: a field near Downham Market, Norfolk

It was that point in the evening which the poetic might call crepuscular. To the four men, unloading dogs and other equipment from two battered pickups, it was the perfect moment between dark and light. Dark enough to obscure their presence, light enough to set up the course. One of the pickups, the black Ford Ranger, drove off across the wide, gently rolling field, the driver careless of the extraordinary damage the tyres were doing to what had been intended for a future as garden turf. Over by the hedge, the dark grey Toyota had been joined by two more 4×4s and more men got out. Cans of beer were passed around, and voices raised as the men relaxed. Two brindle greyhounds and a large grey lurcher were released from crates in the back of the Toyota and inspected. Bets were placed.

The three dogs were pulling on their leashes, eager to get going on their evening's 'sport', when the scene was suddenly floodlit by a large spotlight mounted on a tractor approaching at speed along the lane by the field's edge. Some of the men got back into their cars in a hurry and prepared for a rapid departure. The two by the Toyota pulled what could only be described as cudgels from the back of their vehicle and approached the tractor, swinging the thick, wooden clubs gently to and fro. The three dogs, kept in the background by a thickset man in a torn camouflage jacket, were still pulling on the leads and the lurcher uttered a sharp bark.

The two men with the cudgels stood boldly in the bright spotlight, side by side. Both wore dark jackets and trousers and had pulled balaclavas over their faces. The man, or men, in the tractor were invisible behind their bright light. A voice spoke from behind the light.

'I'm filming this, and I've called the police. Get your dogs and get off my land. And don't come back.'

One of the men outlined by the brilliant light suddenly swung his cudgel harder, then round in a loop and let go. It flew through the air, hit the tractor-mounted light with a crash, and plunged the scene into a relative darkness, now lit only by headlights. The small crowd observing in the background cheered and laughed, emboldened by alcohol and anonymity. In the new dim light, the two men walked forward. Across the wide field, the black Ford pickup turned and began to move toward them, lights out but engine roaring menacingly.

'That's two mistakes you've made,' shouted the older of the two men in balaclavas. 'One,' – and he held up a finger –

'coming here at all; and two,' – he held up a second – 'ringing the police, if you have.' He swung his club again, passing it from hand to hand. 'Now, I suggest you back up this lane and fuck off, unless you want both your legs broken and your barn burned.'

A silence fell, broken only by the approach of the Ford. When it drew up alongside in a spatter of mud and grass, the tractor was still sitting silent and dark in the lane. With the spotlight out, it was now possible to see the shapes of two figures in the cab.

'I don't see any blue lights!' shouted the man with the cudgel. 'Time to bugger off.'

Two more men got out of the second pickup and ranged themselves alongside the first two. There was a muttered conversation, then the four of them spread out and moved forward, as though to enfold the tractor in a bracket of menace. As they got closer, the tractor jerked into motion and reversed slowly down the lane.

The men continued to walk forward and were about to scramble through the thin hedge when a shout from the group behind them drew their attention. Now they could all see the flicker of blue lights reflecting on the cloudy sky. With loud curses, three of them turned and piled into the Ford's cab. The fourth, the man with the cudgel, ignored the shouts to him to follow and hurry up about it. He had a last word for the farmer in the tractor.

'Your legs and your bloody barn, don't forget,' he shouted.
'I won't.'

The Ford's wheels spun on the battered turf then, with a flourish of soil, the tread gripped and it bucketed away over the field. The last man ran for the break in the hedge where the Toyota sat waiting. The figure in camouflage gear was still holding three dogs, now baying like the hound of the Baskervilles.

'Shove 'em in the crates, quick,' said the burly man as he headed for his truck, keys in hand. 'Come on. Hurry it up.'

The dog man rushed his task, then ran for the passenger door, but too late. With the tractor blocking one end of the lane and the police approaching from the other, the burly man made a snap decision and drove the Toyota across the field as fast as the terrain would allow, to make an escape over the hedge at the far side. As it jolted over the ruts made earlier by the Ford, the incompletely fastened crate door in the back flew open and the lurcher jumped out. The dog handler, abandoned by his mates, stood irresolute for a crucial moment, and realised that the opportunity to leg it across the field had passed. When the police cars pulled up in the lane, they were joined by one tractor and one friendly grey lurcher. Blinded by their own lights, they didn't see the remaining man slide slowly, with all the guile of the practised poacher, into the nettle-bounded ditch.

2

July 2020: Norfolk Police HQ, Wymondham

There were three faces round the table in the Chief Superintendent's office. All were equally gloomy. DCI Greg Geldard, head of Norfolk Serious Crimes, opened his mouth to say something, then closed it again and heaved a huge sigh. He flipped over the list of cases-pending on the table in front of him. At the far end of the conference table, his boss Chief Superintendent Margaret Tayler waited with bated breath. She didn't bate it for long.

'You were going to say something, Greg...' she prompted.

Greg took a breath to sigh again, caught Margaret's eye just in time and converted the sigh into words.

'I think we've said it all before,' he said. 'The situation was bad before Covid. It's now a hundred times worse, and opening a few courts, with serious limitations on what they can do, isn't going to make it much better.'

'At least Norwich Crown Court reopens this month,' said Frank Parker from the other end of the long table, trying to look on the bright side.

'Using two courts for each case, if what I hear is correct,' replied Greg. 'That's not going to make much difference to our backlog. Is there no chance we might get one of these new Nightingale courts in the east?'

'Not as far as I've heard.' Frank sighed too. 'And even if we did, it wouldn't help these cases.' He tapped the files in front of him. 'The advice is that they can't be used for cases where the defendants are in gaol or likely to be sent there, because of the lack of secure cells. So that excludes all these.'

'Not our problem.' Margaret summed up her point of view briskly. 'I appreciate that you in the Crown Prosecution Service are having a bad time, Frank, but from the police point of view, we've done our bit. In every one of these cases, we've got the evidence to convict, and we've taken dangerous felons off the street. I agree, these delays in delivering justice are unfortunate but there's no point stressing over what we can't help. We didn't create the pandemic, and it wasn't our fault there were already a lot of delays in the system before Covid made things worse.'

'To be fair,' interrupted Frank defensively, 'there have been a lot of cases, particularly at magistrates' court level, where things didn't go as smoothly as we'd all like because of mix-ups over paperwork or prisoners.' He was careful not to catch Margaret's eye and hunched his, already round, shoulders as though anticipating an aggressive response.

Margaret glared. 'Be that as it may,' she said, 'that's not the case here. And you can take my word for it, Greg will make sure that all his ducks are in a row when the Red Pentney murder cases do eventually make it into court.'

Greg noted that she made that sound more like a threat than a prediction. Investigating the murder and attempted murder committed by 'Red' Pentney had not been straightforward; not least because of his involvement with a civilian member of Norfolk police staff. He was now languishing in gaol, but Greg could understand Margaret's worry about the potential embarrassment of procedural cock-ups!

'In the meantime, we hear what you say, but we have a lot of work on, and if there's nothing we can help you with immediately...'

Frank took his dismissal with good grace and not a small helping of relief.

Once they had the room to themselves, Margaret turned to Greg. 'As you're here and we don't meet face to face very often these days, bring me up to date on your current workload,' she requested.

Greg had been anticipating the request. At his location, halfway down the long side of the conference table, he had the advantage of acres of shiny wooden space. He used it now to spread out the piles of files he'd brought with him.

'I've grouped them into four categories,' he responded. 'We've touched on the first already: the cases where we've prepared the evidence for court and are just waiting for a slot. These include the two Pentney murders, the associated charges for the unauthorised disclosure of information and aiding and abetting blackmail, and the drug and blackmail cases against Helen Gabrys. The two women are out on bail, Pentney himself is safely tucked away in the Bure prison.

'The second pile is the priority cases, top of these being the hunt for the missing Mirren children. As you know, they both disappeared the day their father set fire to the family home in an attempt to hide the death of their mother. Were the father still with us he would be facing a charge of manslaughter at best, and murder at worst, as well as arson and aggravated assault. As it is, I'm very worried about those two children. They fled the family home in the early hours of 27th March, got on a bus to Greater Ormesby, and haven't been seen since.'

'And they're how old?'

'Eight and six. The girl, Karen, is the elder. Her brother is named Jake. We've searched the surrounding area with and without dogs, done as much of a house-to-house as we can in a village where half the inhabitants seem to be shielding and refuse even to open the doors let alone let us in, and we've been in touch with relatives and friends. Nothing. I plan to—'

Margaret interrupted again. 'Take me through the rest of your workload first, Greg, and we'll come back to that.'

'OK. Well, some areas have gone quiet, thanks to lockdown, and others are worse. In short, the local county lines operations are, temporarily I fear, quiet for lack of customers. On the other hand, we have two serious case reviews in hand. One where children have died in suspicious circumstances, and the other where the mother has been hospitalised several times and is alleging risk to her child. I said back in March that the lockdown would drive violence indoors and, unfortunately, I've been proved right,' he added. 'On top of those, we have one case of fraud related to bitcoin which is making my brain leak out through my ears, and I heard this morning of a farmer complaining about vandalism on his property.

'And, if you don't mind me mentioning it, with Chris's departure and Jill's promotion, I am still a man down.'

'Which is why I'm going to give you some advice you won't like,' replied Margaret. Instead of running her fingers through her hair - her trademark move - she seized the lower edge of her jacket and pulled it firmly down. Greg decided that if this was a new tic, he preferred the older version. This one looked threatening. Like a knight of old adjusting his chain mail.

'You need to put the search for the children on the back burner,' she said. 'Prioritise the new enquiries where you can make a difference and move on.'

'It's only been a few weeks,' Greg protested. 'I can't give up on two vulnerable children!'

'It's been three months since there was any sign of them,' corrected Margaret. 'The sea is less than a mile from where they were last seen. And there are three large Broads close by. I'm not saying give up altogether, but unless you get some new evidence that they're still alive, I'm saying prioritise the other cases. You can't do everything.'

3

That evening: by the Bure.

It was Greg's turn to cook. Grating cheese for a sauce, Greg still couldn't drag his thoughts from the lost children. Going over their current workload with his DI, Jim Henning, and newly promoted DS Jill Hayes, he'd had to acknowledge that Margaret had a point.

They made a disparate trio. Greg, university entrant to the police and ex-rugby player, had the stature and build that went with his old sport, brown hair cut tidily rather than stylishly (and then only when his partner, Chris, nagged him about it), and still tended to dress more for the city than the field. Especially when it came to his shoes. Jim was both a Norfolk man and a policeman, born and bred. He'd made his way up through the ranks with native wit and shrewd common sense. His thinning hair had been cut by his wife, and he was comfortable in tweedy jacket and nondescript trousers that bagged at the knees. Jill, by contrast, was young, sharp – especially with anything involving IT – and quietly stylish in dark jeans and white shirt, but with an air that said fashion was the least of her concerns.

By the time Jill had briefed him on their involvement with the two children's serious case reviews and Jim had brought him up to date on the fraud case, Greg had to acknowledge that they were seriously overpressed.

'And we haven't yet got back to the farmer alleging criminal damage,' added Jim. 'It's been two weeks since he made his complaint, and we haven't even been able to schedule a meeting with him.'

'Remind me why that's one for us anyway,' said Greg.

'Value of damage done and associated threats,' said Jim succinctly. 'It may be a bit borderline, but it has the potential to turn nasty. We don't want another Tony Martin on our hands,' he added, referring to the farmer who shot a burglar.

'Anything new at all on the missing children?' Greg asked with fading hope.

'Zero,' replied Jill. 'Our current enquiries have completely run into the ground. No one has seen or heard sight or sound of them for weeks. They've disappeared into thin air. I'm sorry, Boss, but I think I'm with the Chief Super on this. Let's put our efforts where we can make a difference. These serious case reviews are really nasty. Those kids are at risk, and we have a chance to make things safer if we do the right thing. And I say that as someone who's going to be in deep shit at home if we give up on Karen and Jake. You remember my partner taught Karen, and she asks me every day how we're getting on.'

'I haven't given up on those two kids yet.' Greg said it firmly, albeit without much idea what he could do about it. 'But I hear what you're all saying. Jill, let me have a spreadsheet setting out the key dates and commitments relating to the serious case reviews.

'Jim, if you're OK with it, I'm going to see if we can get some help from our old friend DCI Ram Trent on the bitcoin case. He used to work in the fraud squad, so he should be well equipped to help, and I think Margaret owes us one. That frees you and me to go and see our farmer friend.'

'And the Mirren kids?' asked Jill.

'Margaret's challenge was to find some evidence they're still alive. I'm going to give that some thought, then we'll have another chat.'

By the time his fiancée, DI Chris Mathews, got home, a baked macaroni cheese was waiting in the oven and salad stood ready on the kitchen table.

'Lager or wine?' asked Greg as she came in through the door.

'A glass of white would be great,' said Chris, throwing her acid yellow bag onto the sofa and ruffling Tally's feathers as she perched on her shoulder. 'Oops sorry, jealous cat,' she said to Bobby twining round her ankles. 'Here, give a girl a chance to sit down.'

'Supper smells good,' she said to Greg. 'What have I done to deserve the special treatment?'

'Nothing yet,' said Greg, then hurriedly amended the statement with, 'apart from the normal, obviously. But I admit, I am hoping to pick your brains over supper.'

'More shop talk!' said Chris in mock horror. 'OK. Just let me have a bit of a freshen up, then we can eat and brainstorm to your heart's content.'

Not for the first time, Greg reflected on the sheer joy of sharing both interests and careers with his other half. He'd had the opposite experience, with his first wife, of trying to divide himself in two in order to satisfy competing interests. Now, with Chris, he could be confident she was as interested as him in the cases he had underway. It wasn't so long ago that they would have been her cases. He knew she welcomed his input on her investigations too, and the mutual sharing was great for them both.

Through mouthfuls of what he couldn't help but feel was a rather good macaroni cheese, rich in flavour and just on the right side of runny, he laid out his problem.

'So, unless we can find evidence that the kids are still alive, I'm pretty much forced to push their case into the background. And nothing we've done so far has coughed up anything new.'

'I take it the house-to-house and so on have all run into difficulties with our new normal,' said Chris.

'Quite. It's obvious we need to find a new source of evidence. I thought, if you're up for it, we might start by brainstorming where the children could have ended up.'

'OK, you go first,' said Chris.

Greg leaned back, and Bobby jumped on his lap, turning round and round before settling down. 'Starting with the worst option,' he said. 'They could be dead, with possibilities ranging from drowned in the sea, drowned in one of the local Broads or buried somewhere.'

'Or, hidden in a deep freeze,' added Chris.

'Thank you for that.' Greg grimaced. 'If they washed out to sea, we may never find them. If they drowned in one of the Broads, I would have expected the bodies to float to the surface by now.'

'Unless weighted down or somehow trapped on the bottom,' said Chris.

'So essentially, we can't do anything about the sea other than be aware of anything that washes up on the beaches, and we can't do any more with the freshwater options unless we have some evidence that they did go that way. So let's discount those two possibilities for now. Which leaves us with ... they're dead, and the bodies deliberately concealed in some fashion, either in the ground or elsewhere. Or they're alive.' Greg refilled Chris's glass, then his.

'Just to wind up the "dead" options,' he went on, 'we've checked woodland and farmland in the vicinity of where they were last seen. No signs either of bodies, or of disturbed ground. No sign of any of their possessions.'

'If we go with the "still alive" option, where could they be?' asked Chris.

Greg picked up his glass of wine and moved over to the sofa by the French windows. Chris joined him and sat down with her legs curled up beneath her.

'Let's start with the obvious possibilities,' she suggested. 'First, they ran off to London or another big city and disappeared into the mass of homeless.

'Second, they're still somewhere in the vicinity of Ormesby, hiding or being held against their will.

'Third, they've been abducted by stranger or strangers unknown.'

'Trouble is,' responded Greg, 'we have no evidence for or against any of those options. No sign they got on any form of transport to travel anywhere. In fact, no sighting of them at all.'

'Let's tackle it another way,' suggested Chris. 'If they have been abducted, or held against their will, whether in Ormesby or elsewhere, why? Why would anyone hold two children in secret?'

'You know the answer to that,' said Greg grimly. 'And we've also checked with everyone on the sex offenders register for miles around. That got us nowhere either.'

They both drank in silence for a while, gazing out over the garden and the slow river beyond.

'Sorry,' said Chris. 'I don't seem to have been much help. All we've done is rule out stuff you've already done. The only thing I can think of to suggest is a wholescale review of CCTV in the area and as far as Norwich, using that new facial recognition software to see if they can be spotted.'

'Jill suggested that too,' said Greg with a ghost of a grin. 'At least that way she wouldn't have to spend the next week or two with her eyes nailed to a screen.'

Another pause, then Greg said, 'Pursuing that thought, there is one thing we haven't done. In the worst of all possible worlds, what often happens to children taken prisoner by paedophiles?'

'Video,' replied Chris, a dreadful light dawning.

'Exactly. And as you so rightly say, we now have a new tool. Has anyone used the facial recognition software on material from the dark web?'

'I don't know,' said Chris. 'But I can't see any reason why it wouldn't work.'

'And if it did,' said Greg, 'there's the possibility of evidence both that the children are alive, and even, if we're really lucky, some clues as to location.'

4

July 2O2O: a field near Downham Market

The Toyota pickup with muddy licence plates coasted to a quiet halt close to the hedge. A thickset man got out and stood for a moment, apparently listening. All that was audible were the night sounds of wind in the hedge, the distant bark of a vixen and, had his hearing been sufficiently acute, the high-pitched cries of the hunting pipistrelles overhead. He nodded to himself and, shouldering a pack from the back of the pickup, set off across the field. To save effort he walked down a conveniently orientated tramline until he reached the far boundary, marked by a substantial ditch. It was a bit of a scramble into the ditch and even more so getting out the other side. He was breathing heavily by the time he reached the shallow screen of tall trees on the edge of the farmyard.

The grass was long under the trees, and he tripped twice on brambles but didn't dare turn on his torch. He was swearing under his breath and switching the heavy pack from one shoulder to the other by the time he reached the first building, a dilapidated old byre. He edged round the corner cautiously, on the lookout for either staff or cameras or – worst case – a farm dog! He saw no one and nothing, missing the one camera pointed his way because it was well hidden in an owl box.

He switched shoulders with the pack again, wondering if he should have brought a bagman with him. He'd decided against it for reasons of secrecy, and on balance he still thought that decision was right. Not far now!

His target was the big pole barn in front of him. At the far end it had walls of corrugated metal topped by space-boarding. Obviously, it was used for animal housing in the winter. At this end the sides were open, and the space would, in a few months, be full of wheat and barley straw. There was still a substantial stack of the previous year's straw, and the remaining space was filled with farm machinery: a couple of trailers, a tractor and, to his delight, a modern and expensive combine harvester. He edged over for a better look and noted that the combine engine seemed to be stripped down for pre-harvest maintenance. Couldn't be better.

He moved into the shadow of the straw stack and took a last look round. Silence, except for some traffic noise in the distance and the subdued rumble of a plane far overhead, heading for Norwich airport perhaps.

He unloaded the can of petrol from the pack and splashed around half of it at the base of the straw stack. Scrabbling on the earth floor, he picked up an oily rag left behind by some farm mechanic and stuffed it into the top of the can as a makeshift fuse. Then pushed the can under the combine. The smell of petrol rose strongly on the gentle breeze. He paused again to listen, before removing a box of matches from his pocket.

The first match went out immediately, but the second stayed alight long enough to be thrown onto the petrol-wet bales. As there was a *whumph* and a gust of hot air behind him, he moved swiftly to the combine and reached under to light the oily fuse. This had to light first go, or not at all. He couldn't hang around here now. The flame flickered, seemed to go out, and he couldn't stay any longer. He ran for the cover of the old byre, throwing the shoulder bag behind him as he ran.

Feeling safe in the shadow of the dilapidated old shed, he turned and watched. The bales were well alight, an edifice of flame with a black heart. As he watched, there was a violent explosion under the combine and a gout of fire flung parts of the huge machine's components into the air. He knew that he should get out of there, and fast, but couldn't drag himself away from the red glory that was his fire and had once been a building filled with goods and machinery. Only when loud cries from four or five men running into the yard disturbed his concentration, did he turn and slide as unobtrusively as he could into the belt of trees. Even then, he was slow to head back to his Toyota. The flames drew him like a magnet, and the tiny match glow that had seeded an inferno burned in his mind's eye.

5

July 2020: Greater Ormesby

The day started the same as all days. The dim overhead light was turned up to something approaching daylight, and around half an hour later the door at the top of the short flight of steps creaked open. Aunty Jo would appear carrying a tray and the door would swing to behind her with a click.

Ever since the day they'd woken up in the basement room after the self-styled 'Aunty' Jo had fed them sandwiches and fizzy drinks, Karen had repeatedly wondered if she could push Aunty Jo off the steps and make a dash for the door, but two things put her off. First, she knew her little brother Jake was too frightened to come with her. Second, she couldn't think of a way of getting Aunty Jo off the steps. Whichever way she pushed, the woman was likely to land sprawled across the stairs, blocking the escape route.

Early in their confinement, she had hunted through their underground room, and its annex with the sink and cassette toilet, for anything that might make a weapon. If she was strong enough, she supposed she could pull a leg off the bed and use it as a club. But if she was that strong, she could deal with their captor without a weapon. Then, over the weeks, as marked in crayon on the wall above the toilet, she had come to feel a grudging affection for the self-styled Aunty Jo.

No matter how grumpy Karen was, Joanne never failed to bring them food and drinks, three times a day. She had supplied them with a comb for Karen's long fair hair and Jake's shorter version, a TV, games and books. Not enough books, in Karen's opinion, but it seemed she was doing her best.

According to her, it simply wasn't safe for children out in the world. Looking at what was happening, as reported on the TV, Karen felt she had a point. As the death rate climbed and climbed, every news report or presentation by the prime minister reinforced the message. *Stay home. Stay safe.* And if that wasn't enough, Karen had only to remember what her father had done.

For the first few weeks after the local news reported her mother's death and the fire that had destroyed their home, Karen had existed in their hidden room, nursing a frozen nugget of hope in her chest. Jake seemed oblivious to everything, perhaps just relieved that he was out of reach of their father's bullying. But Karen had kept on hoping that it was all a dreadful mistake. That their mother was safe somewhere, perhaps with her friend Tim. Or if she was indeed dead, it was from some sort of terrible accident and that, in time, their father, or even Tim, would appear and claim them from Aunty Jo.

It was only when their father's suicide in the River Waveney was reported, that the hope died, finally and irrevocably. If he had killed himself, then it could only be that he had killed Mum and burned their home. No one was going to come and rescue them. All they had was Aunty Jo.

It was at that point she gave up trying to call for help via email on their secret iPad. She had never, so far, managed to get any phone signal in their hidden room, and the Wi-Fi she could pick up was password-protected. But she'd kept writing emails reporting on their situation and pleading for help. She'd kept hitting Send, and the messages hissed away into the outbox. And there they sat. No signal, so no departure to the Sent folder. She hoped that someday, somehow, a signal would make it through the ground and walls, and the messages would depart. But so far nothing; and now she'd given up. Or, almost given up. She'd stopped typing messages, but she kept the iPad charged and occasionally she checked to see if the messages had gone.

6

March 2018: Clapton, London

Joanne stared at her husband with a sick feeling in her stomach that, for once, had nothing to do with her current condition or the early hour. He carried on pushing clothes any old how into the suitcase on the bed.

'You can't go,' she said in a fierce whisper. 'You can't just leave, just like that.' He looked up, his big gnarled hands falling still for just a moment.

'Try and stop me,' he said briefly, then pointed a finger into her face. 'Just try. You know what'll happen.' Behind the pointing finger with the dirty chewed nail, his bristly face loomed grim and dark. He held the Kitchener pose for a moment, then turned back to the wardrobe behind him. In seconds he'd swept an armful of clothes off their hangers and they too went into the case. She sank down into the bedside chair behind her and tried to think of an argument that would persuade him. *I could give him my news*, she thought. *But would that make him stay or hurry him away?*

While she was thinking, he left the room, then came back with toiletries gathered off the bathroom shelf and threw those in the case as well. Then he closed the lid on their life together and with some effort, got the clasps to fasten.

'Right,' he said, lifting the suitcase off the bed and dropping it beside his feet with a bang she feared would wake their son, Frankie, asleep in the next room.

'Shh, you'll wake Frankie,' she started to say, but he spoke over her.

'Goodbye, Jo. I won't say it's been fun, because it hasn't. The rent's paid until the end of the month. After that, it's up to you.'

'What about Frankie? What will I say to him? Where are you going?' So many questions filled her head her tongue stumbled over them.

'Never you mind where I'm going. None of your business. As for Frankie, tell him whatever you like.'

'But he's your son. You have a responsibility. You have to look after him. And anyway...' She hesitated, still not sure whether to tell him or not. Still not sure whether it would make things better or worse.

'I can't give him what I haven't got,' he said. 'The well's dry, Jo. You and that brat of yours have had it good for the last few years, but now I'm out of work there's nothing. You'll have to get off that lazy arse and find a job yourself. It'll do you good.'

'I'm pregnant,' she burst out, without stopping to think further.

'How convenient! I don't believe you, Jo. And if you are, who's to say it's mine?'

'I am,' she insisted. 'And of course it's yours. Who else's could it be?'

But he was ignoring her. He picked up the case in one hand and shouldered past her, out the bedroom door and over to their living room-cum-kitchen. She followed him, noting with relief that the door to Frankie's room was still shut.

'I tell you, I'm pregnant. I can't work. So how are we going to manage? You have to look after us. It's the law.' She was hissing the words at his back as he filled a glass with water at the sink then downed it without turning round. She sank into a kitchen chair, still watching him, silhouetted against the uncurtained window. The light from the streetlamp shone in, creating a shimmering nimbus around his shaved head. Still facing the window, he rested both hands on the edge of the sink and sighed heavily.

'That's low, even for you, Jo,' he said. 'You got pregnant with Frankie and used that to trap me into marriage. Then when I'm leaving, you're suddenly conveniently pregnant again. What happened to you taking the pill?' He turned round and leaned back on the draining board, dislodging a cup which fell into the sink with a clatter.

'Takes two to tango,' she said. 'Frankie's as much your responsibility as mine, and so is the new baby.'

'If there is one,' he said sceptically. 'And if there is, it's your fault. You were the one taking the pills. No, sorry, Jo, but I'm not going to be trapped again. I've fed, clothed and housed the two of you for eight long years and I've had enough of being broke and miserable. It's your problem now.

'Don't see why you want me to stay anyway,' he said over his shoulder as he headed for the stairs to the shared hall and freedom. 'You're as miserable as me, don't deny it. You do enough moaning about being poor and bored. Well, a spot of work should remove the boredom, and if you get tired of being poor, you could go home to mummy.' With that, he waved a final farewell and closed the door, quietly but firmly, behind him.

7

July 2020: Welsh Farm, near Downham Market

When Greg and Jim climbed out of their car at Welsh Farm, it was hard to say which was smoking more: the ruined barn or the owner.

He marched over the semi-flooded and smoke-stained farmyard, his florid, square face livid with rage, the once-tidy jeans and green sweatshirt smudged with smoke and soot. Greg reckoned he was probably in his late fifties and in the current circumstances looked every one of his years.

'Hello! It's the "better late than never" boys,' he snarled. 'Well, not this time. I've lost a stack of straw and a John Deere combine harvester worth around £800,000 – never mind tools, trailers and the barn that was going to house straw and livestock this winter. It's sheer luck the combine header was the other side the yard, or you could add another £120K to the total.'

'If I could figure out a way of suing you lot for criminal negligence, believe me I would. Haven't you anything to say?' he added, shouting.

Greg waited, patiently, for the shouting to stop.

'Well?' the farmer bellowed. 'Now you're here, say something!'

At Greg's side, Jim shifted restlessly, but on receipt of a firm look from his boss, kept his mouth shut.

'I take it you are Mr Wyatt,' said Greg in a deliberately quiet voice.

'Of course I am,' interrupted the farmer. 'Who the hell do you think I am?'

Greg introduced them, still in a quiet voice. 'I'm Detective Chief Inspector Geldard, and this is Detective Inspector Henning. We'll need to take a good look round shortly, and our forensic team are on their way.' His attention was attracted by the arrival of a van at the gate, where it was stopped briefly by one of the uniformed team then waved through. 'Ah, here they are now,' he added. 'Excuse me for a moment while I have a quick word with them, then it would be helpful if we could sit down somewhere for a discussion.'

'Come to the house when you're ready,' said Mr Wyatt, still grumpy but beginning to moderate the volume a little. He stomped off across the yard, and Greg went over to the Forensic Services van, where Ned, his crime scene manager, was getting out, already clad in paper overalls.

'Doesn't he realise we have a lot else on our plates and no time to dance attendance on every farmer in the county who's threatened by hare coursers?' groused Jim, fortunately in a low voice.

Greg glanced over his shoulder to check the farmer was out of earshot. 'Clearly not,' he said. 'But I don't think it will help to let him hear you say that. Poor chap's had a big shock and lost a lot of valuable equipment. Not surprising he's angry. Not like you to be unsympathetic, Jim,' he added. 'Are you OK? You look tired.'

'Mother-in-law's got Covid,' he said. 'The wife's round there looking after everything, and no doubt she's going to get it too, so she can't come home. Bit of a bummer, actually,' replied Jim.

'Worrying,' agreed Greg. 'Say if you need some time off.'

'No point,' said Jim. 'Nothing I can do except worry more. Better in work, and I'll watch my tongue, honest.' He essayed a smile.

'Ned,' said Greg to the tall, lean man zipping up his overalls. 'Thanks for coming so quickly. I'm just off to have a chat with the owner, but we know from the earlier phone calls that he was threatened by would-be hare coursers recently, and the fire team think an accelerant was involved, so arson is likely.'

'Have you had anyone search the wood yet?' asked Ned, nodding to the belt of trees alongside the farmyard.

'Not yet, no. So far, uniform have concentrated on securing the scene.'

'OK. Good. Leave it to me to organise the search. Arsonists almost always stop to watch their handiwork. So there's a good chance of finding something in there.'

'Thanks, Ned. Let me know if you need more manpower.'

Ned nodded and moved to the back of the van, pulling the hood of his overalls over his shaved head.

Greg turned to Jim. 'OK, let's have that chat with the angry Mr Wyatt,' he said.

The back door of the large farmhouse was standing open when Greg and Jim reached it. Greg knocked on the door frame politely and was rewarded by the swift arrival of an elegant woman in jeans and pale sweater. Her complexion was a good match for her top, and Greg wondered whether her pallor was normal or the result of shock. As he noticed her shaking hands, he concluded the latter.

'Chief Inspector Geldard,' she said. 'Come in. Jeff's in the kitchen, and I've just made coffee. He's stopped shouting,' she added, 'but he's still pretty mad, I should warn you.'

'Not surprising,' said Greg, but by then they'd reached the kitchen.

The farmer was sitting at the far side of a scrubbed wooden table, easily big enough to sit eight. The walls of the warm kitchen were either covered in shelves or hung with utensils and pans. It seemed Mrs Wyatt took her cookery seriously. Greg was sorry to note that the farmer made no move toward the large coffee pot sitting on the bright red Aga and filling the air with a tantalising aroma.

'Mr Wyatt,' he said. 'I can't begin to imagine how distressing and annoying this is for you and your family. The hare-coursing crowd are a nasty bunch at the best of times, but I've never known them go this far. I'm sorry you've been put through this, but believe me, we will do everything we can to bring the culprit to justice.'

'Will you?' demanded the farmer, still angry but his voice now pitched at a volume better suited to a kitchen. 'I thought you tended to give travellers a wide berth. Too scared to go into their encampments!'

'Let's not jump to conclusions,' replied Greg. 'An open mind is the key to good policing.

'I assure you, I'm right,' he added as Mr Wyatt opened his mouth to object. 'If you make your mind up *before* you collect the evidence, you only see evidence that confirms your prejudices. That way you can miss something important. I promise you, we will be thorough in our investigation, and we will go wherever the evidence leads, no matter how difficult that is.'

Mr Wyatt switched tack. 'You the fella who nailed the modern-slavery case, and the terrorism at the science park?' he asked, naming two of Greg's recent cases that had hit the headlines locally.

'That's right,' said Jim before Greg could react.

'Could be you know what you're doing,' allowed the farmer grudgingly. 'OK. What happens now? Coffee?' he asked belatedly.

His wife heaved a sigh of relief and picked up the large pot from the edge of the Aga.

'I'm Jane Wyatt,' she said. 'How do you like your coffee?'

Soon they all had fragrantly steaming mugs in front of them. Greg booted up his iPad and checked the notes he'd made when the call came in.

'I gather you reported a threat two weeks ago,' he said.

'That'd be right,' agreed Mr Wyatt. 'But that was the second threat. The first was when I saw off a bunch of hare coursers two nights before that. That was the usual: *break your legs and fire your barns*, shouting. It's nasty, but I thought no more of it. Your uniformed lot attended when I reported the hare coursing, but by the time they got here they'd all scarpered – some of them straight through my crop. All we got hold of was one grey lurcher.

'Then two weeks ago, I got an anonymous email that told me either I had to let the hare coursing go ahead, or I, and my family, would pay. I told whoever it was to eff off, but then, afterwards, I had second thoughts and reported it to you lot.'

'Do you still have the message?' asked Jim.

'Yes. On my phone.' He scrolled through several screens, breathing heavily with concentration, then held out the phone to Greg. 'See?'

Greg looked. 'Can you forward that to this address?' he asked, and pushed his card over. They all waited while the farmer found his glasses and used his thick fingers, better suited to larger tools, to type slowly on the small phone screen.

'We'll want to go over the details of your encounter with the hare coursers,' said Greg. 'But first, talk me through what happened last night.'

'Normal evening at first,' replied Mr Wyatt. 'Had a quick word with the farm mechanic at the end of the day. He was servicing the combine,' he explained. 'Wasted effort that turned out to be! Anyway, I saw him just before he went home, around 6pm, then came in for a glass of red before supper. We were both watching TV when the balloon went up.

'First it was my farm manager, Frank, hammering on the back door shouting about a fire. He lives in the cottage the other side the farmyard,' he added. 'He'd seen the flames and heard the bang. Jane and I, we'd heard and seen nothing, being at the back of the farmhouse here.'

Jane nodded agreement. 'Jeff ran out to see what was going on, and I dialled 999,' she said. 'But Frank had already reported it, and the fire brigade were on the way.'

'Two more of my chaps had joined us by then, from the staff accommodation behind the farm offices, and we all ran around like headless chickens until the fire brigade arrived. It was too late to save any of the equipment in the barn and our hoses were worse than useless. I could have had as much impact piddling on the fire,' Wyatt remarked bitterly.

'Did any of you see anyone in the yard before the fire?' asked Greg.

'No one that shouldn't have been there,' replied the farmer.

'And after?'

'I didn't see anyone except farm staff, and I don't think they saw anyone either. But we have got some blurry images on our CCTV.'

'Then we'll need those as well,' said Greg. 'We can do a lot to clean up video these days. And we'll need to talk to everyone who was here last night.'

'Some of them are out working,' the farmer objected. 'Spraying and such. Work goes on yer know.'

'Then we'll see them on their return to the yard. Is there anything you'd like to add, Mrs Wyatt?' he asked.

'Jane, please,' she said. 'No, nothing. I followed Jeff out into the yard after I got off the phone to the emergency services call centre, but he shouted at me to keep clear, so I stayed close to the house. Then once the fire brigade arrived, I came back in and started making tea. So very British of me,' she said with a faint smile.

'OK. Now talk me through the events of two weeks ago, when you had the hare coursers here.'

***

Once back at Norfolk police HQ, Greg handed the data chip with the CCTV footage over to Jill, and sat down in the office with Jim.

'We need the report from the hare-coursing incident, Jim,' he said. 'And we need to find the vehicles involved in that, if at all possible. Not much else we can do immediately until we hear from Ned and his team. Hopefully by then Jeff Wyatt will have sent us all the photos he and his foreman took that night in June. We can compare those with the CCTV footage and see if the same men were involved.'

'The CCTV footage is very blurred.' Jim was doubtful.

'It is, but let's see what miracles Jill can perform.'

8

July 2020 – continuing underground

The following day, Jake was unusually chatty. He asked Aunty Jo what she was doing that day when she brought their breakfast. She seemed taken aback and didn't know how to answer.

'Just the usual stuff,' she said eventually. 'No one's going out anywhere, as you know from the TV.' She nodded to the set in the corner.

'How did you know our mum and dad?' Jake asked suddenly, just as she was going back up the stairs. 'Were you friends of theirs? Like Uncle Tim? Do you know Uncle Tim?'

'No, I don't know Uncle Tim, and I didn't know your parents,' she said, sounding surprised. She wasn't nearly as surprised as Karen – she'd had no idea Jake had been brooding on such questions.

'Why are we here then?' asked Jake. 'We must be costing you a lot. My mum always said she'd rather feed me for a week than a fortnight. I think she meant I ate too much'. He looked at the plates of eggs and bacon Aunty Jo had put down on the table before she retreated to the stairs.

'That's OK,' she said as she started back up the stairs. 'I always wanted a boy and a girl. Now I have you.'

The door closed behind her, and Karen was left staring at Jake in surprise.

'Don't you remember how we came here?' she demanded.

'Course I do,' he replied through a mouthful of egg. 'Dad was being horrible, and we ran away, but we couldn't find Tim and then we moved in with Aunty Jo.

'I like it here,' he said. 'She's kind, and there's no one to throw balls at me any more or shout at me for not being the sort of boy they wanted.'

'What about Mum?' asked Karen. 'Don't you miss Mum?'

Jake looked confused. 'S'pose I do, a bit,' he said. 'But if she wanted us, she'd have come for us by now, wouldn't she? At least Aunty Jo wants us.'

Karen opened her mouth to explain that their mother was dead, probably killed by their father, then shut it again. She couldn't bring herself to drag Jake's world crashing down. He was too young. He wouldn't understand. But it felt even more lonely, being the only one who remembered their mother and remembered what freedom felt like.

That afternoon, Aunty Jo returned with an armful of clothes. 'I thought you might be finding it a bit boring, it not being safe to go out,' she said. 'When I was a girl, I used to like playing dressing up. I brought you some clothes to play with.'

She dropped the armful of clothes on the bed and went back to the stairs.

'Have fun,' she said.

Jake wasn't very interested to start with. *Clothes were for girls* was the expression all over his face, and he carried on playing with his trains. Karen turned over the pile with some curiosity. There were dresses, an old feather boa and a moth-eaten fur stole. She put that down quickly, as she was fairly sure the fur was real.

At the bottom of the pile was something different. It was a cowboy outfit – bought in a supermarket, judging from the label in the neck – and attached to it was a belt with two holsters and toy guns. That caught Jake's interest immediately.

'Oh wow,' he said, waving the guns around and pretending to shoot Karen. 'Bang, you're dead!'

'You can't shoot me,' said Karen, entering into the spirit of the game. 'Not if I'm your moll!'

'What do you mean, a moll?' asked Jake.

'Cowboys always have a gangster's moll,' said Karen. 'Come on, get into your cowboy outfit properly, and I'll dress as your moll.' She sifted quickly through the dresses and found a sparkly shift dress. Much too big, on her it draped from neck to ankles.

Both the children shed their clothes quickly, dropping them any old where on the floor, and dressed up for the new game. Jake pulled on the mock-leather chaps and the beaded jacket but paid more attention to the belt and the guns. Karen burst out laughing when he turned round. Without his usual jeans, his pants-clad bum stuck out between the chaps and the belt.

'You need your trousers on,' she said, still laughing. He took no notice.

'Hurry up and get your fancy dress on,' he said. 'Or I'll shoot you.'

He threatened her with the guns and, pretending to be afraid, she cinched the sparkly dress at the waist with a scarf. Then she tossed the feather boa round her shoulder with an air and said, 'I'll have a whisky, if you're buying, mister!'

Upstairs, Aunty Jo was watching on her laptop. The feed from the camera in the corner of the cellar was clear. She checked it was recording and smiled.

9

July 2020 – frustrations and plans

When Greg went home, he was dispirited. So far, huge effort and many hours of recordings from CCTV and ANPR had delivered a big fat nothing. Jill had trawled the available camera footage from the Welsh Farm CCTV and nearby. A couple of possible ATVs had been spotted but lost again as they neared Norwich. The AI-driven facial recognition screening was underway, but again – zilch, so far. The only benefit was that no human had had to put up with the filth that trundled past the computer screens.

Now he was home, fending off the combined attentions of a cat and a parrot, and wondering what to give his father for supper, given the non-arrival of his supermarket food order. He was just tending in the direction of something with eggs – precisely what, he had no idea, given the absence of salad, potatoes and bread – when there was the welcome sound of two sets of wheels approaching down the gravel drive. The first set belonged to the delivery truck; driver very apologetic about missing his designated time slot. The second was Chris's. She helped Greg and the driver carry the shopping into the kitchen, rescued the driver from a predatory beaking by Tally, then sat down with a sigh at the kitchen table surrounded by piles of groceries.

'You sound how I feel,' remarked Greg. 'Hard day?'

'Frustrating one,' said Chris, taking her jacket off and flinging it in the general direction of the sofa. It missed, and Greg reached over to pick it up as she went on. 'I have at least three women on my books who are showing every sign of being abused but refuse to make a complaint or move to a safe place.'

'Can they? Move out, I mean?' asked Greg. 'In the current circs, is there anywhere for them to go?'

'There is if they're willing to take the leap. There are special dispensations for someone in their position, but it's looking horribly as though there's going to be a death or serious injury before anyone can be convinced to get themselves to safety. One of them did move out for a while. Moved to Norwich. Then, would you believe it? She moved back. On top of that, I checked the new rules on marriages, and I think we're scuppered. Again!'

'In what way?' asked Greg, putting a large glass of white wine on the table beside her and deciding his moans had better wait until later.

'The biggest issue is the reception. The old rules limited it to two households. In other words, we could have had your father or my parents but not both. That was never going to work, was it? Which was why we put things off. Now, I think we can plan a socially distanced celebration outdoors and risk the weather, or indoors and risk the rules changing again, in which case we lose a lot of money. And I mean a lot! Some people are thousands out of pocket.'

'I thought we were allowed up to thirty socially distanced guests,' said Greg.

'That was part of the old rules for the ceremony itself. But my biggest fear is that we just don't know what's going to happen later this year. We still have no vaccine, and we could end up with another winter locked down tight! I'm sorry Greg, but I just don't see a way of planning anything with any confidence.'

They were interrupted by the sounds of a car door banging, and the arrival of Greg's father.

'Thank you,' he was saying through his own face covering to the masked taxi driver. 'Please be prompt to pick me up at 9pm. I promise I'll be ready.' He turned to greet his son with a wave and blew a kiss to Chris. She blew one back, thinking, as she did every time she met Greg's father, that if she needed to know what Greg would be like in thirty years, she had the perfect image in front of her: still tall and upright, eyes still clear, hair a little faded and thinner, voice still warm with intelligence and affection.

'Lovely to see you both in person,' he said. 'I've been looking forward to this for weeks.'

Settled down in a large armchair at least two metres from his hosts, he leaned back with a big smile on his face and took a sip of his gin and tonic.

'So, what's for supper?' he asked. 'I'm looking forward to that too, now I've got my tastebuds back in working order.'

'Thanks to a last-minute delivery,' said Greg, 'it's steak, salad and chips followed by lemon tart and strawberries.'

'Brilliant! Since I don't have to drive, I'll have a glass of red to wash it down too, if that's OK.'

'Of course,' said Greg, getting up to forage for a suitable bottle. 'I'll open one ready. How've you been? Fully over the Covid?'

'Yes, thank goodness. Still a bit wobbly, but that's from lack of exercise. I don't seem to have been hit by this so-called long Covid. How about you two? Still going infection-free?'

'Touch wood!' said Chris, matching the action to the words. 'I'm glad you arrived when you did, James. I was just getting into my stride with a mega-moan, and I needed to be interrupted.'

'Moaning about what?' asked James. 'Not the new job, I hope.'

'Not really, or at least, not mainly,' replied Chris. 'It's petty, I know, given what some people are going through, or have been through,' she added, mindful that James had lost his wife, and Greg his mother, to the disease. 'But I was whingeing about not being able to plan our wedding.'

'Talk me through the problem,' suggested James as Greg started to prep salad and put a griddle pan on to warm.

Chris did as she was told, easing her frustrations with the second telling. James thought for a moment then put his gin glass down with a determined click.

'Seems quite straightforward to me,' he said. 'Either you postpone your marriage for the foreseeable future until the world goes back to normal, or you plan something small and low key which limits your risk. You notice I said marriage not wedding,' he went on. 'Looking at you two, I think it's your marriage that's important to you, not a lot of fuss and flummery on a particular day. Although I doubt I'd have been saying that if your mother was still with us, Greg.'

Greg thought, not for the first time, how well his father knew him and how quickly he had assessed Chris.

'Yes, that's right,' said Chris, 'but we do want to celebrate all the same. There are some family and friends it's important to have with us.'

'And, from what you've just told me, even when the rules were stricter you could have up to thirty of them with you on the day. Looking back at my marriage, I wish to God I'd been able to restrict attendance to the most important thirty,' he said with some feeling.

'Yes, that's OK,' said Chris. 'And I suppose we could postpone our reception and have a party when things settle down.'

'Of course you could. If I were you,' said James, 'I'd arrange for a simple reception back here on the day for your thirty guests, with champagne and canapes or something similar. Then have another, bigger party later.'

'That's all very well, and fine by me,' commented Greg. 'I've had the big day with all the trimmings and to be honest I didn't enjoy it very much. I don't think many men do! But even though she's being very brave and reasonable, Chris might actually want to be princess for a day in a big fluffy white dress.'

There was another silence while they all contemplated this picture. Then James and Chris spoke simultaneously.

'No. Can't see it myself. Not white,' said James, just as Chris said, 'Red dress, please!' They all fell about laughing and Chris topped their glasses up again.

Chris was quiet while the steaks arrived on plates and they took their seats at the table, Greg's dad at the far end in compliance with social distancing. As they picked up their knives and forks, she pronounced suddenly, 'I like it. If we'd gone with our original idea of a wedding in Mexico or somewhere, we'd only have had a chosen few anyway, so thirty at the ceremony is more than enough. Let's make a list after supper. And a big party later is a much better idea than planning a big reception now and getting an ulcer stressing about having to cancel. Just one proviso. I still want the big red dress!'

At the end of the evening, the taxi arrived on time and Greg waved his father off, thinking with slight guilt how very much easier everything was without his mother present.

'Especially the wedding planning,' said Chris when he mentioned the thought to her. They finished clearing stuff into the dishwasher, with the usual minor disagreements over what best went where, then headed for bed.

'Now tell me what was troubling you earlier,' she said.

'Same old, same old,' he replied. 'No progress on finding the Mirren children, and not much on the arson case out at Downham Market.'

'Sometimes it's like that,' she said. 'You know that. Sometimes everything seems to go nowhere, then suddenly you'll get a breakthrough. It will happen, I'm sure of it. There is one bit of good news for you,' she added. 'That battered wife who went home after escaping to Norwich... Home is in Suffolk, so that's one less for you and one more for me.'

'Swings and roundabouts,' agreed Greg. 'As for a breakthrough on the Mirren kids, I wish I had your confidence.' He looped a towel over his shoulder and headed for the shower. 'I really wish I did.'

10

2020 – profit from fire?

It was a random chat in a village pub garden that gave Nick the idea. That and the memory of just how much devastation had been wrought by one simple fire.

The conversation with his hare-coursing contacts had strayed from sport to financial matters. The lad with the facial tattoos and stubble, Jacko, had been boasting about where he got his stake money for the bets he'd laid on his grey lurcher.

'It's a bugger, losing that dog,' he'd complained. 'Best lurcher I've had for a year or two.' If his listener had privately thought that, even a year or so ago, the lad was probably still at school then, he kept the thought to himself.

'Still, getting a new one tomorrow. Trained and ready,' he boasted. 'So, we'll be at your next meet, no problem. Cost me a pretty penny too, but the car job works well,' said Tattoo-Face. And he winked.

'What've you got on your list now?' Nick asked.

'Now that'd be telling.' The lad was pretending a discretion he didn't really have. In reality, he was desperate to boast how smart he was. 'High-end Mercs, Jags and Beemers are always in demand.' He was obviously quoting someone.

'What about farm stuff?' Nick asked.

'You mean like Discoverys or Range Rovers? Can always find a home for Range Rovers—' He was interrupted.

'No, I mean farm stuff like tractors, machinery, quad bikes and so on. Maybe the odd four-by-four?'

'I'd have to ask about tractors. They might need some warning, if you know what I mean. But quad bikes, now. Always a market for them.' The two of them fell silent as a man walked past on his way to the gents.

'OK.' Nick stood up and downed the last of his pint. 'I'll be in touch about the quad bikes. And maybe a tractor or two.'

His mind was made up before he reached the car park. Instead of turning his pickup for home, he turned the other way, toward Thetford and the Breckland estates. He was vaguely aware that a lot of land was owned by one estate and noted a marked similarity of style across a number of farms. Many were uniformly neat, with machinery tidily parked either in yards or in barns, signage clear and gates both well maintained and secured. The classic signs of farming under pressure – old silage wrappings and fertiliser sacks dumped just anywhere, farmyards that looked like graveyards of defunct machinery, gates held up by baler twine – were rarely seen here.

After a couple of hours' driving around, he stopped in a garage, topped up with diesel and bought a road map, then turned back north. This time he had in mind the rich Norfolk estates owned by titled landowners and the Crown. On his way, he made particular note of a farmyard with large modern barns, visible from the A11, and added a scribble to his map as soon as he had the opportunity to pull over into a lay-by.

By 8pm he had covered a lot of miles and was tiring. The light was fading and he decided to pause for a meal and to make some more notes.

Faced with a choice of battling into King's Lynn or looking round in his immediate vicinity, he opted for the latter and stopped at the next village pub he saw, pulling up in a car park beside one of the many pubs called The Rose and Crown. He took the map in with him, and moments later was lucky enough to secure a comfortable leather armchair in a corner near the bar when its middle-aged lady occupant decided her evening was over and dragged her reluctant husband to the exit.

He ordered a pint of bitter, a bar meal of scotch eggs with chips and salad, and settled down with his map and a biro. The former exhibited a distinct tendency to flutter in the strong draught from the open windows. By the time he finished his meal, spared both the conversation of the bar manager and distractions from fellow drinkers by the rule that kept everyone at a distance, his map was covered with notes recording what he had seen that day. When he left the pub and headed home to Norwich, he had a priority list in his head. And a second list, of all the details he needed to research further.

Jacko, the lurcher enthusiast, was clearly surprised to be contacted again within the week. This time, confidentiality being key, Nick used the hare-coursing WhatsApp group to arrange a meeting in a lay-by. Had he known it, he was but a few hundred metres from the turning to Greg Geldard's home near the Bure. When he reached the spot, a strategic ten minutes late, Jacko was already waiting, perched on his motorbike and consulting his watch irritably.

'You said—' he began, but Nick interrupted without hesitation.

'Where do the orders come from?' he asked.

'Wha?' Jacko was never very quick on the uptake.

'The orders for the vehicles.' Nick was impatient. 'You told me the cars were ordered. How do you get the orders? Who from?'

'Dunno,' replied Jacko. 'I get them on WhatsApp. They tell me what and when, and where to take them.'

'Which is where?' asked Nick.

'Usually somewhere near Felixstowe, on the A14 somewhere. Sometimes near Tilbury, but that's not so often.'

'Give us your phone,' commanded Nick.

'Wha?'

That seems to be his favourite exclamation, reflected Nick. 'Just open WhatsApp and hand it over.'

Jacko looked sulky, but years of doing what Nick said held good, and he handed over his phone. Nick looked at the cracked and smeared screen. 'You need a new one,' he remarked. 'If business is that good, you can afford one.' He tapped for a few moments, then handed the phone back. 'OK. That's done,' he said.

'Wot you done?' asked Jacko.

'Put myself in touch with your car contact, that's all,' said Nick.

Jacko was examining his phone. 'But you've left me out of the chat,' he complained.

'That's right. And that's the way I like it, OK?' Jacko muttered something, and Nick decided to let it pass. 'OK. That's us done.'

He got back in his pickup, and as soon as there was a gap in the traffic he swung round and headed toward the A47 and Norwich. In his rear-view mirror, he could see Jacko getting back on his bike, dissatisfaction evident in the way he pulled his helmet on and gunned the throttle. Then he was out of sight beyond the bridge over the Bure, and Nick turned his attention to the road in front of him.

He didn't go straight home to the Norwich terraced house he shared with Cissy and her toddler son. He went first to his lock-up garage a few miles away. It had been a few weeks since he'd been there, and it was as cluttered as he remembered. Sighing heavily, he hauled out a range of boxes and bags. Some, with a look over his shoulder, went into the waste skip just down the road. Others he piled into the bed of the pickup, for retention in the garden shed behind his terraced home. After the best part of an hour, sorting and hauling, most of the garage was clear of clutter and the remaining goods he didn't want at home, and couldn't bring himself to throw out, were stacked neatly against the back wall. They included some of the kit for the hare coursing, together with some items that, having fortuitously fallen off lorries, had proved difficult to shift. Then, before the evening wore away, he went for a chat with his brother, Ade.

***

To start with, Ade wasn't too keen. 'I thought you were sticking to the hares and the betting,' he objected. 'This is a bit of a stretch for you, isn't it?'

'Not as far as you think.' Nick threw the rest of his garage sandwich into the river for the ducks and looked at Ade, sitting at the far end of the bench. 'All you have to do is turn up with your tow truck, load up a few bits and pieces, and drop them where I tell you. Not so difficult, is it?'

'What sort of bits and pieces?' demanded Ade.

'Tools mainly.'

'Why d'yer need a tow truck then?' asked Ade.

'There may be a couple of quad bikes, stuff like that,' said Nick. They both fell silent as a couple walking a dog went past on the tow path.

'An' how d'yer know I won't be followed off the farm?'

'You won't,' said Nick. 'They'll be too busy, I promise you that. Do exactly as I say, and you'll be clean away before they've dealt with my little surprise. They may not even realise the stuff has gone.'

It took a while longer to convince Ade, but the promise of cash up front 'for his trouble' was very persuasive. After Ade left, Nick set off for home, calling in at a random garage on the way, to fill up his petrol can.

'Don't put it in your diesel, will you, mate?' asked the garage hand facetiously.

11

April 2018 Clapton, London

The first few days after her husband left, it was all Joanne could do to get Frankie up and off to school. She spent most of the morning either being sick or wanting to be sick. She wasn't sure which was worse. She told Frankie his dad had gone away to look for a new job. He was a bit upset he hadn't said goodbye, but apart from that, he seemed to accept the explanation. He was used to his dad being absent, after all. Then came the familiar cramping sensations in her belly, and she knew that the latest baby had gone the way of the last two.

Perhaps it was just as well, she thought. But she struggled to feel anything – either grief or relief.

That first weekend, she spent Saturday in bed, explaining to Frankie that she was ill and that he'd find food in the fridge. He moaned a bit about the lack of crisps, but for an eight-year-old, he'd done a good job, on the whole, of looking after himself. On Sunday he'd wanted to go out to play with friends in the park, but she'd persuaded him to stay home and read. She stirred herself to make beans on toast for his supper, then went back to bed, noting that she needed to go shopping while he was at school on Monday. He was running out of clean clothes too, so she put a wash on.

On Monday, at Tesco, she checked the bank balance at the hole in the wall, and noticed, without much surprise, that the balance had fallen by half. She drew out £200 before any more disappeared and cursed herself for not taking action sooner. She stocked up on loads of tinned and packet foods while she could and paid for that with the debit card too. Then faced with the problem of how to get it home, she looked left and right as she emerged from the shop with her full load, and headed up the road as fast as she could, expecting every second to be tapped on the shoulder and accused of stealing the trolley.

To her immense relief, she got it all home and spent what seemed like ages ferrying bags and bottles from the trolley in the hall to her kitchen.

Just as she finished, her downstairs neighbour came out and stared at the trolley. 'I hope you're not thinking of leaving that there,' she snapped.

'No. Of course not,' Joanne replied. But once it was empty, she wondered where she could put it. The garden, such as it was, belonged to the ground-floor flat. The hall was clearly a no go. In the end she left it until the evening, then pushed it down the road to the small crescent at the end and abandoned it in the tiny garden behind the railings.

That night she opened the accumulated post of the past few days, then stared at the results. An electricity bill was due. Together with the rent she would need to pay in the middle of April, that would take all the money she had. Frankie was reading a library book from the school, so she had the peace and quiet to do some thinking. Twice she picked up the phone to call a very familiar number from the past, and twice put it down without ringing.

The third time she picked up the phone, she rang him. There was no answer, except his answerphone telling her to leave a message.

Frankie looked up, hearing his dad's voice. 'That's Dad. Can I talk to him?' he asked.

'It's just the voicemail,' she said. Then she got up and left the room. Shut in the bathroom, she rang him again, and this time left a message.

'Bob, please ring me,' she pleaded. 'I've no money and the leccy bill is due. You know I've no money. You took a load from our bank account. I'm not cross, honest, and I won't give you any grief, but you need to look after Frankie. Please ring us. He wants to talk to you.'

There was no callback that night or the next day. When she tried ringing again, she found her number had been blocked.

The following weekend, she reviewed her rapidly dwindling financial resources and her options. She nearly rang the familiar family number again, then decided against. The answer might be no. Better to just turn up. *She wouldn't throw me out onto the street. Would she?*

On Monday she waved bye to Frankie at the school gate, arranged with the mother of one of his friends that she would see him back, then headed for home with her mind made up. A quick search on her phone and she found what she wanted. The cheapest and nearest car hire deal was a Fiat 500 to be collected from Edgeware. She could do that. She arranged to collect it the following morning, and spent the rest of the day packing, piling her remaining two suitcases and a load of plastic carrier bags in her bedroom. The only things she left for the next day were Frankie's stuff and the obvious kitchenware. She didn't want any questions from Frankie until they were ready for off.

At the end of the day, as she cooked sausages ready for Frankie's return home from school, she suddenly realised she felt better than she had in months. Perhaps it was the activity, or the relief of having a plan.

Frankie picked up on her improved mood, and was quite silly and giggly that evening, telling her about some event at school that had amused him a lot, then settling down with a book again.

He was reluctant to go to bed, but she bribed him with a promise that he could read in bed for half an hour, and eventually got him off. She spent the rest of her evening packing her clothes and deciding what to leave behind, then she too went to bed early.

The following morning it was Frankie off to school, then buses to Edgeware to pick up the car. If she checked she had her driving licence once, she checked five times.

After so long not being behind a wheel, she drove off from the garage with exaggerated care, convinced that if she stalled the Fiat they'd come and snatch it back again. But all was well. By the time she arrived back in Clapton she was feeling quite confident. She was lucky that at that time of day there were few cars parked in their street and she found a spot right by their gate.

Rather than start any hares running too soon, she decided to have some lunch first and, as an afterthought, made some sandwiches for the journey. Then she lined up the boxes and bags by their front door, adding at the very end the bags of Frankie's stuff, clothes, toys and books.

An hour before Frankie was due home, she started ferrying their worldly goods out to the little car. It didn't take long before the boot and back seat were piled high. The last couple of bags she put in the passenger footwell. *Frankie will just have to manage with them there,* she said to herself, but softened the blow by making sure one of them was his bag of books.

She was starting to look at her watch anxiously, worried that one of the neighbours might come and ask what was going on, when she decided to go to the school early and wait for Frankie there. She took a last look round the small flat that had been her home for over eight years, then closed the door behind her with a decisive bang and posted the keys through the letter box. *No going back now.*

The car, fully laden, felt different somehow, but she made it safely to Frankie's school and parked up the road from the gate just as a stream of children started to emerge onto the street. It seemed a long time, but was only minutes, before she spotted Frankie. Slightly to her horror, he was with several friends. *Damn. Witnesses. Too bad. Can't be helped.*

She waved vigorously, and he came over, his mates tagging along.

'Hi Tommy. Hi Ryan,' she said to the two she recognised. 'Hurry up, Frankie, get in the car.'

'You've got a car,' he exclaimed, amazed. 'Wow. Where're we going?'

'I'll tell you when we're on our way,' she said. 'Come on. Hurry up.' She more or less pushed him into the car, still exclaiming, then drove off with him waving to his pals. 'Fasten your seat belt,' she said as he squirmed in his seat looking at the stuff piled behind him.

'Where're we going, Mum? he said again. 'We've got a lot of stuff with us.'

'We're going on a visit, an adventure,' she replied. 'We're going to see your grandma.'

12

Late July 2020 – central Ormesby

Jill surveyed her arrangements with some satisfaction. If this was going to be the last big push to break something on the Mirren case, she was going to give it her best shot. When the Chief Super jibbed at the expense of a mobile incident room, she'd substituted a gazebo erected in the car park adjacent to the local garage. Two squad cars with blue flashing lights made sure the display was eye-catching, and a couple of uniformed colleagues were stationed at the crossroads, handing out hastily printed leaflets. Photos of the two children adorned display boards in the gazebo, and Bill sat at the table ready to interview passers-by. A steady trickle of runners, dog walkers and others taking exercise had diverted to sit opposite Bill in the chairs carefully placed the requisite distance apart.

Jill nodded to Bill, shouted, 'Coffee?' then, receiving the thumbs up as he continued to talk to the elderly man with a springer spaniel in tow, headed for the garage and refreshment supplies.

The young man behind the till seemed generally happy with the distraction and the increase in customers generated by the police presence. A pile of their leaflets already lay in front of him.

'Any luck?' he asked Jill as she placed a cardboard tray of four coffees and a handful of KitKats in front of him.

He rang up the total as she replied, 'Not much I'm afraid, but it's early yet. Two children can't have just vanished into thin air. Someone must have seen them.'

'I did,' he said as she tapped her card on the reader. 'But you know that from when one of your chaps talked to me before.' Her interest sharpened.

'I knew someone at the garage had seen them, but I didn't realise it was you. Can you spare me a minute to go over it with me? I've read the report,' she added hurriedly, 'but it's amazing how often people remember something else when they talk about it again.'

'I'm not exactly busy,' he said, waving a hand at the neglected petrol pumps and the one customer prowling the shelves.

'I'll just hand out this coffee, then I'll be back for a word,' she promised.

When she left the coffees with Bill, he was talking to a young woman with a baby. The springer had gone, but a depressed looking Cavapoo regarded her morosely from under the pushchair. Back in the garage, she discovered the till now had an extra stool in front of it.

'Sit you down,' the young man invited.

Nodding her thanks, Jill flicked through her notes. 'I take it you're Ali Haider?'

'That's right.' The young man nodded.

'According to my report, you saw the children in the early morning and sold them,' – she checked again – 'a sausage roll and some biscuits.'

'That's right,' he said again.

'Did you have any conversation with them?' Jill wanted to ask if he hadn't thought it odd that two young children were out and about on their own in a lockdown but didn't want to antagonise him.

'I asked what they were doing out in a lockdown, and where their mother was,' he replied as though he'd read her mind. 'The girl said their mother was just round the corner and they were on their way home after a walk. I said something like "It's a bit early, isn't it?" and she said, "It gets hot later, and Mum's working from home." '

'Did the boy say anything?'

'No, not a word to me, although I think I heard him talking to his sister while they were choosing the biscuits.'

'How did they pay?'

'With cash, as I told your officer before,' he said slightly pointedly, but added, 'And she gave me the right money. Then they went out and sat on the wall over there' – he pointed to the low wall just in front of the police gazebo – 'to eat their sausage roll. Next time I looked they'd gone.'

'Did you see any adult with them?'

'No. That was all I saw. The two kids and them sitting on the wall. Then.' he added.

Jill's interest sharpened. 'What do you mean, "then"? Did you see them later in the day, or since?'

'Well, I've been thinking about it, and I think I might have seen them in the evening. When I was going home.'

'What time would that have been?'

'Around six o'clock. Hamza does the evening shift, and he takes over at five-thirty so it would have been around then.'

'What exactly did you see?'

'I think I saw someone moving around near the bungalow at the end of the road opposite.' He pointed. 'I go home down that road, but to get to it I have to drive round the one-way street around the memorial green.' Jill nodded her understanding. 'It was when I was turning right by the green that I think I saw someone over there. I noticed it because you didn't see many people about. And thinking about it since, they weren't very tall, so it could have been the children.'

13

No comment

Greg surveyed the young man in front of him. He was thin and vaguely scruffy, with a moth-eaten dark beard that failed to hide his facial tattoos and generally did him no favours. His jeans and sweatshirt were covered in pale dog hair and worn at the knees and elbows.

He had declined a solicitor and seemed unperturbed, almost cocky, about an interview under caution. Greg let the silence drag on. He could hear a door slam somewhere in the background and muffled voices. Jacko shuffled in his seat, then took a long, and loud, slurp of his heavily sweetened tea.

'I understand you're a dog lover,' said Greg.

'No comment,' said Jacko.

Greg suppressed a grin. *So this is the no-solicitor plan.* At his side, Steve made a note and looked bored.

'Do you have a dog now?' Greg continued.

'No comment.'

'Because the quantity of dog hairs on your clothes would suggest that's likely.'

Jacko glanced down involuntarily, brushed ineffectually at his fleece sleeve and said, 'No comment,' again.

Greg sighed and ruffled through the folder in front of him, pretending there was more material in it than was actually the case. After a moment, he produced a large photo of the lurcher that had been captured on the night of the hare coursing.

'Is this your dog?' he asked, pushing the photo across the table.

'No comment,' said Jacko, but he looked at the photo for a long moment.

'Because we found your fingerprints on its collar. We also found some human DNA in the same place. It's very likely that will prove to be yours too.'

'No comment.'

Greg looked at Steve, who took his cue. 'Pity,' he said, putting his biro down and closing his notepad. 'Seems a nice dog.'

'What d'you mean, pity?' asked Jacko, provoked into speech.

'It'll be put down soon,' said Steve. 'The pound doesn't keep them for long, you know. If they're not claimed, then...' He drew his finger across his throat.

Jacko leaned back, affecting a nonchalance he didn't seem to feel. 'You're lying. They don't put healthy dogs down,' he said.

'Wrong,' said Steve. 'You're thinking of Dogs Trust. This dog is not with Dogs Trust. It's in the pound. And they only have so much space. When they run out of pens, it's first in, first to die.' He stood up. 'I presume we're finished here, Boss,' he said, and picked up his notebook.

Greg shuffled his papers together. 'Looks like it,' he said.

'Wait,' said Jacko, and chewed a fingernail while he thought hard. Greg, thinking that the smell of burning was almost evident as the wheels turned reluctantly, was reminded of one of Chris's favourite insults.

'OK,' said Jacko eventually. 'Yes, the dog is mine, and you can't put it down. I'll claim him as soon as I'm out of here.' He stood up to go as Steve resumed his seat.

'Just a minute,' said Greg. 'We haven't finished our questions yet. Sit down. OK, we've established that this grey lurcher, captured at the Wyatt's farm on the evening of the first of June, belongs to you. I'll just mention, in passing, that the dog is not microchipped, as required under the Microchipping of Dogs (England) Regulations 2015.'

Jacko looked sulky and muttered something about 'load of old cobblers'.

'Were you present with your dog that evening?'

'No comment,' said Jacko.

'Oh, come on,' said Steve. 'I thought we'd got past that. OK, if you're going to go "no comment" on us again, perhaps we should get your mate Mick O'Hanlon in.' Now, Jacko did look alarmed. 'After all, you went to the meet in his pickup, didn't you?'

'No need to bother Mick,' said Jacko.

Greg noticed Jacko's hands were shaking. 'Seems like you don't want Mr O'Hanlon involved,' he observed. 'Tell you what, Jacko, I'm guessing you want your dog back, and you don't want Mr O'Hanlon to think you dobbed him in. Talk now, and I'll see what I can do about both.'

Greg paused. Then as the silence continued, Steve added, 'Or you have a dead dog and an angry friend. It's up to you, Jacko.'

'OK,' he said. 'I was there for the hare coursing. I'll admit that.'

'Who organised the meet?' asked Greg.

One last hesitation, then Jacko opened the floodgates. 'It was Nick. Nick Waters.'

'You've been to meets organised by him before?'

'Yes. A few.'

'How are they organised? I mean, how do you know when and where to go?'

'WhatsApp,' said Jacko.

'Hand your phone over,' said Greg, holding out his hand.

'Here,' said Jacko. 'But you won't find anything useful. All the WhatsApp messages are deleted.'

'Let us be the judge of that,' Greg said, handing the phone to Steve. 'See what the specialists can mine from that,' he said. 'OK, we've established you and your dog were at the meet organised by Nick Waters. And that you went there in the pickup owned by Mick O'Hanlon, registration number...' He read it out from his file.

'I don't know the number, but it sounds right,' agreed Jacko.

'OK. Let's move on to the fire at the same farm a few days later. How were you involved in that?'

Jacko looked aghast. 'I wasn't,' he said. 'I know nuffin about that. You can't pin that on me. I was...' He hesitated.

'You were going to tell us your alibi,' said Steve. 'Where were you on the night of the second of July?'

'No comment,' said Jacko, and refused to be budged from that.

With the interview suspended, Greg and Steve had a quick word out in the corridor.

'I believe him about the fire,' said Steve. 'That sounded genuine.'

'I agree,' said Greg. 'But his reluctance to say where he was, suggests he was up to something else that night. Zip that phone to the forensic wizards and see what they can find.'

***

In Ormesby, Jill was comparing notes with Jenny.

'That bungalow,' said Jenny, nodding over her shoulder, 'is definitely where Turbo indicated something of interest. But the resident was *not* helpful. She said she was shielding and refused to engage at all – just said she hadn't seen any children. I don't think knocking on her door is going to get us anywhere, without more information.'

'OK, but I think we should at least try,' said Jill. 'I'll give her a go, you get back to base and see what you can dig up on that address. Who lives there, for how long, who's registered to vote – that sort of thing. Don't spend too much time on it. Just a quick check will do.'

'On it,' said Jenny, and headed for her car.

Jill knocked on the door of the white bungalow near the village garage. After several minutes of knocking and no answer, she turned round, surveying the small front garden and the boat on its trailer in the drive. She walked across to the boat, and balancing carefully on the low wall beside it, peered in through the Perspex windows of the canopy. Shading her eyes against reflections and distortions, she could see nothing more than some fitted seating and a central housing, presumably the engine compartment.

A voice hailed her so suddenly she nearly fell off the wall, but she turned round to see a woman standing by the back door of the bungalow.

'What you doing messing with my boat?' the woman demanded. Then as Jill approached with her warrant card held out in front of her, she retreated into her porch and half closed the door behind her. 'I'm shielding,' she said. 'Go away.'

'I'm Detective Sergeant Jill Hayes, and I'm investigating the missing children case,' said Jill loudly and clearly. 'They were spotted near here, and I just wanted to ask if you had seen anything that might be helpful.'

'No. I already told one of your lot that I haven't seen any children,' said the woman.

'And your name is...?' asked Jill

'Joanne Hamilton.'

'Well, perhaps I could have a look in your outbuildings, Ms Hamilton, just to make sure they haven't been in there.'

'They haven't, and I told you, I'm shielding.'

'OK, I understand that,' said Jill, 'but I'm not asking to come into your house. Just to check your garage and any sheds.'

The woman seemed to think for a moment, then shrugged her shoulders. 'OK. I suppose so, if you must,' she said. 'But you won't find anything.'

'Thank you,' said Jill. 'Then I won't disturb you further ... if you could just open your garage door for me?'

It was the work of moments to check the garage, which contained only a chest freezer, a washer dryer and an elderly Ford Fiesta. She took a look in the freezer but, apart from learning that the lady had a preference for ready meals and bacon, she found nothing of interest. The other outbuildings consisted of a small shed and a dilapidated summerhouse. Both were empty of anything except garden furniture and garden tools. She waved to Ms Hamilton as she left the property, and went back to the police gazebo in the garage car park.

'Any luck, Bill?' she asked, taking the seat nearest him.

'A little,' he replied. 'One man, living in what used to be the old pub over there, thinks he saw them get off the bus. He says the view from his window is limited, so he just saw them get off the bus and head off toward the centre of the village. So nothing new but it does support what the bus driver said and the times fit.

'One lady dog walker thinks she may have seen them later in the day, over toward the doctor's surgery, but she's a bit vague. She's sure she saw two children, but she doesn't know if it was them and she's not very sure of the date either.

'And one cyclist, out for his exercise, says he thinks he pedalled past two children matching their description in the early evening, walking down that road toward where we're sitting here.'

Jill's interest sharpened. 'That fits with what the man in the garage says he saw. I think we should concentrate our efforts on the houses around here. Let's try a door-to-door again, but be sensitive to people's concerns about infection. If they say they're shielding then we only talk to them outside, and if we are invited in, it's masks on and keep your distance.'

'Shielding is the perfect excuse to keep us from seeing anything we shouldn't,' complained Bill.

'I know. But we don't have nearly enough to justify a search warrant, so it's all we can do at present. Thanks, Bill. I think we can pack up here. We might still get some useful calls. Our visibility here today and our online presence might spark more memories but, for now, let's concentrate our available manpower on that house-to-house.'

14

April 2018 – Ormesby

Pulling up outside the white bungalow she'd had described to her but not seen, Joanne stretched and yawned, tired from the long drive east in an unfamiliar car. It was just after half past eight and the lights were on in her mother's house. She'd hoped to arrive a little earlier, but by the time they'd stopped to get supper in a McDonald's, then again for Frankie to unload some of the large coke she had unwisely allowed him to drink, her timetable was all to pot. She looked over at the passenger seat. Frankie was still asleep, but stirred when she shook him gently.

'Come on, Frankie,' she said. 'Time to wake up. We've arrived.'

'Arrived where?' he asked drowsily.

'Your grandma's. Come on.' She picked up her tote, came round to the passenger door and opened it. 'Come on, Frankie.' Then she led him, beginning to wake up, to the door at the side of the bungalow.

There was a button by the door, which she pressed and heard some Westminster Chimes ringing in the hall. Through the glass in the door, she saw more lights come on, then her mother was standing in front of her, exactly as she remembered her. Grey hair tied tightly back, glasses astride a fierce nose, scrawny throat rising from a much-washed jumper and thin lips pressed together.

'Hi, Mum,' she said. 'This is your grandson, Frankie.'

'What do you want?' her mother asked.

Joanne would have recoiled but that the response was exactly what she'd expected. While she was considering how to reply, Frankie stepped forward and held his hand out.

'Hello, Grandma,' he said. 'I'm Frankie. How are you?'

There was a tense pause, then her mother said, 'Hello, Francis. I'm very well, thank you. You'd better come in,' she said into empty air somewhere over Frankie's head, and stood aside for them to enter.

An hour later, Frankie now fast asleep on the sofa before the fire in the sitting room, a subdued conversation had established two things. That her mother, and her uncharitable views, had not changed at all. But that she would allow them to stay 'for a while'.

'But you need to keep out of sight,' she'd said. 'I know it's not the boy's fault, and he has lovely manners, I'll give you that, but there's no getting round that you've been living in sin and he's a bastard. I don't want that getting all over the village.'

On the back foot, and with few other options, Joanne had bitten her lip on everything she'd wanted to say and settled for a bitter 'Thank you.'

15

29–31 July 2020

His plans in place, his reconnoitre complete, all Nick had to do was contact his outlet. He messaged via WhatsApp.

2 days from now. 1 Range Rover, 1 Kawasaki Mule The reply was swift.

Yes. ///Juniors.Twin.Flamingo 04.30 01/08

He rang his brother. 'We're on,' he said. 'Meet me on the A11, midnight Friday. You'll be picking up a Range Rover and a farm buggy.'

'On the A11?' asked Ade incredulously.

'Don't be daft,' replied Nick. 'I'll take you to the location and help you load the items, then you bugger off to where I tell you, and I'll see to it there's no comeback.'

Over in Wymondham, a forensic digital expert was startled to see a new WhatsApp message bounce onto the phone he'd been examining.

///Juniors.Twin.Flamingo 04.30 01/08

He put it to one side while he finished his report, then a synapse clicked in his subconscious, and he flicked screens on his iPad to the *what3words* app. He picked up the phone to his boss.

Ned rang Jim moments later. 'One of my bright lads has picked up something on Jacko Green's phone,' he said. 'He thinks it looks like a *what3words* location, plus a time and date. Given Green's history of twocking and the proximity to Felixstowe, he thought it might be a rendezvous. I agree with him.'

Jim jotted the message down in a hurry. 'Brilliant. I'll pass it on to Suffolk,' he said. 'Any idea of the origin?'

'No. It's encrypted,' replied Ned.

Jim picked up the phone to ring Suffolk. With luck, they'd nab the team of car thieves that had been plaguing East Anglia. Worth a try, anyway.

By Friday, Nick was so hyped he could barely sit still. Even Cissy noticed, and her repeated enquiries as to what was wrong with him eventually provoked him into giving her a slap. The resulting crying and moaning annoyed him even more, to the point where he thought he'd better make himself scarce before he did something he'd regret.

He took himself down to his lock-up to make sure he'd got everything he'd need. Then he poured petrol into the wine bottles he'd lifted from next door's green bin, added cotton wicks and pushed corks roughly into the necks to hold them in place. He loaded the second petrol can into his pickup and wondered what else to do while he waited. He checked he'd got his lighter and a box of matches, once, twice, multiple times, then started flicking through images on his phone.

At last, it was time to make a move. The phone's battery was nearly flat by now, so he plugged it into the socket in the pickup, locked the garage and drove off.

Arriving at his destination a little early, he drove past and parked unobtrusively a mile or two up the road. The big smart farmyard he'd originally spotted from the A11 was laid out on the top of the hill. Three big grain stores surrounded an open yard. The farmhouse and what he assumed to be staff accommodation were some distance away on the other side of a belt of trees. Even at this time of night he could hear the humming of machinery which he assumed to be the cooling fans on the stores. Maybe that was why they were built some distance from the houses. They were certainly noisy.

The full-height doors on the big machinery store were open. If his informant was right, the shed would be nearly empty, as the combine and other harvest equipment was busy at work in Breckland. And so would be the farmworkers.

Checking his watch, he drove back down the hill and parked just one field away from the yard, his pickup invisible from the road, behind a tall hedge. Then he set off on foot to the machinery store. Moving as quietly as he could, even though he was pretty sure the yard was deserted, he pulled his balaclava over his face in case of CCTV and slipped into the store. Exactly as he hoped, the Range Rover and the Kawasaki buggy that were his targets for today were parked in the far corner. To his delighted surprise, the buggy was resting on a trailer. That was going to make his task even easier. It was the work of moments to start the Range Rover with the piece of digital kit that had cost him a pretty penny on the dark web. It took very few more to hitch it to the trailer. He was just about to drive it out of the shed when headlights and the sound of an HGV engine alerted him to the arrival of a grain lorry. For a moment he froze in the driving seat, then slid to the floor and lurked below the windows, ready to make run for it.

The grain lorry drove past the front of the machinery shed, then swung round and reversed up to the pit in front of the nearest grain store. There was a lot more noise as it tipped its load into the pit, then the driver secured the back of his lorry and walked into a small cabin at the front of the grain store before emerging a few moments later and climbing back into his cab. The lorry drove off again, and Nick resumed breathing. He realised, first, that regular deliveries of the harvested grain were likely, and second, that his best chance of getting away unseen was now, before the next delivery arrived. He got back into the Range Rover and drove it and the trailer out the store, across the yard and down the next field, arriving at the hedge where his pickup was parked.

As far as Nick could see, no one up at the yard noticed him drive off, and there'd been no cries of rage that suggested their losses had been noticed. Time for the bit he'd been looking forward to.

He picked up the can of petrol in one hand, the box of bottles with the other, and set off back up the field. The latest grain lorry was tipping at the same pit as before, so Nick hung back behind the nearest grain store until it drove off, exactly as the first had done.

It was the work of just a few moments to sluice petrol from the can into the pit still full of newly harvested barley, and then around the walls of the store. He saved some to leave a trail across the yard into the machinery store, then placed five of his bottles strategically around the store. The sixth he kept.

Standing in the yard, near his petrol trail, he took a last look round. This was the bit he enjoyed, nearly as much as that orgasmic moment when the flames leaped into the sky. The anticipation!

He bent down and lit the petrol trail with his lighter. As the flame danced across the yard, he also lit the wick in the bottle he still held and hurled it into the machinery shed. Then he ran for it.

Exactly as he had at the farm near Downham Market, he paused on the edge of the yard, in the shade of the rustling trees, to admire his handiwork.

He heard at least two separate explosions as the flames reached his Molotov cocktails, then the remaining bottles merged into one satisfying bang, and he thought he'd better move a little further away before too much attention was attracted to the fire. He was trotting down the field, still glancing over his shoulder to admire his handiwork, when an almighty blast and a wall of hot air knocked him off his feet.

16

April 2018 – Ormesby, a few days later

Joanne had assumed that when her mother said *keep out of sight*, she meant *keep a low profile*. She should have known that her mother always said exactly what she meant. She surveyed the cellar room with disbelief when her mother told her that was where she and Frankie would be living.

'You can't be serious,' she'd said. 'There's no light, no air; it'll be damp.'

'It's not damp,' her mother snapped. 'There's light... Don't be stupid, I'm not going to keep you in the dark.' And she flicked the light switch to demonstrate. 'There's room for a bathroom in the corner, and there's water there already.' She pointed to an old sink by the washing machine. 'If you give me a hand, we can move the single bed down from the spare room, and I've got a camp bed in the garage that'll do for Francis. I'll even get you a TV,' she said – like it was the ultimate concession. 'You can come up to the sitting room in the evening,' she added, 'if Francis is good.'

'But Frankie needs room to play. And he needs to go to school.'

'That's what I'm offering,' her mother said. 'Take it or leave it. It's no skin off my nose if you want to go. I didn't invite you in the first place. This way, you get somewhere to stay, I keep my life, and there's no gossip.'

Joanne reflected on the unpaid rent she'd run out on, the unpaid electricity bill, the debts probably already in the hands of bailiffs, and looked again at the basement room. It was a no-brainer.

'OK,' she said. 'We'll give it a try, for a bit. Just until I get a job and can afford somewhere to live.'

'Some gratitude would be good,' her witch of a mother said, and Joanne had forced another unwilling 'Thank you' through stiff lips.

17

1 August 2020 – early hours

When Nick came to, he had no idea where he was, what had just happened, or how much time had passed. Sound arrived more slowly than sight. Gradually what he could see, dark skies and a glow reflected in the clouds, was augmented by a roaring sound behind him. Slowly and painfully, he turned over onto his stomach and raised his head to stare back the way he had come. His vision seemed blurred but cleared slowly as he blinked, to reveal a flickering glow illuminating the broken walls of a shattered grain store.

As he stared, he realised the vibration on his hip was coming from his mobile phone. Clumsily he pulled it out and looked at the screen. It was Ade. He held it to his ear, still not entirely sure what had happened.

'I'm waiting where you said,' his brother announced rather irritably. 'Where are you and what's going on?'

Where he was and what was going on suddenly came back to Nick like a tide coming in.

'OK. Slight delay,' he said. 'No problem, but can you meet me at *what3words*...' He gave Ade the current location of his pickup and the Range Rover.

'OK,' said Ade. 'Whoa, hang on, are you sure it's OK? A couple of fire engines have just gone past me.'

'It's OK,' said Nick. 'They'll be too busy to bother with us.'

That was a slight exaggeration, but he thought the chances of them noticing two dark vehicles several fields away, with all they had to deal with at the farm, were slight to non-existent.

He struggled to his feet and set off down the field, stumbling over the rough grass in the darkness which his shadow cast in front of him, but not daring to get out his torch. The glow behind him was augmented by blue flashing lights by the time he reached his pickup. Turning to look back, he saw more blue lights arriving, the later ones apparently belonging to police cars.

'Time to get out of here,' he muttered to himself just as Ade drew up in the road the other side of the hedge. Rather than shout, he had recourse again to his phone.

'Ade, I'm just the other side this hedge. Lower your ramp and I'll bring the goods round to you.'

Under cover of the noise from the blaze and the efforts of the fire service, he started the Range Rover's engine and drove it to the field entrance and onto the road just behind Ade, the trailer towed behind.

Ade cast his eye over the combination. 'Range Rover on my transporter first, and I'll tow the buggy on the trailer if I can't get both on board.'

Nick let Ade drive the Range Rover onto the flatbed, then looked at the space left. 'If you squeeze it up a bit, I think they'll both go on.'

Ade paused in strapping the car down. 'OK, you bring it up,' he said.

Heart in his mouth, as this wasn't a task he was familiar with and his head was still buzzing from the blast, Nick drove the buggy onto the ramp. The tracks were not an ideal width apart, and he inched slowly up, hoping for the best.

'Watch out,' Ade said sharply as the buggy started to tip.

Nick corrected his direction. For a moment it hung in the balance then, between them, the two men got it onto the flatbed. Ade secured it behind the car and jumped off to raise the ramp.

'I'm out of here, Nick, and so should you be,' he said.

'You know where you're going?'

'Yes.'

Nick waited while Ade drove off, then got into his pickup. His head ached and his vision, especially in his right eye, seemed blurred. He rubbed it, then remembered Ade's final comment and drove out of the field toward the A11. Just as he rejoined the dual carriageway heading north, he was passed by two more police cars, blue lights flashing. They took the turning toward Leyton Estate Farm.

***

Some miles further south, Ade was driving steadily toward his rendezvous near Felixstowe, muttering under his breath and swearing he would never, ever, let Nick involve him in another carry-on like this. Gradually, as his distance from the burning buildings increased and his heart rate slowed to something more normal, he started to feel hungry and thirsty.

Stress, he thought. He checked the time and, reckoning he was making good progress, decided to take a short break. On the outskirts of Thetford, he stopped at an all-night McDonald's and bought a large, sweet coffee and a Big Mac meal. The coffee was too hot to drink straight away, so he parked it in the cup-holder, scoffed the burger and chips, then resumed his trip to Felixstowe.

Around an hour later he pulled up in a lay-by some miles outside a village, and turned his engine off. He got out of the cab for a pee, then checked his phone to make sure he was in the correct location. He was, but he was also alone. He could neither see, nor hear, any other vehicle. He was, however, clearly visible against the skyline to the two men who were waiting down the road. They nodded to each other, then started up their curtain-sided lorry to drive it to the rendezvous.

They pulled up just past Ade, and both got out of the cab. Ade couldn't help but notice that they walked like two very heavily muscled men – somewhere between a swagger and a waddle. That was all he could see, as they were dressed in dark clothes and pulled black balaclavas over their faces as they came toward him.

He started to open his cab door, but the first of the men slammed it shut again. 'Lower the ramp and stay put,' he said. Ade had no intention of arguing.

The two men walked round to the back and glanced over his load. One of them reappeared at the driver's window. 'Keys,' he said, and snapped his fingers. Ade handed the buggy keys over, then in response to a gesture, wound the window back up and stared fixedly in front of him.

Before long the Range Rover and the Kawasaki were unloaded and driven round to the lorry.

'You can go,' said one of the dark-clothed men, and waved him off. Ade put his transporter in gear and drove away. It was some time before his heart stopped pounding.

18

May 2018 – Ormesby

Job hunting was difficult with no car and no home address. Joanne had returned the hire car to a local branch the day after they arrived in Norfolk. Much as she would have liked to keep it, it was an expense she couldn't afford. Restricted to bus travel and an ever-diminishing pot of cash for bus fares, Joanne had hunted for a job, any sort of job, in the village, in Caister, but no further afield than Great Yarmouth. She'd rapidly had to revise her ideas downward from office job, through shop assistant, to care worker, and only narrowly avoided what she felt to be the bottom of the pile: veg picking.

Working in a care home in Caister was poorly paid and the hours were long, but at least she had some money in her pocket now and she could look around for something that suited her better. Her main worry was leaving Frankie on his own, but as luck would have it, her mother seemed to be developing a little warmth for him. To describe it as affection was perhaps going too far, but she liked his manners and also his enthusiasm for reading. Now, when Joanne got home, she often found him curled up on a corner of the sofa, a book from her mother's extensive collection in his hands. Admittedly the curtains were all drawn so no one could see in and wonder why old Mrs Hamilton had a young visitor, but at least it was better than finding him alone in the basement.

A few days later, when she went to make a sandwich for Frankie's lunch as she normally did, her mother pushed her aside.

'I'll give Francis his lunch,' she said. 'He eats too many sandwiches. He's getting pasty-faced.'

Joanne had opened her mouth to point out that if Frankie was getting 'pasty-faced' it was because of a lack of fresh air and sunlight but thought the better of it and managed a grudging thank you. Perhaps if Frankie continued to charm her mother like this, things would improve. And when she got a better job, she would move them both out and never speak to her mother again.

When she got home that evening, she asked Frankie how he'd enjoyed his lunch.

He pulled a face. 'Salad,' he said. 'With corned beef and bread and butter. But I did say thank you, like you said,' he reassured her.

The salad theme continued that whole week, with, occasionally, added fruit. Joanne had to concede, in the face of Frankie's complaints, that her mother did seem to be trying her best.

Then came the day she got home and Frankie wasn't in his usual corner of the sofa.

'Where's Frankie,' she asked, her coat half off, half on.

'Downstairs,' her mother said. 'He seemed a bit off colour after lunch, so I told him to go and have a lie-down.'

'What do you mean, a bit off colour?' Joanne asked, heading for the door to the stairs down to the basement.

'Wheezing,' her mother replied. 'You didn't tell me he was asthmatic!'

'He isn't,' said Joanne, wrenching the door open and heading down the stairs. As she took in the silence, she was relieved that she couldn't hear any wheezing. Then she saw Frankie, lying across the bed.

19

31 July 2020

Jill was disappointed with the resources allotted to the house-to-house, but there was no arguing with the combined exigencies of budget and Covid-related sick leave, so two uniformed constables, Bill, and herself were all she had. She decided to start at the village centre, near the garage, and work outwards, on the assumption that the possible sighting of the two children by the garage hand was genuine. She allocated the white bungalow with the boat on the drive to herself, since she'd already spoken to the occupier, Joanne Hamilton, as recorded in her notes. However, despite repeated knocking and ringing of the doorbell, she couldn't get an answer at that property and moved on to the next.

This householder was up and about, and more than happy to chat.

'I'd ask you in, but I'm not sure we're supposed to,' said the lady in jeans and jumper and with wild curly hair dyed an unrealistic red. 'These rules are so confusing, aren't they. How about I bring you coffee in the garden?' She gestured to the small back lawn bearing a table and two chairs. 'Bryce has gone for his morning bike ride, but I expect he'll be back soon. I'm Anne,' she added belatedly.

Jill accepted the offer of coffee and went to sit on one of the chairs, which, as she soon discovered, was a little damp from the morning dew.

'You're here about those children, I imagine,' said her hostess as she returned with a tray laden with coffee mugs, milk, sugar and biscuits. She put it down on the table with a sigh, then sank into the other chair. 'Oh dear, it's a bit wet, isn't it,' she said, fidgeting. 'Not to worry, we won't dissolve.'

Jill, aware of the damp seeping through her trousers, agreed politely that the chances of dissolution were slight.

'I realise you may have answered these questions before, but there seems to have been a sighting of the children near here later on the evening of the twenty-seventh of March. Do you remember what you were doing that evening?'

'Given we were in lockdown, probably watching the depressing news and eating supper,' replied Anne. 'Which is pretty much what we did every evening, except when we were outside clapping the NHS.'

'Did you see anything of the children back in March, or have you seen them at any time since?' asked Jill.

'No, and no,' said Anne. 'I'm sorry, I'm not being much use, am I? I doubt Bryce will be any help either. He tends not to notice anything that doesn't have an engine.'

'What can you tell me about your neighbour?' asked Jill, changing tack. 'I mean the one in the bungalow on the corner.' Seeing the expression of surprise on Anne's face, she added hastily, 'Nothing sinister, it's just that I haven't been able to talk to her this morning and the last time I saw her, from a distance, she said she was shielding.'

Anne opened her mouth to answer but was interrupted by the arrival of a burly man in ill-judged Lycra, on his bike.

'Oh, here's Bryce. You might as well talk to us both at once now. I'll just get you a coffee, luv,' she said to the slightly sweaty Bryce, approaching the table and removing his bike helmet as he did so.

'Detective Sergeant Hayes,' said Jill. 'We're doing a house-to-house, asking if anyone spotted the two missing Mirren children back in March. Or any time since, for that matter. I'm sure you saw us this week in front of the garage, and you'll probably have seen the case reported on the news too.'

'I saw you, yes, as I pedalled by,' replied Bryce. 'Hang on, I'll just fetch another chair.' He went over to the garden shed and reappeared with a third chair, which he plonked down by the table.

'Keep your distance, Bryce,' said his wife automatically. Judging from his reaction, it was a routine reminder.

'As I was saying, I'm afraid I can't help. I haven't seen the children at all.'

'She was just asking about her next door,' Anne commented, putting another mug of coffee on the table. 'How she can't get a word with her and that she's shielding.'

'No surprise there then,' said Bryce. 'I'd say she's been shielding for the last couple of years. We never see sight nor sound of her. And I don't think she's an early riser either.'

'That's what I was about to say,' said his wife. 'Curtains drawn till all hours round there.'

'Probably on account of her midnight gardening,' remarked Bryce, somewhat undermining his claim to never see her. He took a gulp of his coffee. 'Wow, that's a bit hot,' he said, spluttering slightly and put the mug down again.

'What do you mean, "midnight gardening"?' asked Jill, her antennae on full alert.

'Not recently,' said Bryce, 'but a year or two ago, she went through a phase of digging her garden at night. You can see through the hedge from our bathroom window. A couple of times I saw her having a real good dig in her back garden late at night. I concluded she was a poor sleeper, and it was her way of settling down. If I could've had a word, I'd have offered up our garden for her efforts,' he added with a laugh, 'but I haven't seen her to speak to for at least two years.'

Jill settled back in her seat. If it was that long ago, it couldn't have anything to do with the Mirren children. Perhaps she *was* just a poor sleeper.

'I will say, she digs like a good 'un, for her age that is. I hope I'm as fit when I'm that old.'

'How old is she?' asked Jill, thinking that the woman she'd seen in the doorway had, if anything, looked ageless.

'Must be pushing seventy if she's a day,' said Bryce, and his wife agreed.

'I'd say around that too,' she said. 'She's been a pensioner all the time we've lived here, and that's been at least eight years.'

'And always reclusive?' asked Jill.

'Always,' they affirmed in chorus.

'Well, I'll try there again later in the day,' said Jill, rising from her damp chair. 'Thank you for the coffee.'

***

On the phone in his office, Jim wasn't faring much better. Now on his second day of attempting to speak to an opposite number in Suffolk, he was back on hold while yet another 'I'll see what I can do' merchant disappeared for a lengthy period. After ten minutes he gave up and rang Chris on her mobile.

'Sorry, Chris,' he said. 'I know this isn't protocol, but I'm having real trouble contacting anyone in your neck of the woods to respond to an important tip-off. Can you help?'

Judging from the background noise, Chris was driving. There was a pause, then she said, 'Sorry, Jim, I'm just trying to think who would be the best bet. I know we're a bit thin on the ground at the moment, both in CID and in uniform. Between people isolating and people actually ill, finding anyone is a bit of a bummer at present.'

'So I've just discovered,' he replied. 'Thing is, we've got some intelligence that points to something going off in a very precise location near Felixstowe in the early hours of Saturday morning. Could be linked to hare coursing, but the timing looks wrong for that. If it was on our patch, I'd be checking it out, but as it's not...' He left the thought hanging.

'Try talking to DI Richards. I know he's on duty, but I think he is pretty hard-pressed. That's the best I can do.'

'Thanks, Chris. Will do. You OK?'

'Fine, thanks,' she said. 'Just worried about one or two of my domestic cases that lockdown didn't help, but you know how it is.'

Jim rang off and tried DI Richards. At least this time he got through, but he struggled to get much engagement.

'So, in short, you picked this intel off a suspect's WhatsApp messages, you don't know what it relates to, and all you have is a date, location and time.'

Put like that, Jim had to agree it sounded thin. The trouble was, it was hard to articulate instinct without sounding like a wally, and instinct was what was telling him this was worth checking out.

'Thank you for passing it on,' said DI Richards. 'If I've got a team anywhere near there on Saturday morning, we'll check it out. But you know how it is.'

Again, Jim agreed he knew how it was, and rang off with the certainty that nothing would be done.

***

At the end of the day, Jill ran a check round all her small team to assess what they'd learned. As she reported to Greg, it wouldn't take a big piece of paper to summarise it all.

'Only one thing,' she said. 'I'm still not one hundred per cent happy about the resident in the bungalow with a boat. There's something not right there, but I can't put my finger on it. She still denies seeing the children, but so does almost everyone else in the area, so that's not it. She still won't let me over the threshold, but she maintains she's shielding, and her neighbours say she's a recluse at the best of times, so possibly that's not a great surprise.

'I did start to get excited when her neighbours said she'd been spotted digging in her garden at night, but it was a couple of years ago so, while odd, it can't have anything to do with the Mirren children.

'All we've got, really, apart from the itch between my shoulder blades, is the half-hearted signal Turbo gave near the boat. And that's not enough for a warrant, is it?'

'Nowhere near,' said Greg. 'OK, wind up the house-to-house, and we'll have a rethink.' He knew that feeling between the shoulder blades, and respected Jill's instinct. 'One other thought,' he added. 'You could try a chat with the local surgery and see what they can tell you about – what's her name now?'

'Mrs Joanne Hamilton,' supplied Jill.

'Mrs Hamilton. Explain that she says she's shielding, and that while you obviously don't want to put her at risk, you would really like a proper chat with her. You know how to put it.'

'Will do,' said Jill. 'Although the likelihood is, they'll just stand on medical confidentiality and give me the brush-off.'

'Worth a try,' said Greg, and turned back to his paperwork with a sigh. He was due a day off tomorrow, and it couldn't come soon enough!

20

May 2018 – Ormesby

Frankie's face was congested. His lips were swollen and, when she took up his hand, she realised his fingers were too. Then she took in the cold and screamed. When her mother rushed downstairs, Joanne was rocking Frankie in her arms and keening.

As soon as her mother came into view, a flash of pure rage filled Joanne to bursting point.

'Look what you've done, just look. He's dead. You evil old bat, he's dead and you left him to die alone.'

Gently Joanne put Frankie back on the bed and stood up. She felt seven feet tall, and still growing as the anger swelled inside her. Her mother backed off until she was hard up against the stairs. As her heels met the first step, she sat down abruptly. Her face was white, the lines either side her nose even deeper than normal.

'I didn't do anything,' she said. 'I didn't. I gave him his lunch as usual, crab salad, then he didn't feel very well so he came down here to rest. How was I to know he was asthmatic? You hadn't said anything. I didn't do anything. I liked Francis. He was a good boy. I didn't—'

By now eight feet tall, judging by how she loomed over the wizened old woman on the stairs, and unable to bear any more chatter from the evil witch, Joanne seized her by the throat and shook her like a terrier shakes a rat.

'Crab! Allergic reaction!' were a few of the words she managed to choke out through the black mist that filled her sight.

When the mist cleared and she'd shrunk back to her normal size, her mother was lying broken on the stairs, livid red finger marks on her throat and blood leaking from her ears.

21

---

30 July 2020 – Norfolk police HQ

Greg stood in his usual place by the whiteboard and surveyed his team, spread around the unusually draughty ops room, papers fluttering in the breeze from all the open windows.

'First of all,' he said, 'can I just say how great it is to see you all in person. Zooms are all very well, but they're a poor substitute for a proper team meeting.' There were nods all round the room. 'However,' he went on, 'don't get too used to it, because this will clearly be the exception rather than the rule, until this pandemic runs its course...'

'Or they get a vaccine out,' added Bill.

'Quite,' said Greg. 'But until then, we're stuck with working under constraints, and I know it's not easy, believe me. Now, let's not waste this valuable time together. We have two cases to consider and at least one of them seems to be linked to other crimes locally. Jim, let's take you first with the arson and hare-coursing incidents.'

Jim stood up in the corner by the window. 'At least I won't be mouthing at you silently this time,' he said. 'In summary, Mr Wyatt of Welsh Farm, near Downham Market, reported a hare-coursing incident on the evening of the twenty-eighth of June. He had been successful in scaring his unwelcome visitors away and uniform attended swiftly enough to catch a grey lurcher, but no human participants. On the second of July, on the same farm, a barn was burned down with loss of some valuable farm machinery and stores. This was arson.

'Fingerprints and DNA taken from the collar of the lurcher indicated involvement of one Jacko Green. At interview he admitted to being present at the hare coursing, which he says was organised by Nick Waters, and he travelled there with a Mick O'Hanlon. All three are known to us: Jacko for twocking, Hanlon for generalised violence and theft – albeit he hasn't yet been convicted on any count thanks to alibis provided by his travelling neighbours – and Waters for handling stolen goods. Jacko denies being present on the occasion of the arson attack, but has refused to explain where he was that night. That's where we stand at present, pending any further forensic evidence and a chat with Messrs Hanlon and Waters.'

Ned waved a hand. 'And then there's the data from Jacko's phone,' he said. 'He's in various WhatsApp groups, at least two with Nick Waters, so that's another link. Unfortunately, the messages have been deleted and can't be recovered, so we don't know what they were chatting about or, in most cases, when. However, as luck would have it, we do have one message that arrived while we were researching the phone. It was from someone labelled X-RayDelta and read as follows: *Yes. ///Juniors.Twin.Flamingo 04.30 01/08.*

'Thanks, Ned,' said Jim. 'Sorry, I should have mentioned that. We think it's a rendezvous for something, but it's out of our patch so I've been trying to pass it on to Suffolk. Without much luck so far.'

'Thanks, Jim and Ned. OK! Next steps on this case,' said Greg. 'Jim, get Waters and O'Hanlon in, and we'll interview them both. Steve, do some checking. See if you can identify any crime reports for the second of July. If Jacko is refusing to say where he was that evening, it may be because he was up to no good. Also, see what you can find on any known associates other than Waters and O'Hanlon.

'Now, Jill, would you like to report on the Mirren case?'

Jim sat down, and over on the other side of the room, Jill stood up. Everyone turned their heads as though at a tennis match.

'A little more information as a result of the outdoor evidence event in Ormesby,' she said. 'Mainly thanks to Bill's efforts in waylaying all passers-by.' Bill took a mock bow but was clearly pleased to be thanked.

'First, confirmation that the two children did definitely get off that bus in the early morning of the twenty-seventh of March and bought some stuff in the garage. Since then, we have some reasonable sightings back in the same area in the evening of the same day. They wouldn't stand up in court, but they come from two different witnesses, and I'm inclined to believe them. I've just initiated a further door-to-door in the immediate vicinity of the garage, to see what we can flush out.

'Next, last thing before we packed up the gazebo, Bill stopped a dog walker and they said they'd seen two children matching the Mirrens' description in Braeburn Drive around early afternoon that day. It's the street that Tim Simmons lives on and where he would have been if he hadn't been in hospital recovering from the attack by the children's father. It reinforces the idea that they were looking for their mother and her boyfriend.'

Jill sat down. Greg turned round from adding to the whiteboard summary. 'Anything from the facial recognition software?' he asked.

'Not so far.'

Ned interrupted. 'Last update I had,' he said, 'it had more or less completed reviewing old data and hadn't found anything. Once it's gone through the more recent stuff, we'll be done.'

'OK,' said Greg. 'It was a good idea, but I must admit my hopes are fading. OK, Jill, what's the focus for the door-to-door?'

'Mainly, to take people back over what we now suspect was the children's route later in that day – especially the possible sighting near the garage. Did they see anything? What were they doing that evening? Have they checked outbuildings, etc, and can we do another check? I'm hoping for something that might justify a closer look by Ned's team.'

'Especially as that was where Turbo gave me a sort of alert,' chipped in Jenny.

'Trouble is, it's all a bit *sort of*,' said Greg. 'Don't get me wrong, Jill. I don't disagree with what you're doing, but we're really going to struggle to get a warrant for any sort of detailed search unless we have something more concrete. Especially with people using the "shielding" excuse.

'OK. We all know what we need to do. Let's get on with it, and stay safe everyone. Distance, masks and handwashing are still the order of the day!'

***

Thirty-five miles east-northeast of police HQ and a few feet underground, Karen and Jake were both bored. Karen and Jake were therefore squabbling. It had started with an argument over what they watched on TV, progressed to a tug of war over the remote control, and ended with an all-out fight. Jake adopted his preferred windmill approach to a physical tussle: arms rotating and fists flying. Karen responded with her scientific two punches to the biceps, then laughed scornfully when Jake sat down in tears, literally dis-armed.

'You never learn, do you,' she taunted him. 'Stupid!'

'Not!' said Jake through tears. 'You're bigger'n me. S'not fair. I'll tell Aunty Jo on you.'

'Tell away,' said Karen. 'See if I care.'

'Tell me what?' said a voice from the top of the stairs. 'Let's have less row or it'll be no lunch for you. And if you carry on, no supper either.'

The door slammed to behind her so hard it didn't latch properly. Karen was quick to notice. She waited in silence for Aunty Jo to reappear and lock the door properly, but there was no sign of her. She waited some more. Still nothing.

'Jake, shut up a minute,' she said over his whining. 'The door's open.'

'So what,' he snivelled.

'So, we can go out. Go outside and maybe find Tim,' she said.

'I don't want to go outside. I don't want to go,' he said, sounding astonished that she would feel differently. 'I don't like it out there. It's dark and cold, and people catch things and die.'

Karen took no notice. She was putting a few clothes into the bag she'd arrived with. It was a bit tattered, but it would do. She pulled the old iPad from its hiding place, checked its battery – nearly full – and pushed that too into the bag. Then she started up the steps. 'Come on, Jake,' she said. 'Hurry up.'

'Not coming,' he said. 'Told you, I don't want to.'

'Look.' She came back down the steps and crouched down to him. 'I'm sorry I called you stupid. But we have to take our chance. We may not get another. Come on, Jake. Trust me.'

He pulled out of her grasp and went back to sit on the bed. 'I told you, I'm not coming,' he said. 'I think *you're* stupid. You're going to make Aunty Jo mad.'

Karen hesitated, but telling herself that she could always come back for him, or send help, she went back up the stairs and listened at the top by the partly open door. She could hear a TV or radio, and something like a washing machine. That was all. She looked back at Jake one more time, then pulled the door open a fraction more and slipped through, the bag of clothes and iPad on her back.

The door opened on the sitting room she vaguely remembered from the night they had arrived. Beyond that was a passageway, and at the end of it the door to the kitchen. That was where the noise was coming from. She tiptoed down the passage and suddenly realised the front door was on her left. It appeared to be locked, but there was a key in the hole. She was just trying to turn the key, when Jake put his head around the door from the cellar and shouted.

Aunty Jo, Aunty Jo, Karen's being naughty!

Karen froze. The radio in the kitchen suddenly fell silent and the door opened. Then a whirlwind swept her up and threw her down the cellar stairs to the room at the bottom. Back where she'd started from.

22

June 2018 – Ormesby

Thinking about it later, weeks later, Joanne concluded that she'd gone a little mad that evening. Not the killing of her mother. That was right and justified after how she'd treated her all her life and then what she'd done to Frankie. But the aftermath – that was perhaps a little deranged.

She had considered ringing for an ambulance, but *What is the point?* Frankie was dead and nothing would bring him back. And his killer had been punished. She didn't want to go to gaol for that.

Her first move had been to wrap her mother's body in bin bags, then push her into the chest freezer in the garage. That solved that, at least for now.

Frankie had been a different matter. It was hours before she could even bring herself to hide his face in the sheet she'd wrapped round him. There was no way he was going in any freezer. He deserved better.

Once darkness fell, she went out into the back garden and looked around. There was a moon so she could see clearly, but the high hedges and the loom of the garage hid her from the road and neighbours. There was a small square of lawn between the summerhouse and the heating-oil tank. She fetched a spade from the garage, and started to remove turf. By morning she had a shallow grave measuring roughly five feet by two feet, and she was shaking with exhaustion. She went indoors and turned the heating off in the basement. She noticed that the lower sides of Frankie's body were turning dark red, and the rest of his skin was grey. He didn't look like Frankie any more. More like a mannequin with Frankie's face.

As soon as it was late enough in the morning, she rang the care home and reported she was sick and wouldn't be in work for a day or two. Then she went and sat with Frankie until it was dark again.

Just before she carried him out to the garden, she realised that some of her giddiness and headache was probably down to dehydration and drank two large glasses of water as she stood at the kitchen sink. Then she went into the basement and picked her son up in her arms for the last time.

The grave was long enough but a bit narrow, so she had to lie him on his side. She buried him with one of his favourite books in his hands – *The Tiger Who Came to Tea* – then replaced the turf she had removed. The spare soil went on one of the flower beds, then she went to sit in the summerhouse. The dawn was just creeping over the hedge when she woke, and she went back into the bungalow, carrying the spade. Under the lawn, Frankie slept in peace.

23

31 July–1 August 2020 – still underground

It took some minutes before Karen could work out what had happened. She remembered making it as far as the hall and the noise of a television. Then she remembered a fall down the flight of steps, but not how it happened. When she became aware of her surroundings again, she was lying half on the floor and half on the last few steps. Her legs were higher than her head and it was uncomfortable. She started to wriggle round, stopped because it hurt in all sorts of places, then managed to roll over and pull her legs down to ground level. She turned her head and saw Jake sitting back on his heels, watching her.

'Are you all right, Karen?' he asked in a soft voice. He looked frightened, and her priorities switched from solving her problems to reassuring her little brother.

'I'm OK,' she said, and realised as she spoke that yes, she probably was. She was sore and bruised but didn't seem to have broken anything. She wriggled some more, suppressing a series of *Ow*s to avoid alarming Jake, and managed to end up sitting with her legs stretched out in front of her, her back to the last step of the stairs.

'Your head's bleeding,' said Jake in a little voice that reflected his concern. She put a hand to her forehead and brought it away with blood on the fingertips; but not a lot, she realised with a rush of relief.

'It's OK,' she said. 'It's just a scratch.'

'You should wash it,' said Jake, with memories of his mother's concern for him when he fell down and scraped his knee.

'I will in a minute,' said Karen. 'What happened?'

'You broke the rule,' said Jake with absolute certainty.

'What rule?'

'The rule that says you can't go out because of Covid,' he replied. 'You broke the rule, then you made Aunty Jo mad, then you fell down the stairs.'

'Did I?' She needed to think about that.

'Do you want a drink of water?' asked Jake. 'When people have accidents on the telly, they always have a drink of water. I could get you a drink of water.'

'Yes OK, Jake, thank you,' she said, as much to give him something to do as to quench her thirst. It wasn't a bad idea however, and after he'd brought her a glassful, spilling some of it on the way, she had a drink and decided that she'd had enough of sitting on the floor. She got up with a bit of a struggle and went to sit by the TV. The pictures flickered but the sound was off. She realised her head ached and put her hand to her forehead again. It was still bleeding a bit and she realised the blood was trickling down her neck. *I'll have to do something about that.*

'Where's the iPad?' she asked, struck by a sudden thought.

'Where you dropped it,' said Jake, and he brought it over to her unasked. It was still in the bag, and she had to dig through the contents before she could pull it out. It seemed to have survived the drop, and she heaved a sigh of relief. Perhaps it was the relief that made her careless. Sitting where she was, in front of the TV, she opened it, booted it up, and noticed something that made her very excited. She nearly said something to Jake, but caution made her hold her tongue. He might blab to Aunty Jo, and she didn't want her to know about the iPad.

Karen didn't realise that that bird had already flown. Upstairs, on her monitor, Aunty Jo could clearly see Karen holding the iPad she hadn't known they had.

'Much good that'll do you,' she muttered, well aware that there was no phone signal in the cellar and that her Wi-Fi was password-protected. Luckily, she couldn't see the screen of the iPad. Couldn't see that it was announcing an email had left the outbox.

***

Karen slept badly that night, partly from the bruises and headache, partly from excitement. Once Jake was asleep, she went to the screened corner where the toilet was and opened the iPad again. No, she hadn't imagined it. One of the emails that had been sitting in the outbox for days had left. It was now securely in the Sent folder. *How did that happen? What can I do to make the others send?* She'd tried holding the laptop up to the window over the toilet and it had never had any effect before. She realised, with a gasp she had to stifle to avoid waking Jake, that it had to be because she'd got out into the bungalow above. The iPad had been with her, and it must have got a signal and sent the message before she'd been pushed back down the steps.

So, how could she do it again? Aunty Jo wasn't going to leave the door open again; she wouldn't make that mistake twice. Revolving plans for stealing keys, or rushing the door, Karen eventually went back to sleep.

24

1 August 2020 – by the Bure

Greg was woken from a deep sleep by the rasping sound of his mobile phone simultaneously vibrating along the bedside table and ringing with, what he now felt to be, a poorly chosen ringtone. Making a note to change it soonest, he picked it up. Next to him, Chris stirred sleepily then rolled over, burying her face in the pillow.

'Geldard,' he said, then stiffened. 'I'll be there in about an hour. Alert Jim Henning and Jill Hayes. No, on second thoughts, Jill has more than enough to do on the missing children case. Jim and I will deal for now. Have you rung Ned? Good.' He rang off.

Chris pulled a tousled head from the pillow. 'Emergency?' she asked without much hope that their planned day off was going to happen.

'Fire and explosion at a farm grain store near Silfield. One casualty so far, and it's suspected arson. Could be the same chap that set light to Welsh Farm. Sounds like a similar MO. Sorry, Chris, our day off is off.'

'So I assumed,' she said, resting back on the pillow. 'Take care, and let me know how you get on. I'll get some shopping in. Apart from that, I plan to be here all day.' She was speaking to Greg's back as he headed for the shower.

'OK, thanks,' he replied.

By the time he got back, Chris was up, and in her dressing gown, and had laid out trousers, a short-sleeved shirt, and pants on the bed.

'Thought this might speed you up,' she said. 'I take it time is of the essence, as always, and I won't get back to sleep now.'

He dropped a kiss on her head as he passed. 'Thanks again,' he said, dressing swiftly. 'I'll let you know when you can expect me back.'

He picked up his phone and wallet, and clattered down the stairs, past Tally asleep on the back of the sofa with her head under her wing, and out the back door, almost tripping over Bobby on her way in. He noticed that she seemed to be carrying a small rodent of some kind and hoped it was dead. Otherwise, he'd certainly be hearing about it from Chris. In less than twenty minutes from his phone call, he was on the road and heading southeast on exceptionally quiet roads.

His phone rang again as he joined the A47. 'Hi, Jim,' he said into the hands-free. 'On your way?'

'Yup.' It was apparent Jim had his mouth full of something.

'Don't tell me your long-suffering wife got up to make you a bacon sarnie!'

'No,' said Jim. 'Toast. And I had to make it myself. Can't start the day on an empty stomach. What've you heard?'

'Just that it's arson, probably, complicated by an explosion and a death.'

'That's what they told me,' said Jim. 'I should be there in half an hour.'

'Me too.'

As it happened, Jim and Greg pulled up beside the police tape almost simultaneously. A uniformed officer checked their warrant cards and held the tape up so they could drive under.

'Park over near the fire trucks,' he advised. They did so and were greeted by the familiar voice of Commander Fisher, Fire Service Command, as they climbed into overalls and pulled gloves on.

'Here we are again,' he said, smacking his hands together.

'Ned here?' asked Greg.

'Over by the barn on your left,' he replied. 'Can't let him go further until we've got everything cooled down. But I can tell you now, I don't think it's Semtex this time. Not like the explosion on the science park.'

'Then what did cause it?' asked Greg.

'Grain dust. At this point, my guess is an arsonist, possibly the same one as last time, starting a fire with an accelerant. Probably petrol. Got more than he bargained for, because grain had very recently been tipped into the store and there was a lot of dust.'

'I knew grain dust was explosive if ignited, but I thought it needed the sort of contained environment you get in a mill,' said Greg.

'Not necessarily,' the fire chief replied. 'It all depends on the concentration of dust in the air. Anyway, that's the current theory. We'll know more about the accelerant, etc when we and your forensic team can take a closer look.'

Greg looked round at the scene of organised chaos: hoses snaking in all directions, tumbled blockwork littering the ground in front of the blown-out grain store and the debris of another building smoking on his right.

'Anywhere we *can* access?' he asked.

'As I told your man Ned, you can have free access to the perimeter and the surrounding field, but we need to carry on damping down this mess for a while.'

An altercation over at the outer tape barrier drew their attention. A well-built man in a logoed fleece had climbed out of a Range Rover and was remonstrating with the officer controlling access.

'Possibly the farmer or farm manager,' said Greg. 'I'll go and have a chat with him. Jim, can you catch up with Ned?'

'Will do,' said Jim, and he set off in the direction of the Forensic Services vehicle.

Greg checked his phone for messages as he went over to the perimeter tape. Nothing, thank goodness. The conversation between the uniformed constable and the Range Rover driver fell quiet as he approached.

'DCI Geldard,' said Greg, introducing himself. 'And you are...?'

'Hamish Grey, farm manager,' said the man. 'What the hell has happened here?'

'Just what we're trying to establish,' said Greg. 'I need to ask you a few questions and I'm sure you'll have some for me. Is there anywhere we can go for a quiet chat?'

'Come down to the farmhouse,' said the man. And he got back into his car.

Greg followed the Range Rover back to the road then round a left turn to pull up in front of a substantial house. There were lights on in many of the windows, so Greg was not surprised to be met at the door by a harassed-looking woman. She appeared to have dressed hurriedly, being somewhat oddly clad in tracksuit bottoms and an inside-out jumper pulled over something that looked distinctly like a nightie.

'What's happened?' she demanded of Hamish. 'Who are you,' she asked Greg.

'The sheds are on fire, the grain store's exploded and he's the police,' replied Hamish. Greg could only wish his staff would report as succinctly.

'Oh God,' the woman exclaimed.

'My wife, Amy,' said Hamish. 'This way.' He indicated a small office near the back door, and sat down at a desk piled high with paper and machinery manuals and rubbed his face.

'Sorry,' he said. 'We're in harvest and it's been a long few days. Now this! Take a seat,' he added. 'Oh Lord, I need to tell the lads where to take the next few loads. And perhaps I'd better stop the combine for the moment, while we figure out what to do. I imagine the stores are going to be unusable for the foreseeable?'

Greg sat down opposite Hamish. 'I'm afraid so,' he said. 'Look, I realise you've a lot on your plate, but I do need to ask a few questions. The early phase of an investigation is time critical.'

Hamish had already picked up a phone. 'Can I take five minutes to stop the combine and redirect the grain lorries?' he said. 'Then I'm yours.'

He took Greg's nod for consent, and within moments was snapping terse orders into the phone. It was well within the five minutes when he turned back to Greg.

'OK, that'll hold things for now,' he said. 'What do you want to know? What's happened?'

Ignoring the second question for the moment, Greg asked, 'Where were you this evening?'

'Up until 8pm I was driving one of our two combines over at...' He named a location unfamiliar to Greg. Seeing the lack of comprehension, Hamish walked to a map on the wall and pointed. Greg noted that it was some fifteen miles away from the farmyard. 'Then I handed over to one of the men and came back here for some supper. Around nine-thirty I went back to the field to check moisture levels. Normally we'd have to stop combining because of the dew, but tonight it was staying dry so I decided we'd keep going while we could. One of the grain lorries hadn't long since returned from tipping, and I was about to send another one over, when Amy rang to say there'd been a big bang and one of the men had rung for the fire brigade. A text arrived from the farmhand almost simultaneously saying the same thing. I told her to stay in the house and I'd be back soonest. That's about it, except I'm puzzled I haven't heard from the grain store manager. I hope he's OK.'

Greg looked up from his notes. 'I'm sorry to say that there has been a casualty,' he said. 'I know no more than that at present. I'll contact the fire service commander in a moment.

'What do you keep in the stores up the road?'

'There are three grain stores. At the moment, one contains wheat from last year, one is empty, ready for this year's harvest, and one was being filled with barley from the crop we're combining at the moment. At least, that was the position earlier this evening,' Hamish said wryly. 'The boss is really not going to be happy! The other big shed up at the yard is a machinery store. Thank God it was almost empty! The combines, chaser bin and lorries are all out working. The other Range Rover and the Kawasaki Mule are in there. And a fortune in tools as well.'

'Are you aware of having upset anyone recently?' asked Greg. When Hamish shook his head, he added, 'Hare coursers, perhaps?'

'We've seen signs of hare coursing on some of our land, but not recently,' said Hamish. 'And I've never managed to catch them at it. We routinely block all the field entrances to vehicles, and that seems to act as a deterrent.'

'Who owns the farm?' asked Greg. 'You referred to the boss not being happy.'

'It's owned by a trust, but the man I take orders from, and as far as I know the sole beneficiary of the trust, is Sir Monty Chevening-Gore. He made his money in the City, and the farms are one of many investments,' replied Hamish. 'I manage all five farms.'

'How many staff do you have?' asked Greg.

'Two foremen, one mechanic, three combine-slash-tractor drivers and two HGV drivers.'

'Is that all? asked Greg, surprised.

'That's right. We're all arable – no livestock at all – so we don't need a large staff. At this time of year we take on extra staff for harvest, including the grain store manager. He's from Romania. Comes here every summer for harvest, then goes home again. I would like to know he's OK.'

'We will need to speak to them all, but later today will do,' said Greg. 'I'll see what I can find out about the grain store manager.'

As Greg rang Jim, Hamish made a muttered excuse and left the room.

'Jim,' said Greg. 'What can you tell me about the casualty?'

'IC1 male, probably aged around forty according to the first responder that attended, who was, you'll be pleased to hear, none other than our old friend Ben Asheton! Found by the fire service, in the yard near the grain store that blew, half covered in rubble. In their opinion he was dead when they found him, and Ben concurs. Probably down to the blast but we'll have to wait on a post-mortem. He's bagged and awaiting retrieval by the mortuary team. As the fire service had already moved him, there was no point leaving him in situ.'

'Any ID?' asked Greg.

'Only that he's wearing a logoed fleece like the one the farm manager was wearing. Nothing in his pockets except a mobile phone, somewhat the worse for wear, as you can imagine. That's been handed over to Ned.'

Greg looked up as Hamish came back into the room with a couple of mugs of coffee. 'Thought this might be a good idea,' he said. 'I certainly need one.'

'I'm afraid it seems very likely that the casualty *is* one of your men and, from what you've said, probably the store manager,' Greg said. 'We'll need you to identify him later today.'

'He's dead then,' said Hamish.

'I'm afraid so.'

'I need to let Sir Monty know what's going on,' said Hamish over the rim of his coffee mug.

Greg, looking at the milky coffee in the one he'd been handed, took a polite sip then set it down. 'I'll leave you to get on with it for now,' he said. 'Thank you for your help. Just a couple of things:

'First, you need to work on the assumption the whole yard is out of bounds for now, both for safety reasons and because it's a crime scene. I'll let you know as soon as we're given access by the fire service, then I'd like you to meet me up there.

'Second, as I said, we need to talk to all your staff. Can you make them available to us, say, from 14.00 today?'

'Yes, to both,' said Hamish.

25

June 2018 – Ormesby

It was two days later when Joanne got a big shock as she walked past the mirror in the hall. She'd just decided she needed to go back to work, or to resign, one or the other, and she couldn't make her mind up which. She was heading for the kitchen and another glass of water – all she'd been able to stomach since losing Frankie – when the mirror reflected her mother.

She choked back a scream and stopped dead, her heart pounding in her throat. Slowly she reached out a hand to the mirror, and the reflection reached toward her, touching her outstretched fingers. And even more slowly, she realised that the reflection was of *her*. She moved toward the mirror and examined what she had become. Her hair, unwashed, untended and dragged back in a ponytail, seemed to have turned grey. Two new lines ran down beside her nose, and the recent starvation, or dehydration, had withered her skin. Disaster had turned her into her mother.

It was the push she needed toward a little more normality. And that meant taking a little more care of herself – starting with her diet. A quick survey of the refrigerator revealed that the milk was off, and the salad drawer was full of tired tomatoes and limp leaves. The cucumber was past resurrection and went in the bin. Joanne drank orange juice from the carton, then made black coffee, toast and marmalade, and plans.

By the end of the day she'd resigned her care job, read through all the paperwork her mother had carefully filed away – still in its envelopes – in the desk drawer, and gone through her mother's wardrobe. Blouses and jumpers had gone in the washing machine in the basement and, with a struggle, she'd brought herself to disinfect the stairs and strip the bed. Once the washing was done, she closed the door on the basement and went to sit on the sofa in the lounge, a notebook and biro in her hands.

The next day she decided she really had to do some shopping. She dressed carefully in some of her mother's clothes, pulled her hair back into the tight ponytail, then twisted it into a bun. Dressed in her mother's overcoat, she paused by the hall mirror, nodded, then picked up her mother's shopping bag and headed for the bus stop up the road.

It was still early morning, and no one seemed to take any notice of her. A reflection, she assumed, of the low profile her inherently unfriendly mother had maintained in the village. In the weeks she had been there, her mother had not been to one single village event, not church, village hall or pub. No one had called round, except the paper boy and the postman, and the latter only occasionally. These facts encouraged her to believe her deception would work. That, and her newly greyed hair.

She completed her shopping successfully in Caister's Tesco, without challenge or conversation with anyone, and returned home with bulging bags of groceries. Then she settled down with the pen and notebook again. The signature still needed some work before she could risk writing a cheque.

26

---

1 August 2020 – evening

Jim and Greg took stock at the end of the day, leaning exhaustedly on the sides of their cars as they chatted. In the background, firefighters were still rolling up hoses and generally clearing away. Ned and his team were close to completing their first search of what was left of the machinery store and no more casualties had been discovered.

'That,' as Greg had said, 'was at least *one* piece of good news.'

Greg and Jim had interviewed all the regular workforce and the two additional harvest workers. Their whereabouts during the evening had been established, which wasn't terribly difficult as all of them had been hard at work driving combines, lorries or chaser bins – roles from which it was pretty difficult to absent yourself without someone noticing, as Greg had also remarked.

'Any news on the post-mortem?' asked Jim.

'Scheduled for tomorrow,' replied Greg. 'The doc was away today and her deputy had already been called out to a suspected drowning in the Yare, so it won't happen now until first thing in the morning. It's unlikely to change anything.

Ah, here's Ned. Anything new?' he asked as Ned approached pushing the paper hood of his overalls back from his shaved head.

'Not much to report as yet,' he said. 'The fire investigator thinks the accelerant was petrol and that Molotov cocktails were used in at least two of the barns. I concur. You can still smell the petrol in places, and fragments of the bottles are scattered around sheds 2 and 3. We've taken samples from a lot of places, and I think we've got some decent fingerprints, probably mostly from the farmworkers. We'll check against the ones taken this afternoon for exclusion purposes and see where we get to. Only one thing new to report, and that's the contents of the machinery store. We can find no evidence of a Range Rover nor of a Kawasaki Mule having been stored there when the fire was set. So, either they were nicked last night, or our friend Hamish is trying to boost his insurance claim.'

Greg looked up quickly. 'Well, well,' he said. 'Word with Mr Grey, I think, Jim, then we'll be off home.'

As they arrived back at the farmhouse, Greg's phone rang. Concentrating on his parking, he was slightly distracted as he answered on his hands-free.

'Jill, can I catch up with you later? We're just about to interview the farm manager again.'

'Of course,' she said. 'It was just an update on what I've managed to dig up on Mrs Hamilton. Some of it's a bit odd, but nothing—'

'OK, thanks, Jill,' he interrupted. 'I need to go. I'll ring later. Thanks for touching base.' He rang off.

When they walked back into Hamish Grey's office he was on the phone, and two other logoed workers were occupying chairs at the small table – one of them half asleep and the other chewing on a bar of chocolate. They looked round at Greg and Jim. Greg recognised them as two of the lorry drivers, and realised, from the half of the phone conversation he could hear, that Hamish was negotiating for grain storage space elsewhere. When he put the phone down there was a tired smile on his face.

'That's OK then,' he said. 'From now on, we'll be taking grain direct from the combine to Perry's, the grain merchant at Thetford. They'll be expecting us.' The two drivers nodded and stood up to leave.

'Have you got some news for me?' Hamish asked of the two detectives.

'Not exactly,' said Greg, 'but we do need a word. May we?' He gestured at the two chairs recently vacated by the drivers, and on Hamish's nod, they sat down.

Hamish joined them. 'What's *not exactly* news?' he asked.

'Can you take me through, again, what was in the machinery store last night?' asked Greg.

'From the top,' said Hamish, 'one Range Rover, one Kawasaki Mule on a trailer, and a long list of tools and spare parts. I've started on a full inventory.' He leaned back in his chair and scrabbled around on his desk. 'Here, this is as far as I've got. It's not comprehensive yet.'

Greg took it from him and ran his eye down the page. 'The thing is,' he said, 'our forensic team tell me there's no evidence that either the Range Rover or the Kawasaki were in the building when the fire began.'

'What!' Hamish exclaimed. 'But they were definitely there when we went off to combine.'

'Do you have any evidence of that?' asked Greg. 'I'm sorry, but I have to ask.'

'Bloody cheek,' said Hamish. 'First some arse burns my buildings down, then the police accuse me of imaginary machinery! You'll be suggesting I set light to the place myself next!'

'We did consider that possibility,' said Greg, unmoved by the display of anger. 'You wouldn't be the first farmer to solve his financial difficulties with a well-timed fire. But this wasn't good timing. There's ample evidence you were elsewhere and none that we've found so far that you stand to benefit from a fire.

'So, there are a number of possibilities. Either the equipment never existed, and you thought you'd inflate your insurance claim, or it's somewhere else and the same applies regarding insurance. Or it was stolen last night. And if the latter, then it's too big a coincidence for it to have been nicked by someone else just before the fire started. Odds on it was taken by the arsonist, either as a side venture or the fire was at least partly designed as cover for the theft.

'So, have you any evidence of the presence of those two vehicles?'

Breathing slightly heavily, Hamish went to a storage rack and selected a box file. It hit the table in front of Greg with a slam, and Hamish opened it to riffle through a pile of papers. He slowly and deliberately selected two, then placed them in front of Greg.

'Proof of purchase of each,' he said. 'If you hang about a bit, I'll find the insurance docs as well, but those are on the computer and I may need my secretary to dig them out on

Monday. As to them being in the building, I suggest you ask my mechanic when he last saw them there. And we can check the CCTV to see if there're any images of them being moved around. Unfortunately the cameras were lost in the fire, but images before that, up to the point the cameras were lost, should be on record.'

'Thank you,' said Greg. 'We'll need all the CCTV footage you've got for the twenty-four hours up to the fire, as a starter at least.'

'No problem,' said Hamish, turning back to his desktop. 'But it'll be a big file. Do you want it on a memory stick?'

'Yes, please,' said Greg.

Out by the cars again, Greg handed the memory stick to Jim. 'Make sure that gets to Jill, will you,' he said.

27

---

2 August 2020

When Greg arrived in the office early Sunday morning, he wasn't surprised to find Jill there ahead of him, already scrutinising CCTV footage from the farm.

'Morning, Jill,' he said. 'I've only just realised I forgot to ring you back last night. What was it you wanted to tell me?'

'Morning, Boss,' she said, turning round from her laptop. 'It's OK. I realise you had a busy day yesterday. It was about the old lady who lives in that bungalow in Ormesby. You know, the one that won't let us in. I had a chat with the local surgery, as you suggested. They couldn't tell me anything about why she's shielding, but not because of patient confidentiality. Just that, as they hadn't seen her for over two years, they had no current knowledge of her health. They said she'd been called for routine checkups and vaccinations but never turned up nor made any appointments. All they could tell me, therefore, was that she was a woman, born in December 1950, and presumably in robust health since she never bothered them. While I was at it, I rang the local dentists as well, four or five of them actually, and none of them had her on their books either.'

'So, what's bothering you?' asked Greg. 'You said last night there was something you weren't happy about.'

'First, I think she looks young for her age. Not exactly in the first flush of youth, but not that old either. Second, if she's so fit she never sees either a doctor or a dentist, why is she shielding?'

'Could just be her age,' replied Greg, hazarding a guess. 'Not unreasonable to protect herself at that age. She's in the high-risk group.'

'Suppose so,' said Jill, but her tone made it clear she wasn't convinced. Privately determined to do some more checking, she turned back to her screens with a sigh.

Late morning, with the post-mortem report on his desk and Ned on his way in, Greg called the team, such as it was, together in the incident room. He looked round his depleted ranks with a sigh. Jill, Jim and Ned sat near the open windows, benefiting from the breeze. Steve sat opposite, drinking coffee from an enormous mug that bore the words 'I used to cough to hide the fart. Now I fart to hide the cough!'

Greg suppressed a grin and turned to Jill. 'No Bill or Jenny?' he asked.

'Bill got pinged and he's isolating,' said Jill, referring to the Covid contact warning scheme. 'It's Jenny's day off, and given the hours she's been working recently, I thought we could spare her for today. Mind you, I didn't know about Bill then,' she said ruefully.

'Still makes sense,' said Greg. 'It won't be any help if we all run ourselves into the ground. This looks like being a long haul. OK, let's review where we've got to with the two main cases.

'I've had the post-mortem report on the casualty at the farm, who has, incidentally, been identified as Andrei Popescu, the grain store manager. The cause of death is given as one, blunt force trauma, with two, a contributory factor being an underlying heart condition. The doc says he may not have been aware of the heart condition, but it certainly wouldn't have helped his body deal with the shock of the blast and the subsequent trauma resulting from him hitting the concrete yard. It seems he was in front of the grain store when it blew up, probably heading out to see what was happening in the yard. He took the full force of the blast when the grain dust ignited. So it seems likely that the death was an unintended consequence of the arson, rather than the primary object. However, we need to keep an open mind on that. In any event, I think we should treat this as a murder inquiry until we can rule anything out.

'I've informed Hamish Grey, who tells me that Popescu's wife has been notified of her husband's death. She's apparently on her way to Norfolk now. Ned, anything from you?'

'Not much yet,' said Ned, looking up from his notes. 'I'm hamstrung by lack of staff too. We put the effort into collecting samples of DNA and fingerprints, and we've got exclusionary samples from the farm team. What I don't have is the manpower to process everything quickly. I'm sorry about that.' He looked intensely frustrated, and Greg could appreciate how he felt. 'I *can* confirm that petrol was the accelerant, and that it was both flung around from a petrol can and deployed in glass bottles. We recovered shards of glass from the bottles, and a petrol can.

'I can also confirm that there is definitely no sign of either the Range Rover or the Kawasaki in the machinery store at the time of the fire.'

'I can add something on that,' interrupted Jill. 'I started on the most recent CCTV images available – those recorded shortly before the blast and fire – and worked my way back. I've got as far as up to an hour or so before the fire, and I can see what looks like someone driving the Range Rover out of the farmyard, towing something behind it which could have been the Kawasaki on a trailer. It heads out of the machinery shed, then turns away from the camera and disappears. I haven't completed my check of all the feeds, but it doesn't seem it went out of the main farm gate. I think it probably went off across the fields.'

'That's great work, Jill,' said Greg.

Jim jumped up with his phone in hand. 'I've already got uniform checking the area around the yard for signs of entry,' he said. 'I'll get them to look specifically for traces of the Range Rover and Kawasaki. If they were nicked, then either they're still around, or they've been picked up somewhere in the vicinity. Anything on the driver, Jill?'

'Not much,' she said. 'Tall man, I think, in dark clothes and with a balaclava over his head. That's all so far, but I'll keep looking.' Her phone rang as she spoke, and she glanced down to turn it to silent. 'Sorry, Boss,' she said.

'No problem,' said Greg. 'As you have the floor, Jill, can you update everyone on the missing children.'

'I'm afraid it won't take me long, and you've heard most of it before. The last confirmed sighting of the children was on the morning of the twenty-seventh of March, by the man in the garage who sold them a sausage roll, amongst other things. There's an unconfirmed sighting by the same man the evening of the same day, when he saw what sounds like the children near the end of the road opposite the garage. Given that he'd already talked to them and knew what they looked like, I'm inclined to take that sighting seriously. Unfortunately no one else saw them after that, and at least one key householder – the lady who lives in the bungalow with a boat, where Turbo signalled some interest – is refusing to engage. She claims to be shielding, but the local doctor's surgery haven't seen her for two years, so who knows?' She shrugged. 'I've done a bit more checking this morning, and she receives a pension from the civil service, and has a passport. There's something just not sitting right with me about that woman, but that's all I've got so far.'

'OK,' said Greg. 'Sorry I haven't anything inspiring to add. It's a case of keep on keeping on, I'm afraid. See you all later, and thank you for coming in. I may not always remember to say so, but I appreciate your dedication and so does the Chief Super.

'Jim, let's have a word about Suffolk.'

The two men went back to Greg's office, leaving Jill in front of her screens and Steve heading over to Silfield.

'I guess Suffolk hasn't followed up our tip-off,' said Greg.

'No,' said Jim. 'I spoke to the DI Chris put me in touch with, and he wasn't keen on committing resource. I've checked, and they didn't. Had something better to do, apparently.'

'It occurs to me,' said Greg, 'that it may have been the location for the handover of the Range Rover and Kawasaki.

The timing would fit, and bearing in mind where we got the intel from...'

Jim nodded. 'I was thinking along the same lines,' he said. 'We pick up details of a rendezvous from the phone belonging to Jacko Green, who already has previous for twocking and is apparently more affluent than his known income would account for. Moreover, we also have him linked to another farm which suffered an arson attack recently.'

'Although his link to the farm was earlier in the year than the arson attack,' replied Greg. 'He was identified in connection with the hare-coursing incident. But don't let me put you off, Jim, I'm just playing devil's advocate. On which theme, it can't have been Jacko at Silfield on Friday night because we still had him at the station.'

'I wish to God that Suffolk had taken us seriously,' said Jim. 'We might have had last night's culprits in the bag *and* the network that takes stolen vehicles abroad as well.'

'You're assuming they were headed for Felixstowe,' said Greg.

'Aren't you?'

'I suppose I am. Which leaves us with what?'

'Let's assume we're right. If it wasn't Jacko carrying out Friday's arson attack, then it was one of his contacts and one, maybe, who was hare coursing at Welsh Farm last month. We could start from there.'

'And at the other end, if the Range Rover and Kawasaki were on their way to Felixstowe that night, we might find them on cameras somewhere between Silfield and the rendezvous point.'

'Good thinking, Jim. I'm also going to have another go at Suffolk police. They may have missed the rendezvous, but they could have a look round at Felixstowe. If that was the intended destination, then the vehicles might be in a container there, awaiting shipping.'

***

Back at her desk, Jill immediately got stuck in to reviewing more CCTV material from the farmyard. As a result, it was after six before she remembered the message on her phone. Dragging her eyes from her screens, she looked down at her phone and flicked through to voice messages. What she heard electrified her. She glanced round the room, but she was the last one there. Steve hadn't come back from the farm, and no one else had arrived. She grabbed her phone and headed for Greg's office.

'I'm sorry, Boss,' she said as she went in. 'I've had a message you need to know about. I'm afraid it arrived this morning, but I didn't have chance to look until just now.'

Greg looked up from his phone. 'Sorry, Jill,' he said. 'I'll be with you in a moment.' Then, into the phone, he said, 'Thanks, Chris. Anything you can do to prod your colleagues into action would be good. I think they missed an important opportunity Friday night, and if they don't follow up on this, they'll miss another.' He listened in silence for a moment, then said, 'Aren't we all? See you later. I should be home this evening.' He put his phone down and looked up at Jill. 'What is it?' he said. 'Sorry to keep you waiting. Suffolk are pleading shorthandedness, if that's even a word – like they're the only ones! What have you got for me?'

'A message I should have picked up sooner. It's from Tim Simmons, Anne Mirren's boyfriend. You know, the children's mother's boyfriend.'

'Yes, I know', said Greg. 'What's he got to say?'

'He says he's had an email from the children. I've spoken to him briefly, and he's forwarded it to me.'

'He's what?' Greg was galvanised into life. 'Does it tell us where they are?'

'No, unfortunately, and I don't think it's recent. At least, I've read it over and over, and I think it was written sometime ago but only sent today. Here. See.' She held out her iPad.

Greg took it from her and read:

Hi Tim. We've been looking for you but we can't find you. Can you come and get us? We're in Ormesby.

'Why are you assuming it was delayed?'

'Because it reads like it was written the day they arrived. But it didn't arrive in Tim's inbox until yesterday, and then he didn't notice it until today. It was sent from Anne Mirren's email address, using 4G. So, with a bit of luck, we'll be able to find the phone or tablet by checking which towers it pinged while it was sending.'

'Well done, Jill. Do you need some help getting on to that?'

'About that. It occurred to me, I could use Bill working from home. He could do this while still isolating.'

'Good idea. Go ahead, Jill.'

She hesitated in the doorway. 'I'm sorry I missed this earlier,' she said. 'We could have actioned this earlier if I'd picked up the message.'

'Noted, Jill. But we can't do everything. You're on to it now. Has anyone spoken to Tim Simmons yet?'

'I have, over the phone. I'll go and see him now, once I've got Bill started on the phone network providers.

'Let me know as soon as you have a location.'

28

2 August 2020 – outskirts of Norwich

Nick was still reeling in more ways than one. Getting flattened by a wholly unexpected explosion had not been part of his plans. Hearing on the news the following day that someone had died in the blast was also a bit of a bummer. His head still ringing, both from leftover concussion and his wife's repeated remonstrations about his failure to show up for a family party, he'd heard the *BBC Look East* announcement with a strong sense of disbelief. He left the room a moment later, ignoring his wife's shrill complaints, and took refuge in the bathroom. Seconds after that, his phone rang, and it was no surprise to see it was his brother, Ade. He left the call to go to answerphone while he tried to soothe his aching head under the cold-water tap. It did help with the aches and pains. It didn't do much about the seething thoughts.

As he took the stairs down two at a time his phone pinged with a message, once, then twice.

'And where d'you think you're goin'?' his wife demanded from the sitting room just as he reached the front door.

'Out,' he said, and made his escape.

Sitting in his pickup, the doors locked and windows up, he examined his phone. The first ping had been Ade demanding he ring back. The second was the unknown contact on WhatsApp.

Delivery received. Payment made.

Hands shaking slightly, Nick checked his banking app. He had just sufficient Wi-Fi signal from the house to log on. Sure enough, his balance had increased by eight thousand pounds. Bit disappointing, given the risks he'd taken. And he still had to pay Ade. If he was going to do this again, it would be with a higher-value target. Otherwise, it just wasn't worth it. He texted Ade to meet him at the lock-up, and put the pickup in gear.

Ten minutes later, he was facing a torrent of complaints from his brother that reminded him, uncomfortably, of his wife's nagging.

'For God's sake, Ade,' he said, when he could get a word in edgeways. 'Stop being such an old woman. Here,' – he handed over a wedge of notes – 'a thousand pounds, as we agreed. Not bad for one night's work.'

'Not nearly enough, given the risks,' his brother said. 'You never told me anyone was going to get hurt.'

'Try a bit louder, why don't you?' Nick snapped back. 'I don't think the old girl three doors down could quite hear that.'

The two brothers stared at each other, chests heaving, temporarily silent. The familial similarities stood out, the jutting chins and glaring eyes clearly wrought from the same DNA even though hair, height and weight varied.

Ade started again, only this time a bit quieter. 'I was OK with a bit of twocking. I didn't even object to a spot of arson – those rich farming bastards can afford it. But I never signed up for murder.'

In Nick's view, Ade was still talking too loud, and he made haste to pull the garage door closed before he turned to answer.

'Grow a pair, Ade,' he recommended. 'All you did was transport two vehicles from A to B. All *I* did was create a distraction and deliver them to you. The rest was in the hands of the gods. Accident or fate. Nothing you need to get your knickers in a twist about. If you don't want the cash, I'll have it back.'

Ade took a step back and pushed the roll of notes into his pocket. 'I took the risk, I'll take the money', he said. 'But don't ask me again.'

'As you like,' said Nick. 'Now push off. I've got things to do.'

The things included a message to Jacko Green. But he got no answer.

29

December 2018 – Ormesby

Christmas fell on a Tuesday, and for over a week Joanne saw no one at all. She ate party food from Tesco and watched television, read books and examined her, or rather her mother's, bank account. *No, I have to stop thinking that way. My bank account.* She was now Joanne Hamilton, retired recluse, and quite well off, thank you. The civil service pension arrived in the bank account every month, without fail, and she was spending so little it was mounting up nicely. She supposed she could maybe take a holiday or move abroad. *No, I couldn't move, ever. Not and leave Frankie behind.* But she could have the occasional break from the cold of England and the lonely life.

But first she needed to do something about the contents of the freezer. She couldn't go away and risk a power cut exposing what she'd done. She finished her coffee and, gathering her courage around her, went out to the chest freezer in the garage. It took several deep breaths before she was ready to lift the lid. When she did, it was with a convulsive movement, not far removed from panic.

She peeled back the top bin bag. Over the six months or more that had elapsed, frost had formed on the contents, obscuring all the details of the upturned face. She suppressed a shudder that was now wholly caused by the cold in the garage, and closed the lid again. Then looked round her for inspiration.

There were a couple of old suitcases and a trunk. She considered, briefly, dismembering the body and dumping the parts into the sea or the Broads but abandoned the idea as too messy and too risky. *No, the body will have to be hidden somewhere on the property, but not buried in the garden – there is no way the evil old witch is going to join Frankie under the lawn.*

She was turning to go back into the house for another think and, to be frank, to get warm again, when her eye was caught by an odd round shape in the corner. It looked like a cross between a hatbox and an umbrella stand. She went over to examine it properly, and with a little effort managed to pull it into the centre of the floor. It was about four feet tall and three feet in diameter. It seemed to be made from curved plywood, and she had no idea what its original purpose might have been. Presumably it had stored or transported something, sometime, but Lord knew what. It had, however, given her an idea. She walked round it several times, then went indoors to do some research online.

Two days later, her order from the hardware superstore arrived: some heavy-duty waste sacks and bags of instant cement.

'You got some DIY planned, missus?' asked the delivery driver.

'Just a bit,' she said as she gave him a tip for moving the bags into the garage for her.

That evening, she pulled heavy gloves on and moved the body out of the freezer. She guessed that if it took a whole day to defrost a turkey, it would be similar for another scrawny old bird.

In fact, she'd miscalculated badly. It took two days before the body had even defrosted enough to become malleable. She guessed that it was probably still frozen in the middle, but that didn't matter provided she could bend the arms and legs.

She took the precaution of covering the narrow window at the back of the garage with an old sheet; then that night, lit only by the single strip light, she laid out the body on the floor by the cylindrical box and compared the relative dimensions by eye.

It was straightforward enough to fold the arms over the body, and she strapped them in place with an old belt. Folding the legs up was more difficult and, in the end, she had to use quite a lot of force, dislocating the hips in the process. She was breathing heavily by this point, and would have liked to stop for a rest, but didn't dare leave things half done. She slid the folded body into one of the extra-large refuse sacks then pulled another over from the opposite direction, so they overlapped. She sealed the join with tape, then did the same thing again twice more. That would have to do. She stepped back with her hand on the ache in the small of her back and thought the bags should be sufficient to contain any liquid.

The next step was easier. She laid the plywood cylinder on its side and, with some help from a sack barrow, managed to push the wrapped body inside. Some screwed-up newspaper helped wedge it in place, then she tipped the whole thing upright. Using the sack barrow again, the final step was to move it into the garden and position it, like a truncated column, near the back fence. She stepped back to survey the effect, then hurried to fetch the large, shallow planter that was to form the lid. With that in position, she felt she could breathe again.

The following day she started on the concrete. A couple of bags at a time, she layered it up the side of the cylinder then left it to cure. By the end of the week, her garden had acquired a concrete column supporting a planter containing cascading plants. At this time of year, they were all foliage plants, but later, she thought, she could add colour. A fitting, if wordless, tribute to her son.

30

---

3 August 2020 – Norfolk police HQ

Greg arrived at work in a bad temper, slamming his car door and stomping into the office. The black cloud over his head was almost visible.

'Whoa,' said Jim, watching his approach through the window of the incident room. 'Storm clouds on the horizon. I recommend caution and heads down.' Behind him, Jill was on the phone, Steve was clutching his usual giant mug of coffee and Jenny was just taking her jacket off.

'The boss?' asked Jenny.

'Yup,' said Jim. 'Looks like a bull amongst bumble bees. If he gets any hotter under the collar his shirt's going to burst into flame.'

'Nice mix of metaphors,' remarked Jenny. 'And you can tell all that from here?'

'Mark my words—' Jim started, but at that point the door flew open so hard it bounced off the wall and swung back, nearly hitting Greg in the face.

'Morning,' he said. And went straight to his office.

'See,' said Jim to the room at large, and headed for the coffee machine.

A judicious ten minutes later he pushed Greg's office door open and put a mug of strong black coffee on his desk. 'Bad start?' he asked. Then added into the silence, 'Is there something I need to know?'

'No,' said Greg rather shortly. Then he took a breath and with an obvious effort said, 'Sorry, Jim. That's part of the problem – no news. I'm just so frustrated we haven't found those children. It should be simple, but it isn't. Then an arsonist on the top ... it's getting to me, I suppose. On top of all that, Chris and I came this close to having words this morning...' He held up a finger and thumb just a fraction of an inch apart. 'And I hate being at odds with her. I nearly got one of her creative insults,' he added with a wry smile.

'What did you do?' asked Jim.

'I suppose I was banging on about Suffolk police,' Greg admitted. 'No, if I'm honest, there's no suppose about it. I *was* banging on about Suffolk and their inability to respond to hot tip-offs. Chris felt obliged to defend her colleagues, and it went from there. Plus, I was meant to be having today off. We had plans. But there's no way I can take time off at the moment.'

'Chris understands that, I'm sure,' said Jim,

'Yes, she does, but it doesn't stop us both being disappointed and ... oh never mind, Jim. Let's not dwell on it. We have a lot to do, and the sooner we get on, the sooner we might get a bit of life back. I need to shift some of this.' He gestured at the pile of paper on his desk. 'Then let's put our heads together about next steps on the arson case.'

As Jim was leaving the office, Greg called him back. 'Hang on,' he said. 'I have had one thought. Can we pick Jacko Green up again?'

'He was charged with hunting a wild mammal with a dog and with permitting a dog to be used for hunting and released pending a hearing at the magistrates' court. God knows when that will be. It shouldn't be too difficult to find him,' replied Jim.

'I'd like a chat with the other two blokes involved in the hare-coursing incident as well.' Greg scrabbled in the pile of papers. 'One was Mick O'Hanlon and the other was Nick something.'

'Nick Waters,' Jim said. 'I'll get the word out. Do you want them in here when we find them?'

'Yes, Jim. Thanks. We'll interview them together.'

A few hours later, just as Greg was starting to think about lunch, Jim returned with the welcome news that Jacko Green was in Interview Room 1, and that Nick Waters was on his way in the back of a squad car.

'Unfortunately, we haven't been able to get hold of Mick O'Hanlon,' said Jim. 'We found him at the travellers' camp in Broadlands, but the two constables attending were unable to get onto site. They were stopped by a homemade roadblock and the news that the camp had Covid and was self-isolating.'

'How very convenient,' remarked Greg. 'OK. We'll have to live with that for now. We don't have enough for an arrest warrant. But let's keep a discreet eye on it. If they suddenly stop isolating, we might need to seize the opportunity and grab him while we can.

'Let's have that chat with Jacko Green, and by the time we've finished with him Mr Waters should be here.'

Jacko was righteously indignant. 'What now?' he demanded before they had fairly got into the room. 'You've already charged me with hare coursing. What more d'you want? You're just picking on me now. Just because I have a lurcher, I'm suddenly public enemy number one, is that it? I tell you, that dog is as mild and gentle as a ... as a...' He was lost for a simile and Greg seized the opportunity to step in.

'Just a few questions, Jacko,' he said. 'If you've kept your nose clean, you've nothing to worry about. But I think we'll do this under caution, just in case.'

'Am I under arrest?' demanded Jacko, leaning his elbows on the table in front of him. 'Because if so, I want my brief.'

'You didn't have one last time we had a chat,' remarked Jim. 'You refused one. Are you expecting trouble today?'

'No, that's not what I meant. I'm entitled, aren't I?'

'You're not under arrest, anyway,' said Greg. 'At least, not yet. So, do you want a solicitor or don't you? We can sit around and wait for one, if that's your choice, or we can get on with it and you can answer a few questions. As I said, if you've stayed on the straight and narrow, you'll be free to go that much sooner.'

The number of expressions flitting over Jacko's face illustrated the difficulty of thought, then he came to a decision. 'OK, let's get on with it,' he said.

Jim switched the recorder on, and Greg administered the caution.

'OK, we're good to go,' he said to Jacko, who was currently engaged in picking his nose then inspecting the result on the end of his finger. 'Where did you go on Friday after you were released from custody?'

'Home, a'course.'

'What time did you get there?'

'Latish, thanks to your lot being very slow and stupid about letting me go,' said Jacko.

'How late?'

'Don't know exactly. Around nine or ten, I think. The news was on when I got in,' he added.

'And after that?'

'I had a few beers and went to bed.'

'Down the pub or at home?' asked Jim.

'At home. The pub just isn't the same after all the Covid stuff. Miserable bastards,' he added. Jim assumed he meant the government.

'Can anyone vouch for you being at home?'

'Ma and Dad were in,' he said. 'They'll tell you I was there.'

'But they couldn't vouch for you being in all night, I assume?' said Greg.

'They'll tell you when I went up to bed, because I watched the late film with me old dad, and I 'spect the old girl will bang on about having to get me out of bed in the mornin',' said Jacko. 'She's always moanin' about that. Just cuz she wakes early, she thinks everyone should bounce out of bed at sparrow's fart.' He shook his head at the unreasonableness of her attitude. 'Hang on,' he said suddenly. 'Why're you askin' me about Friday night? You're not trying to pin that explosion on me, are you? I was home. I was nowhere near there. I'm not having this!' He stood up to go.

'Just a moment, Jacko,' said Greg. 'I told you at the start, if you're clean, you have nothing to worry about. So why don't you sit down again?'

'No way,' said Jacko. 'You're trying to set me up.'

'Just the opposite, actually,' said Greg. 'I'm giving you the chance to prove it wasn't you, so we don't need to bother you again.'

Jacko sat down again, slowly and reluctantly.

'That's better,' said Greg. 'You see, even if you weren't directly involved with the arson at the farm, and I have to say it doesn't seem your sort of thing, you must admit that arson attacks seem to follow you around. First there's one at Welsh Farm, shortly after you're there for a hare-coursing event. Then there's another last Friday, just after you come out of custody. Now, if it wasn't you, then perhaps it was one of your mates. Mick O'Hanlon, say, or Nick Waters? They were both at Welsh Farm, weren't they?'

'No comment,' said Jacko.

Greg noticed that, just as the last time Mick O'Hanlon was mentioned, Jacko started shaking. Greg and Jim exchanged glances.

'Never mind,' said. Jim. 'We can ask Mick when he gets here. And Nick Waters too.'

Jacko looked up. 'Now don't you drop me in it with Mick,' he said. 'Not unless you want another body on your hands.'

'So Mick *was* involved with the explosion,' said Jim.

'I never said that! No. That's not what I meant. I just meant that Mick has a nasty temper, and I don't want him turning it on me. Big hands too.' And he shuddered.

'You're afraid of Mick O'Hanlon?' said Jim.

'Too right, I am. And so would you be if he'd ever thumped you.'

'Let's talk about Nick Waters then,' said Greg. 'What do you know about him?'

'No comment,' said Jacko.

Jim banged his hands on the table theatrically. 'Well, that's it then,' he said. 'If you won't talk, we'll just have to ask Mick what you've been up to with him.'

'Now hold on, DI Henning,' Greg intervened. 'We can't expect Jacko here to stick his neck out with someone like Mick O'Hanlon. On the other hand, if he won't talk about Mick, we can expect him to talk about Nick Waters. That would be fair, wouldn't it?'

Jacko was looking from Jim to Greg and back again, as though watching tennis. He nodded eagerly. 'Look,' he said. 'I don't know much, really I don't. But I did get this message yesterday from Nick...' He fumbled in his pocket then drew out a phone in a battered case. 'Here. Look!' He flicked through a couple of screens then held out his phone. It was a WhatsApp message, apparently from Nick Waters.

Job 4 u. Meet same place tom?

'Who's Tom?' asked Greg.

'He means tomorrow,' said Jacko with a hint of a sneer.

'And the place?'

'A lay-by outside Acle. Near the river. That's all I have,' he repeated. 'Now I want to go. Arrest me or I walk out.'

'OK, OK.' Greg held his hands up. 'You can go. But don't leave the country, will you?'

'Like I would,' said Jacko. 'Full of foreigners, ain't it, abroad.' Jim held the door open for him, and he slouched out of the room. First checking there was an officer waiting outside to see Jacko off the premises, Jim returned to his seat.

Greg was staring at the ceiling. 'Not sure where we're going with this, Jim,' he said. 'Forgive me if I think aloud for a bit.

'What do we know? Jacko was involved in the hare coursing but probably not with the arson on either occasion. He is probably up to something, but it isn't starting fires. He's terrified of Mick O'Hanlon and has some connections with Nick Waters.'

'Mick is as thick as a workhouse butty and a bully,' said Jim. 'I can well believe he'd beat the shit out of anyone who upset him, but arson seems a bit too complicated for him. It involves planning for a start, and Mick is all fists and no brains.'

'What about the Waters chap? What do we know about him?'

'Not a lot, really,' said Jim. 'Last time we interviewed him, Jacko said Nick organised the hare coursing, but we can't prove it. All we have is Jacko's accusation, and Nick's wife is emphatic he was at home that evening so it's Jacko's word against hers. ANPR hasn't picked up any vehicle registered to Waters anywhere near the farm that evening, and we have no forensics that tie him to it either. Not yet, anyway.'

'Could be driving round with false plates,' said Greg.

'Very likely,' said Jim. 'But we still need to catch him at it.'

'And the message Jacko just showed us?'

'Given Jacko's favourite pastimes, I'd say either we're looking at another hare-coursing event or Waters is wanting a driver.'

'That would fit with the possible Felixstowe connection,' agreed Greg. 'But it doesn't seem possible that it was Jacko driving the Range Rover away from Silfield on Friday. God, I do wish Suffolk had attended that location!'

'Now let's not go there again,' said Jim hastily. 'Nick Waters must be here by now.'

'True. Let's take a short break, and then see what we can get from him.'

***

Renewed both by a tuna sandwich and a quick telephone conversation with Chris, during which each had apologised to the other, Greg returned to Interview Room 1. Jim was waiting outside, chatting with the uniformed constable who'd brought Waters in.

'Did you get a look in the lock-up?' he was asking.

'No, sir. He was just locking the shutter door when we arrived. I had no reason to ask him to open it up again, so I just brought him on here.' The young officer was uneasy that he had made a mistake.

'That's fine,' said Jim. 'I just thought that if you'd had an opportunity to look around, it would be interesting to know what he's got in there. I don't think we were aware he's got a lock-up.'

'No. I don't think he was too pleased to be picked up there,' said the constable. 'We went to his home address originally but he wasn't there, and when we asked his wife where we might find him, she pointed us at the lock-up. I think she was pretty cheesed off with him about something,' he added.

Greg and Jim went into the interview room and sat down at the table. Nick Waters was sitting on the far side, his back to the window high in the wall behind him. He was neatly dressed in shirt and jeans but was sweating more than the temperature justified, and when Greg looked closely, there seemed to be bruising both on the side of his face and on the arm that showed below the short sleeve. Greg glanced round at the uniformed officer still in the corner of the room.

'I wonder if Mr Waters might like a tea,' he said.

'Already offered him one,' said the officer, 'but he said no.'

'I'm good,' growled Nick. 'And I'd like to get out of here without wasting any time.'

Greg nodded to the officer that he could go as Jim switched the recording equipment on. 'OK, fine by us,' he said. 'I just thought you looked a bit under the weather. Where did you get those bruises?'

'What bruises? Oh, these? Walked into the bathroom door,' he said.

'Bit unimaginative,' said Greg. 'Can't you do any better than that? Now, if you'd said your wife had clouted you, I might have believed you, judging from how cross she seemed to be this morning.' He paused. Nick remained silent. 'Nothing to say?' asked Greg.

'Didn't think you'd asked me a question,' said Nick.

'How about this one? Just so you're clear, question coming up, Mr Waters. Where were you on Friday night?'

'Out with mates,' said Waters.

'Out where?'

'Just round and about,' said Waters. 'Don't expect me to get anyone into trouble with these mad Covid rules.'

'So, no corroboration then,' said Greg. 'OK, what time did you get home?'

'Around twelve, twelve-thirty, I guess,' said Waters.

'And will your irritable wife confirm that?'

'S'pose so. You'll have to ask her, won't you?'

'We will, believe me on that,' said Greg. 'Where were you on Saturday morning?'

'Still home. Then ... let me see ... I think I went down to my lock-up to do some work on my car.'

'That would be the pickup you drove to the hare-coursing incident at Welsh Farm in June?'

'No comment.'

'And if we told you we had your vehicle on camera near the A11 on the night of the thirty-first of July?'

'I'd say you were mistaken, or lying,' replied Waters.

Greg looked at him for a long silent moment. Despite the calm denial, he looked, if anything, even sweatier, and Greg had a strong feeling that they were on to something. On the other hand, it was true, he was lying. For now, he had no data from the ANPR cameras that implicated Waters.

'What were you doing at your lock-up today?' asked Greg, changing tack.

'Minding my own business. Pity you can't say the same,' replied Waters.

Greg glanced at Jim, who took up the thread. 'Let's go back a bit, to the first of June. What were you doing that evening?'

'No idea,' said Waters. 'Too long ago. I expect I was at home watching the TV like the rest of the country.'

'And the seventeenth of July?'

'Same, I expect.'

An hour later, repeated questions had elicited nothing more useful and Waters was starting to look both more impatient and more comfortable.

'If that's all you've got, you're wasting my time and yours,' he said eventually. 'Either arrest me, or I'm off.' He stood up to go.

Jim and Greg exchanged a glance, then Greg shuffled his papers together. 'Thank you for your time, Mr Waters,' he said. 'Inspector Henning will see you out.'

Back in his office, Greg dropped the paperwork on his desk with a sigh and stretched to the ceiling to work some of the kinks out of his backbone. He heard the door behind him open and said, without turning, 'Well that was a waste of time.'

'Sorry, Boss,' said Jill's voice. 'I've got something you need to know about, but if it's a bad time...'

'No, sorry, Jill, I thought you were Jim. What've you got?'

'That email from the children... The signal pinged a couple of towers and places the location in Ormesby.'

'Only two? Not three?'

''Fraid so.'

'So not enough for a definitive triangulation?'

'Well, it does give us Ormesby and probably the centre. So, can I go and get a proper look at Ms Hamilton's place?'

'Not without her permission, no. Sorry, Jill, I realise you're excited about this, but we already knew the children had been in Ormesby around that time. I don't think this moves us forward. And it certainly isn't enough for a warrant in the face of someone shielding from Covid!'

31

4 August 2020

Diana Grain, Jill's partner, was worried on two counts. First, she was, of course, worried about the young girl she'd taught until Covid had messed up schools and the child's parents had messed up her life. Karen and Jake were at the forefront of her mind every day, and the failure to find them bugged *her* almost as much as it did Jill. However, the operative word was 'almost'. Diana was now beyond worried about the impact the case was having on Jill. It was occupying her every waking moment and, judging by the way she talked in what little sleep she got, occupying her few sleeping moments as well. She had tried to get Jill to take a break, but without success. She'd tried to get her talking about the case, but with little more to show for it than a few words. And from what Jill had let slip, Diana was now concerned that she was starting to obsess about one specific possibility.

'But I thought your boss, Greg, had said you didn't have enough to get a search warrant,' she said. 'He's very experienced, isn't he? Do you genuinely think he's wrong?'

'No, I'm sure he's right about that,' Jill replied. 'But don't you see, that's why I need to find the evidence that will justify a warrant. I'm certain that woman knows more than she's saying.'

'Might it not be possible...' Diana was phrasing her question as carefully as she could. '... that the reason you haven't found enough evidence is because it isn't there to be found? That she's just a recluse who is scared to death of Covid?'

'You haven't met her,' said Jill. 'I tell you, there's something screwy about her. And Turbo found something round there too, don't forget.'

'The dog,' said Diana sceptically. 'And didn't his handler say his signal was doubtful?'

'Well I'm going to check it out some more, one way or another. See you later, but don't wait up for me – it might be a long one.' And Jill left for the office.

She spent the morning trawling online databases. She knew she was good at that, better than most was not too much of a claim, and by lunchtime she'd amassed a pile of data on Joanne Hamilton. She knew where she had worked as a civil servant, when she'd started collecting her pension and what day of the month it was paid by bank transfer. The date she'd bought the bungalow in Ormesby was on record, as was her marriage, the later divorce and the birth of a daughter. She got excited about that for a moment, but swiftly realised the daughter would now be in her fifties and long since left home. Certainly none of the neighbours had mentioned seeing any family visiting Mrs Hamilton. Neither the divorced husband nor the daughter appeared in any census return she could find, nor in any other database that she'd been able to mine so far. Frustrated, she went looking for Ned.

She found him on the phone, as usual, still chasing analytical chemistry.

'I hope you're not going to ask me for those DNA results,' he said when he put the phone down. 'I'm spending my life on this damn thing,' – indicating the phone – 'and all I'm doing is taking up the time of the few staff they *do* have in the lab. So I'm probably holding things up, not speeding them up.' He sighed, leaned back in his chair and rubbed his hand over his shaved head. 'What can I do for you, Jill?' he asked. 'Anything, provided it doesn't involve the laboratory!'

'Can I borrow someone to do some sampling for me?' she asked, adding hurriedly, 'not DNA! I want someone to check around for me, in Ormesby, for fingerprints. We already have the kids' prints on record, don't we?'

'Yes, from their home,' said Ned. 'Have you got a lead then?'

'Something I'm working on,' said Jill. 'At the least, I want to exclude a possibility. So can I borrow someone to do some checking for me?'

'I don't have many people in,' said Ned. 'Most of my team are still working the arson case. They should be finished there this evening. Will tomorrow do?'

'I was hoping for this afternoon,' said Jill.

'In that case, the only person I have available is one of the new recruits. He's coming in at lunchtime. He should be OK for this job, but keep an eye on him for me, will you? Actually, he'll benefit from the experience so it's a win-win. His name's Alan Thorpe. Goes by Al.'

'Thanks, Ned. I owe you one.'

It was late afternoon by the time Jill had all her ducks in a row, of which the most important was, of course, her new assistant. Al was young, dark and earnest. His slightly receding hair was cropped short, as were his beard and moustache. Lanky and leaning as though slightly embarrassed by his height, Jill concluded that he had been designed for the word gangling. He was also as enthusiastic as a cockapoo puppy and very keen for a new experience. He chatted non-stop from Wymondham to Ormesby until Jill had to plead for a few moments' silence to give herself a break. By then she'd already been briefed on his family (eccentric), his training (fascinating) and his love life (non-existent).

When they pulled up in the garage forecourt where the children had last been seen, she turned in her seat for his final briefing.

'You know the background,' she said. 'The last confirmed sighting of the children was here and there are other, unconfirmed, sightings placing them in this area later that same day. We also know that the police search dog picked something up over there – by the bungalow with the boat in the drive.' She pointed. 'Now, there's no reason to do any more work over here by the garage, that's already been covered by your colleagues. What I want to do now is check out the area by that bungalow.'

'We're unlikely to get anything from surfaces out in the open,' objected Al. 'Too much elapsed time and too much weather.'

'Yes, I realise that,' said Jill with ostentatious patience. 'What I'm interested in are the outbuildings and so on, in the immediate area round that bungalow.'

'Not inside the bungalow?' asked Ned.

'No. The lady's shielding,' said Jill.

'Don't we need a warrant to go into her property?'

'You can let me worry about that,' said Jill. Then added, as Al was still looking worried, 'Stuff like a boat or shed that's open is OK. You have my authority for it.' She hoped that Al couldn't see her fingers crossed behind her back – metaphorically speaking.

They started with the boat. Jill opened the canvas cover and gave Al a boost up into the cockpit. Unsurprisingly there were fingerprints aplenty on the edge of the gunwale. Al found a few more under the edge of the bench seat at the back and some good prints from the steering wheel.

Outside the boat, Jill was becoming nervous about how long he was taking but strove hard to hide it. So far, there was no sign of movement in the house. When Al emerged at last, she led him round the corner of the house to the back garden and the small summerhouse. While he was working in there, she tried the back door of the garage. It was open.

'Al,' she said quietly, 'last job is in here.'

He nodded and replied, rather more loudly than she liked, 'Sure thing. I've just finished here.' He picked his equipment up and followed her into the garage. As he did, the overhead strip light suddenly came on and an old lady was visible in the side door that led to the bungalow. She was masked and holding something in her right hand.

'I've rung for the police,' she announced in a voice that was only slightly muffled by the mask.

'We are the police,' said Jill, stepping forward and holding out her warrant card. She stopped several metres from Mrs

Hamilton. 'We've spoken before Mrs Hamilton. I didn't bother you because I know you are shielding. We're just pursuing our enquiries about the two missing children, there's nothing to worry about.'

'Get out, right now,' the woman shouted, making Al jump. 'You have no right to be in my property without my permission. Get out. And I'll be making an official complaint, you can be sure of that.'

Shaken and, in Al's case, chastened as well, the two of them left the garage and crossed the road to Jill's car.

'Are we in trouble?' asked Al once they were on their way back to Wymondham.

'You're not,' she reassured him. 'Everything we did this afternoon was on my authority. Don't worry, I'll make that clear if there's any comeback. You just concentrate on checking those fingerprints against what we have on file.'

'Got it,' he said, but he still looked worried and was noticeably quieter on the return journey.

***

When, at last, he got home from police HQ, Nick Waters was not best pleased to find his wife had gone out. He'd been more than ready for a showdown about loyalty and discretion, but the house was empty except for a single line scrawled on the back of an envelope to say she had gone to see her sister. Muttering, he clattered round the tidy kitchen – for all her faults, he couldn't call her lazy – and got a beer out of the fridge. Spotting a packet of ham, he decided on a cheese and ham toastie, and took a malicious pleasure in leaving the kitchen looking as though a bomb had hit it: dirty cutlery, greasy plate, messy grill pan, cheese and breadcrumbs everywhere. His phone pinged just as he sat down with the toastie and another beer. Flicking through screens he saw he had a message from his new clients.

New merch wot & when?

He took a bite of cheese and ham and thought while he chewed. Then, wriggling a little on the battered sofa, he managed to extract his notebook from his hip pocket, and flicked through the notes he'd made several weeks earlier. He was still ruminating on the possibilities when his phone pinged again.

??

'Hold yer horses,' he muttered to himself, not happy with the impatience on display but, swallowing the last of his beer, he wiped his greasy hands on his jeans and picked up the phone again.

Range Rover 21/8, he replied. Surely he could get hold of Jacko by then.

OK. 7/8, was the answer.

Damn! *2 soon*, he messaged back.

7/8 or 0, came back.

He sighed, thought again, and messaged: *OK 7/8*. If he couldn't get hold of Jacko at short notice, he'd have to drive to the collection point himself.

The notes he'd made when he scouted out the possibilities were adequate for him to work out timings. If the collection was at or near the last one, in time and geography, he would need to start the distraction at around 10pm Thursday night.

At least his target was a bit closer to the collection point this time. Only snag was, if *he* had to make the delivery, he had a long journey home on Friday morning. Judging by the experiences of today, the cops would be round at his within hours. Briefly, he considered whether the risk was too great, but decided he wanted to do it. Needed to do it. He'd just have to set up some sort of alibi. Perhaps Mick could help with that.

32

---

4 August 2020 – evening

Greg was on his way home when his phone rang. He answered on hands-free, and if anyone had been in the car they would have noticed his lips thin and his knuckles whiten on the steering wheel. At the next opportunity he left the dual carriageway and crossed over to take the lane travelling south, back toward Wymondham.

Once parked outside Norfolk police HQ again, he sat for a moment considering his options and giving himself time to think through what he wanted to say. Then he stalked into the building and straight to his office. One of the Chief Superintendent's secretaries was hovering in the corridor and followed him in.

'Before you say anything,' he said, holding up a hand, 'I know. Margaret wants to see me. I'll be along as soon as I've established the facts.' The girl looked as though she was minded to argue, but took a second look at Greg's face and thought the better of it.

'OK,' she said. 'I'll tell her.'

Greg picked up his phone. 'In my office, now!' he said when his call was answered. Then he put the phone down. He heard the footsteps coming down the corridor, the moment when they hesitated outside his door, then the quiet knock.

'Come in,' he said. And Jill entered, looking rather pale. She stood to attention in front of his desk.

'Take a seat, Jill.'

'I'd rather stand, Boss, if you don't mind,' she said, staring straight in front of her.

'OK. As you will. Now explain to me what you thought you were up to.'

'As you know, sir, I'm convinced that the woman in that property, Mrs Joanne Hamilton, knows more than she's saying. I recognise that we don't have sufficient evidence for a search warrant, nor enough to justify a search without a warrant, so I went about collecting more evidence.'

'And in doing so, you conducted an illegal search,' said Greg. 'You're too experienced to make such a rookie mistake. You have years in the force, even if only months as a sergeant. You know you can't just follow instinct or your gut! I concede either might help steer you. I agree that sometimes what we call instinct is a subconscious recognition of what the evidence is telling us. But, we do nothing without evidence. And we follow due process. Otherwise, we're no better than a lynch mob. You know that!

'Worse, you not only put yourself in the shit, and damaged the good name of Norfolk police, but you took a raw forensic scientist with you and put his career at risk too.'

Still at attention, Jill was holding it together, just. There was a suspicious moistness forming in her eyes.

'No blame lies with Alan Thorpe,' she said. 'I take full responsibility. He acted solely under my orders.'

'Which might help a bit,' conceded Greg. 'But not a lot. He's still going to come in for criticism, even if *you* know and *I* know it's unfair. I warn you, Ned's going to be out for your blood. And I have to see Margaret now. Do you have anything to tell me that will help?'

'No, Boss,' said Jill, still staring at the middle distance.

Greg sighed and stood up. 'Go home, Jill,' he said. 'I don' t want to see you for at least two days.'

'Am I suspended, Boss?' she asked.

'Not yet. We'll see what Margaret has to say.'

'I'm sorry, Boss,' said Jill, then shut up before she lost it.

'Go home,' Greg repeated, and headed for the stairs to the next floor and Chief Superintendent Tayler's office.

'Go straight in,' said the same secretary he had seen earlier. 'She's expecting you.'

Margaret swung round from facing the window as Greg entered, her fluffy brown hair in its usual chaotic state.

'This is a mess, Greg,' she said. 'If this Mrs Hamilton goes public with her complaint, it's going to attract all sorts of attention, and none of it wanted. What on earth was DS Hayes thinking? She's experienced enough to know better.'

'I know,' said Greg. 'Just what I told her. In all honesty, Boss, I blame myself. I knew her partner had taught one of the children and I should have seen she was too close and getting too involved personally. The Covid pressures haven't helped either, and I should have seen that too.'

'Stop with the self-flagellation,' ordered Margaret. 'Or you'll have to get in the queue. I probably put too much pressure on your team too. But none of this helps. What we need now is a plan to deal with the fallout.'

'Do you think it would help if I went and apologised to Mrs Hamilton,' asked Greg, but whatever Margaret's reply might have been was interrupted by the door opening precipitously.

'He wouldn't wait,' said the secretary as Ned stood framed in the doorway, the lanky Al Thorpe lurking self-consciously behind him.

'You need to know this,' said Ned. 'The children's fingerprints are all over the inside of that boat.'

33

Later that same evening

Ned's announcement landed in their midst like a B-52 with failed engines.

'You're sure?' asked Greg.

'I'm sure. Al may be new to this, but he's thorough. And I've double-checked his comparisons with the prints we lifted at the children's own home. There's no doubt. There are clear palm and fingerprints from the boy, Jake, on both the steering wheel and the engine housing. The girl's prints are smudged on the gunwale but clear on the engine housing and under the rear seat. The children were definitely in that boat.'

'Thank you, Ned,' said Margaret. 'Let me have a copy of your report on my desk asap, please.' Ned took that as his dismissal and started to usher both the secretary and Al out of the room before him.

'Ned, stick around a bit, will you?' said Greg. 'We may need your team tonight.'

'Got it,' said Ned, and closed the door behind him.

'Oh boy,' said Greg. 'Jill was right.'

'Yes,' agreed Margaret. 'But in all the wrong ways.'

'Where does this leave us?' asked Greg. 'We now have evidence that the children were on that property, and the second sighting of them by the garage hand was probably right too. We need entry to that property and we need it now. Am I OK to conduct a Section 17 search?' he asked.

'Your justification being...?'

'To save life,' he replied. 'The children have been missing for one hundred and thirty days and this is the first evidence we have of where they went after the last confirmed sighting. Given the message received by Tim Simmons, and the fact that they only seem to have had very limited access to the telephone network, I think it's reasonable to conclude they're being held against their will, and that means they're at risk.'

'We can run it past the legal team,' said Margaret, 'but much as I would love to say yes, I'm not sure it holds up. There are too many assumptions and guesses. OK, the children were in that boat, but where they went after that is anyone's guess, and even that is evidence we came by improperly.

'I think you should make an application for a warrant. If you can persuade the duty magistrate, then you're good to go. Make that your priority for now, and put Ned on standby for crack of dawn tomorrow.

'And don't do a Jill on me, Greg. Don't put *your* career on the line as well.'

Reluctantly, Greg had to acknowledge the sense of her advice. He nodded his acquiescence, and went off to write the most persuasive application for a search warrant of his entire career so far.

In fact, back in his office he decided two phone calls were his top priorities. First, he let Chris know that he wouldn't be home that night. At least he left a message for her, as she wasn't picking up either the landline or her mobile. He remembered she'd said something about a busy day, and assumed she too was still on duty. Making a mental note that they really must schedule some rest time together soon, he dialled again.

'Jill,' he said, 'you were right. The children had been in that boat.' He listened in silence for a moment then added, 'I'm afraid that doesn't let you off the hook. You're still in trouble for breach of the rules, but I thought it only fair to let you know. I'm now drafting an application for a warrant.' He listened again, then added, 'It won't be until tomorrow. I'll let you know what's happening.'

It took some time to set out in precise detail the background to the children's departure from their family home and the reasons for it, what was known about their journey to Ormesby and the sightings in the village. That left him with the tricky bit to draft. He had at least three goes at describing Turbo's 'evidence', the incomplete data from the phone masts and, most sensitive of all, the explanation of how and why the outbuildings and boat had been accessed and fingerprint evidence collected. At the end he read it through again, and sighed. He felt that he had, at best, only a fifty–fifty chance of getting this past a magistrate. He picked up his phone to the duty legal adviser.

'I believe Margaret may have warned you this was coming,' he said. He could hear a TV in the background and the sound of muted voices.

'Yes,' was the response. 'Hang on, let me go to my study.' The background noise faded as Greg listened. 'Have you forwarded your form to me?'

'Yes, just now,' said Greg. 'It's urgent, I'm afraid. I'll need to knock up the duty magistrate.' There was silence for a while, then the lawyer came back on the line.

'Worth a try,' he said, 'but I have to warn you, I think you only have a fifty–fifty chance. Some of it is a bit thin. OK, you have my go-ahead. The duty magistrate is...' There was a pause, and then he said, 'That's not good. It's Terence Batley-Shaw.'

'Oh damn.' Greg knew the man. Honest, hard-working, but pernickety over detail. 'It would be, wouldn't it.'

'Good luck. I'll send the form on to him and give him a ring to let him know a decision is needed asap. Stick close to your phone; he'll probably have questions for you.'

'I don't have to go and sit in his kitchen then?' said Greg.

'Not now. You can thank Covid for that.'

On his way through the office to brief Ned on developments, phone firmly clutched in hand in case of calls, Greg was surprised to see Jill at her desk, earnestly scrolling through images on her three screens.

'I thought I'd sent you home,' he said, only part of the stern tone actually real.

She looked up, startled. 'Sorry, Boss,' she said. 'Yes you did, but you didn't actually suspend me and I had an idea I wanted to check out. So...' And she waved at the screens.

'I should send you straight back home,' said Greg, but relented at the look of horror on her face. 'OK, you can stay as long as I do. As soon as we have a decision from the magistrate, I'll be away and so will you.'

'OK, Boss. It's a deal.'

While he was waiting, Greg made himself a super strong mug of black coffee and, with a bit of foraging, found some chocolate hobnobs. Suitably armed for a long wait, he didn't know whether to be pleased or worried when his phone rang and the number on the display was that of Mr Batley-Shaw JP.

'I've read your application,' said the senatorial voice on the line. 'I have some questions. I can see that the children were in that boat at sometime, but I don't see why you've concluded they're in the house associated with it. Talk me through your evidence.'

Greg went through everything they had, making as good a case as he could. He had a sinking feeling that it wasn't going to be enough.

'Yes,' said the magistrate. 'All that's in your application, and I understood it all. I'm sorry to say, Chief Inspector, that I don't think you've made your case. I'll have one last look through all the paperwork, but I think it has to be no.'

Greg put the phone down, wondering how he was going to break the news to Jill. But he found he didn't need to. She was standing right behind him and had clearly heard every word. That being so, he was surprised she didn't look more depressed. If anything, she looked excited.

'I've something you need to see, Boss,' she said. 'Come this way, quick.' She seized his arm and almost hustled him along to her desk. 'There,' she said, and pointed at one of her screens. 'Look there.'

He peered at the slightly blurred image. It seemed to be of a boy, filmed from above, dressed in a cowboy outfit. The lighting was poor, but there seemed to be a girl in the background.

'Now watch,' said Jill, and she pressed play. The image became a video, and after maybe half a minute, the boy looked up toward the camera. Jill froze the image and pointed to one of her other screens. 'I captured that image and put it through the facial recognition software. It's Jake Mirren. Confidence rating over eighty per cent.'

Greg sat down beside Jill and looked from one screen to the other. 'Anything to identify the location?' he asked. 'Any markers?'

'One. The image is taken from a mummy website club. Not Mumsnet but quite similar. The person who posted the image has the username *frankiesmum135*. But the IP address is Joanne Hamilton's.'

Greg shot to his feet. 'You're sure about this? Because if you're wrong, it won't be just you that's toast, it will be me as well.'

'I'm sure,' said Jill.

Greg fumbled with his phone and rang Mr Batley-Shaw. 'Before you make a final decision, I have another piece of evidence which has just been identified. I think you'll want to see it. May I send you that further information?'

There was a certain amount of humming and hawing at the other end, then the answer was 'Yes. But make sure all the paperwork is correct before I sign it off. You're sure it's significant?'

'It's game-changing,' said Greg into his phone, and rang off. 'Jill, come with me. Help me summarise what you've got, then I'll send it off to Batley-Shaw.'

***

Organising a complex raid is always demanding. Organising a raid when significant numbers of your forces are either isolating or sick adds a whole new dimension. By the time Greg had uniformed officers, plus as many of his immediate team as he could muster – which came down to Jill, Jenny and Steve – plus Ned and the SOC experts, it was pushing midnight.

'If you're wrong, the timing will make the whole exercise look even worse,' Margaret warned.

'And if we're right and something happens to the children while we delay, it would be a disaster,' countered Greg.

Margaret held up her hands in surrender. 'Just want to make sure you're confident of your grounds,' she said.

'I am,' said Greg, and devoutly hoped that was true.

With a local team keeping what he hoped was a discreet surveillance on the property, and the emergency safeguarding contact at the local council on speed dial, they all set off for Ormesby and a rendezvous by the village green. Close enough to the target, but not so close that their presence would be visible to Mrs Hamilton – always supposing she was up at this late hour.

'No blue flashing lights, no sirens,' Greg had warned. 'You know the plan.'

Shortly after the cars and vans arrived by the green, Greg got out of his car to check everyone was present and correct, then sent two squad cars to seal off the approaches to their target. Next he checked the readiness of the sergeant with the big red key. Jenny was accompanied by Turbo, and the rest of his team were all appropriately equipped and protected by stab vests. They'd reviewed risks and concluded that firearms support wasn't justified.

In the second rank were Ned and his experts, which on this occasion included Alan Thorpe. Ned reckoned he deserved the opportunity but had taken the precaution of administering a severe warning about no chatter. Pale with excitement, Al had taken it on board and remained mute.

As they neared their target, Greg noted that it was in total darkness, not a light showing anywhere. He nodded to Jenny and Steve to deploy to the back garden, just in case anyone made a run for it, then he and the man with the ram approached the front door, followed by Jill. Just as they stepped forward, light flooded the front garden with brilliance.

'Damn! Motion sensors,' said Greg. 'Too late for the quiet approach now. Go for it.'

The shout of 'Police! Open up!' rang out almost simultaneously with the bang as the ram hit the front door just below the lock. It didn't take two tries. As the door flew open, in his peripheral vision Greg saw the backup from the nearest squad car deploy into the road. They barrelled into the house, Greg first, followed closely by the sergeant and Jill. To their right was a door which, according to the plans on Rightmove, should be the sitting room. It was, and it was empty.

'Clear,' shouted Greg.

Jill headed past him to the door at the back of the hall, which turned out to be a bathroom.

'Clear,' she said, and they both moved down the hall toward the remaining three doors. Jill checked the one on the left. Another bedroom.

'Clear,' she said. The door on the right opened to reveal a terrified woman holding a walking stick in her hand. She brandished it and screamed.

'Get out! I've rung the police. Get out!'

Greg took a step back as the stick whistled past his face, then leaped forward under the next swing and wrestled it off her. With a push, he precipitated the dressing gown-clad lady into the arms of the sergeant, who wrapped her in a bear hug.

'Calm down,' he said into her ear. 'We *are* the police, and we have a warrant to search these premises.' If anything, this galvanised her into further activity and Jill had to come to the rescue to help subdue her.

Greg emerged from the room behind. 'Bedroom and en suite,' he reported. 'Clear. No sign of the children so far. Get Jenny and Turbo in.'

Mrs Hamilton had been pushed into the spare bedroom, the uniformed sergeant standing over her ready to quell any signs of rebellion.

'Where are the children, Mrs Hamilton?' demanded Greg. 'Where are Karen and Jake? We know you've posted photos of them on the internet.'

She sat in stony silence.

Steve pushed his head round the front door. 'Jenny thinks Turbo has found something in the back garden,' he reported.

Greg's heart sank. *Don't say we're too late*, he thought.

Jill had been scouting the kitchen. 'Also clear,' she said. 'Should I get Ned in for a closer look?'

'Yes,' said Greg, watching Mrs Hamilton closely for a reaction, any reaction. But he realised bleakly that she'd reacted more to the news about the back garden than she had to the prospect of a forensic examination of her property. His heart sank still further, and he followed Steve out of the house and round to the back garden.

It was currently as brightly lit as three powerful police torches could make it. The focus of all the light was the furiously wagging rump of an excited springer spaniel and a rough concrete pillar. As he approached, the dog sat and pointed at the pillar with his nose. Jenny, responding to the canine prompt, stepped forward to lift a large, and evidently heavy, planter off the top of the pillar with her blue-gloved hands. She put it down beside the dog, then redirected her torchlight into the interior of the apparently hollow construction. Greg reached her side just as she pulled at something in a heavy-duty plastic bag.

Thinking that it looked as though it had been there some time, Greg was about to divert attention to the interior of the bungalow, when Turbo broke ranks and jumped up at the pillar. It fell back under the impetus of his sudden weight and the concrete shattered to reveal a plywood tube containing an amorphous shape wrapped in plastic. In the light of the torches they could see a split in the wrapping, and what it revealed of the contents froze the words on Greg's lips. His first thought was at least it wasn't the children. He vocalised the second.

'Tell Ned we need him here, and ring the pathologist,' he said, looking at the partially skeletonised body under the wrappings.

In the sitting room, Ned was busy organising his troops when Al coughed nervously to attract his attention.

'This cupboard door's locked,' he said.

Ned came over to inspect the door, then walked through the hall and into the bathroom to examine the wall from the other side, as best he could with a walk-in shower in the way.

'Get the ram,' he said. 'We need this door open.' Then he called for quiet. 'If there's anyone there, stand clear, we're coming through,' he shouted at the door. Then he nodded to the sergeant. 'The rooms don't measure up,' he said. 'There's something behind here. Can you open it, please?'

'No problem,' said the sergeant, and swung. The door flew open to reveal a flight of steps going down.

'Get Greg,' Ned said to Steve, who was hovering by the back door, and reaching out, he flicked the light switch by the door. At the bottom of the stairs he saw two scared faces, one behind the other.

'Got them,' he said under his breath, and held out his hand. 'It's OK,' he said. 'You're safe now. You can come out. We're the police. We're here to take you to safety.'

34

5 August 2020 – the early hours

Out in the garden, everyone was staring at the body, so abruptly decanted from the pillar.

'Don't touch anything else, secure the scene and wait for Ned,' Greg instructed Jenny. 'And get Turbo back in your car. We don't need any more help from him!' Then he turned and followed Steve back into the bungalow.

He found Ned sitting on a flight of steps leading down to a cellar. He was talking to someone out of Greg's line of sight.

'It really is all over, I promise,' Ned was saying. 'Come on, you can leave the cellar now and we'll take you somewhere safe.'

'Are they both there, Ned?' he asked.

'Yes, both safe and sound,' said Ned over his shoulder.

Greg looked round at Jill. 'I think it might be a good idea if you go and give Ned a hand,' he said in an undertone. 'I'll ring that safeguarding lead. Is an ambulance on its way?'

'Yes, Boss. First thing I did, as agreed,' she replied.

Jill joined Ned on the stairs. 'Hi,' she said, 'I'm Jill. You know my best friend, Diana Grain, don't you, Karen?'

'You mean Miss Grain my teacher?' said a small voice from the bottom of the stairs.

'That's right. She lives with me in a little cottage in Thorpe. Look, I've got a photo of her on my phone.' She held out her phone to Karen, who came a couple of steps up to study the photo of two laughing faces with a cottage garden in the background.

Karen looked from the photo to Jill, and back again. 'That's you, with Miss Grain,' she said. 'We really are safe now.'

'You're safe now,' repeated Jill.

In a sudden rush, Karen ran up the stairs and into Jill's arms. 'Thank you, thank you,' she cried. Then she turned and looked over her shoulder. 'Come on, Jake,' she said. 'It's safe now. We can come out.'

'No,' said a voice in mulish tones. 'It's not safe and I'm not coming out. We have to stay home. It's the law. You heard it on the TV. We have to stay home.'

Jill glanced at Ned then back at Jake. 'It really is OK,' she said. 'Honest. I'm with the police, and if I say you can come out, then you can come out.'

'No,' repeated Jake. 'It's not safe. I'll get Covid and I'll die. I'm not coming out.' And he started to cry. 'I want Aunty Jo,' he sobbed.

Jill looked at Ned again, at a loss what to do next.

'I've an idea,' muttered the father of three and, taking out a mask from his pocket, he went down a step toward Jake, who retreated backward across the small cellar until his legs came up against the bed behind him.

'Look,' said Ned, holding out the mask. 'You put this on and I'll put mine on, then you'll be safe, I promise. You've seen people on the TV wearing masks, haven't you? I'm even wearing full protection.' He gestured at his coveralls. 'Come on, lad,' he added, 'it's very late and your sister's waiting for you.'

'She hasn't got a mask on,' said Jake, pointing to Jill.

'Quite right,' said Ned. 'Jill, put your mask back on like a good girl.'

Jill pulled her mask back up as instructed, her other arm still round Karen, and Jake came slowly up the stairs. All four of them backed away from the steps and went to sit on the big sofa – the one where the children had sat, on the first evening that Aunty Jo had found them in the boat, had Jill and Ned but known it.

'Where's Aunty Jo?' asked Jake again.

'She's talking to my boss,' replied Jill. 'Don't worry about her. Very soon we'll take you to somewhere you can have a rest and a meal. Is there anything you'd really like, and I'll see what we can do?'

'Ice cream,' said Jake straight away. Karen didn't say anything. Jill looked down at her with concern and noticed the child seemed to be in shock.

'Are you all right, Karen?' she asked quietly.

'Yes,' she replied. 'But I need to tell you something. Jake's "Aunty Jo" has been keeping us prisoner. Jake doesn't understand, but she has.'

'Yes, we know,' said Jill, under cover of Ned's ongoing, ice cream-related conversation with Jake. 'We're dealing with Aunty Jo, don't worry. Did she hurt you?'

'Only when she pushed me down the stairs,' said Karen. 'I was trying to escape and she didn't like it.'

Jill's expression hardened, but anything she might have said was interrupted by the arrival of blue flashing lights in the road outside. 'I think that's the ambulance,' she said to Karen.

'Why?' The girl was startled. 'We're not ill.'

'It's normal,' said Jill. 'We just need them to check you over, make sure you're all right, then we'll find you somewhere safe to stay. Don't worry. They're nice, and I'll stay with you.' She could hear the sounds of paramedics arriving and running the gauntlet of the officers securing the scene, then a young man clad in green came in with bag in hand.

'So, are these my two customers?' he asked, putting his bag down on the floor and surveying the children, hands on hips. 'Doesn't look much wrong with you, I must say. But how about you come out to my ambulance and we'll have a proper look at you?'

Jake looked up. 'Are we going for a ride in your ambulance?' he asked.

'That's the plan,' the young man agreed.

'Can I sound the siren?' asked Jake.

'We'll see about that,' said the paramedic. 'Maybe not just now, it's still the middle of the night and you'd wake everyone up. But you can turn the blue lights on and off if you're good.'

Jake stood up with alacrity. 'OK,' he said.

Karen rolled her eyes at Jill, and stood up to follow. As they passed through the hall, Jill noted, with relief, that the door to the spare bedroom was firmly closed. She and Ned stood back as the two children were ushered into the ambulance.

'I'll go with them to the hospital,' she said to Ned. 'I assume social services will take over from there, but we can't leave them on their own till then.'

'I agree,' said Ned. 'Greg's with the so-called Aunty Jo, I suppose. What about the children's relatives? Who will inform them?'

'Either Greg or me, I would think,' said Jill. 'There's only some grandparents and they don't seem to have been involved in the children's lives very much. I don't know what will happen to them now.'

'Poor kids,' said Ned. 'Meanwhile, I'd better take a look at Turbo's find in the back garden. It may be they had a lucky escape.'

In the spare bedroom, Greg was surveying Aunty Jo, now handcuffed and sulking on the bed, her gaze directed at the floor.

'Joanne Hamilton, I am arresting you for the false imprisonment of Karen Mirren and Jake Mirren. We also wish to question you about the body we have just found in the garden. Other charges may follow. You do not have to say anything. But it may harm your defence if you do not mention when questioned something which you later rely on in court. Anything you do say may be given in evidence.' He paused for a reaction, but got nothing beyond one wild glance up at the mention of the body. 'You will now be taken to a police station and questioned further. If you want legal advice that will be arranged.' He looked at Steve. 'Take her to Wymondham and see her processed – I need to join Ned. I'll question her in the morning, which isn't far away by the look of things,' he added, noting the lighter sky in the east.

When he joined Ned in the garden, he could indeed hear the beginnings of the dawn chorus, the voices of blackbirds predominating. A couple of the forensic team were unrolling a tent, preparatory to erecting it over the felled column and its grisly contents. Ned was bent over studying the plastic, the glimpse of bones and partially mummified flesh.

'We need the doc,' he said to Greg over his shoulder. 'And possibly your friends George and Mildred.'

Greg grimaced at the reference to the idiosyncratic forensic anthropologists from Bradford. 'Let's wait and see what the doc says,' he replied. 'I believe she's on her way. Any idea how long it's been there?'

'We'll know better when the doc's had a proper look,' said Ned. 'But I'd guess a couple of years at least. Not much we can do here until then, other than preserve the scene. I'll go back and organise a full search of the bungalow and gardens, now you've got Mrs Hamilton out of the way.'

'Yes, thanks, Ned. Then, I think, you should get your head down for a bit.'

'Same to you,' said Ned, but Greg shook his head.

'When I can,' he said. 'But time is ticking. I can only hold her for so long!'

35

---

5 August 2020 – morning

By 9am their small corner of Ormesby was swarming with activity. Crime scene tape fluttered around the bungalow and the boat on its drive. Uniformed officers were keeping the increasing crowd of muttering onlookers at bay. The doc and a mortuary van had arrived, plus a second forensic science van. Driven out of the bungalow by busy specialists, Greg had retreated to his car. To his relief, he found a text from Chris.

On a callout. All fine. Back later. Let me know you're OK.

He texted back.

All fine here too. Found the kids And a body .

He looked up at a sharp rap on his windscreen, and got out of the car in a hurry.

'Anything for me, Doc?' he asked.

'Not much. Given the way it's wrapped and the state it's in, I can't do much until I have it back in the mortuary and can take a proper look. What I can tell you, from a quick look at the skull, is that it's an adult, probably a woman, and has been there a couple of years at least.'

'So, within the tenure of Mrs Hamilton, but nothing to do with recent events,' said Greg.

'So it would seem.'

'But it might be we got to the kids in the nick of time. Thanks, Doc.'

'I'll ring later when I know more,' she promised. 'This will be a priority.'

Greg checked in with the sergeant controlling security, and with Ned, then decided to leave them to it. He got back in his car, nodding a thank you to the officer who lifted the tape to let him past, and headed for home.

His first phone call was to Chief Superintendent Margaret Tayler, with an update.

'I'll put out a press release saying the children are safe as soon as I've spoken to the grandparents,' she said. 'Thank God for some good news. What about the body?'

'Heading for the mortuary as we speak.'

'Can we keep a lid on that news for a while?' asked Margaret.

'I doubt it, Boss. The locals are already rubbernecking and it's only a matter of time before the media turn up.'

'Then, for the moment, I'll say that some unidentified human remains have been found and that investigations are ongoing. And that the resident of the property is assisting us with our enquiries. When will you be in?'

Greg glanced at the clock on his dashboard. 'I'm on my way home to freshen up. Say around eleven-thirty. That gives Mrs Hamilton time to get lawyered up, assuming that's what she wants. Jill is at the hospital with the children, and I'll check with her in a moment.'

'OK. See you later.'

His call to Jill went to answerphone, not entirely to his surprise, since she was in a hospital and her phone was probably turned off. She rang him back just as he turned in at the long rutted drive to his house near Acle.

'Hi, Boss,' she said. 'The children have been checked over and are fine, if a bit pale and flabby from long confinement. Social services are here and seem to be getting on well with Karen at least. The boy, Jake, seems to have Stockholm syndrome, as well as paranoia about Covid. They've been discussing where to take the children, pending any claim by relatives. In more normal times they might have stayed in hospital for a night or so, but given the Covid pressures, everyone wants them out of here asap. I've stressed the need for confidentiality, to keep the media off their backs, and social services are currently talking to an experienced foster parent about taking them on.'

'Sounds sensible,' said Greg, pulling up outside his cottage. 'If that's what happens, make sure the foster family have a family liaison officer assigned. And that they understand we will need to talk to the children as soon as possible.'

'Will do,' said Jill, and rang off.

By the time Greg had greeted Bobby and Tally, showered, shaved and consumed a hasty slice of toast or two, his eyes were closing. He lay down on the sofa, Bobby curled up alongside, and, taking the precaution of setting a thirty-minute alarm, he tried to stop his mind spinning in circles. When the alarm went off he woke with a jerk, startled to find that sleep had arrived so quickly, but much refreshed by the short nap. He was already ringing Jim as he took his seat in his car.

'I'll be in within the half hour,' he said. 'Anything from the doc yet?'

'Not yet,' said Jim, his voice echoing round the car. Jim always seemed to shout down a hands-free. 'But we're promised at least an interim report shortly. Mrs Hamilton's currently in discussion with a duty solicitor. She apparently said she doesn't have a solicitor and wouldn't know where to go for one, so with luck we can start interviewing her when you are ready.'

'Anything from Ned?' asked Greg.

'Again, an interim report. He says they've been through the whole property, outbuildings and so on, and found nothing else untoward.'

'By which I take it he means no more bodies.'

'That's right. But there's every sign the children have been kept in that cellar ever since they arrived in Ormesby. The cellar had a CCTV camera in one corner and Ned's got a laptop, presumed to be Mrs Hamilton's, which is currently being analysed. They also found a mobile phone in the main bedroom, and an iPad in the cellar which may well be the one Diana Grain loaned to the children for schoolwork. They're all with the techies.

'What Ned describes as "loads" of fingerprints have been lifted from different parts of the property – Mrs Hamilton doesn't seem to have been an assiduous cleaner – and DNA samples have been taken from toothbrushes, hairbrushes and so on. That's about it for now.'

'Good. Jim, I'd like you to join me for the first interviews. I may want to rotate Jill in later, just to get a different perspective, when she's had a break. She's with the children at present.'

'What about you?' asked Jim. 'Have you had any sleep?'

'Some,' said Greg and refrained from elaborating. Jim got the message anyway, as was evidenced by the large mug of black coffee that awaited Greg on his arrival.

Greg took a large swig then rang for Jim. 'Let's have a chat and agree our strategy,' he said, just as the interim report from Doctor Paisley pinged into his inbox.

The body is that of a woman, estimated age somewhere between 50 and 70, height around 1 metre 60. Hair is grey and there has been some dental work on the teeth, so dental records may be helpful in IDing the remains. It has also been possible to take samples that should yield DNA, but they will take a little time to analyse.

Cause of death is tricky, with so little soft tissue remaining unchanged. There is damage to the occipital bone but it's doubtful it would have been lethal on its own. Samples have gone for analysis, but we may never know for certain what was the cause.

There were no clothes, belongings or any other materials enclosed with the body, other than a leather strap used to hold the arms close to the torso. Otherwise it's just bones, and a lot of adipocere, resulting from the anaerobic environment in which the body was stored.

Estimated date of death is 2–3 years ago.

Greg looked up as Jim came into his office. 'I take it you've seen the doc's report,' he said.

'Yes. Not much to go on yet.'

'No,' agreed Greg. 'Let's hope dental records and the DNA give us an ID. I gather Steve's already checked and the former owner of the property not only moved out more than ten years ago, but is alive and well and living in Great Yarmouth.

'Right, let's plan this interview. We have two areas for questions. First, the children, how she came to meet them, how they came to be imprisoned in her cellar, her motives for keeping them, what she was intending to do with them, and so on.

'Then, the body. Who is it? How did they come to die? How did they end up in her garden ornament? Who killed them? How did they acquire the injury to the back of the head?'

36

5 August 2020 – afternoon

Greg's phone rang just before he headed to the interview suite with Jim.

'Chris, everything OK?' he asked.

'Just about,' she said. 'One of the families I've been monitoring had a bit of a bust-up last night and I've been involved in interviewing the wife.' She sounded exhausted and Greg was immediately concerned.

'Where are you now?' he asked.

'On my way home. I'm going to take a break, then write my report up at home. Fingers crossed, but I think this time she may actually support a prosecution. I heard about the children,' she added. 'It's all over the news. I'm thrilled for you, Greg. Such a relief. But what's this about a body?'

'I'm hoping to find out,' he replied. 'Just about to start the interview with Mrs Hamilton. Take care, Chris. I'll let you know when I'm on my way home.'

He rang off and walked briskly down the corridor to the interviewing suite, picking up Jim en route.

'All ready?' he asked.

'Think so,' said Jim. 'Anything more from Ned?'

'Nothing yet.'

They entered Interview Room 2, to find Mrs Hamilton sitting at the table with a duty solicitor they recognised. He nodded as they came in and sat down.

'You met me this morning, Mrs Hamilton,' said Greg. 'I'm DCI Geldard and this is DI Henning.' He held up a hand as she seemed about to launch into speech. 'If you don't mind, we'll just do the formalities for the tape, and then we can get started properly.'

Everyone introduced – the solicitor turned out to be Mr Joseph Streeter, a name Greg vaguely recognised as a regular round the magistrates' courts – and the caution repeated for the tape, Greg paused a moment and looked at Mrs Hamilton. Her grey hair was now tamed into a straggly ponytail, and she'd been provided with a tracksuit from the police stores. Either tiredness or some disaster of longer standing had etched stress lines into her hollow cheeks and engraved deep contours under her eyes.

'You have been charged with the unlawful imprisonment of two children, Karen Mirren and Jake Mirren. What have you to say?' asked Greg.

Somewhat to his surprise – he had been expecting a 'no comment' response – she replied calmly.

'I was not and never have imprisoned the children. They came to me, lost and abandoned, in the middle of a pandemic.

I took them in, looked after them and kept them safe. And this is the thanks I get.'

Jim and Greg exchanged glances. 'How do you explain that the door to the cellar was locked with them inside it?' asked Greg.

'I was keeping them safe and obeying the lockdown rules,' she replied. 'Jake is a good boy and was content to stay indoors, but Karen is wilful and had already tried to wander off. It was for their own good.'

'Why did you not let them stay in the main part of your property?' asked Greg. 'You had an empty spare bedroom. Surely it would have been more comfortable and healthier than keeping them below ground.'

'To start with, it was because I was shielding,' said Mrs Hamilton. 'I wanted to keep my exposure to them to a minimum until I was sure they didn't have Covid. Then, it was because Karen was naughty about the lockdown restrictions.'

'And why didn't you inform the authorities, either the council or us, that you had the children? There has been a major manhunt underway for them that has been fully reported in the press and on the TV. We even held a special event just across the road from your bungalow, asking for help to find them.'

'Oh, was that what that was?' she said. 'I didn't know. I told you, I was shielding. As for the news, I've more or less stopped watching it. It's so depressing.'

'You take the local paper,' said Greg. 'I've seen it in your home.'

'Well, I just didn't see the need to get involved with all that,' she responded. 'I've told you, the children were safe with me.'

'You paint a delightful picture of yourself as their rescuer,' said Greg. 'Unfortunately it doesn't accord with the children's version of events. They say you found them in your boat, took them into your house, doped them, then kept them under lock and key in that cellar, never letting them out even to go to the bathroom, let alone to play in the garden!'

'The children's version, or Karen's?' asked Mrs Hamilton. 'I'm sure Jake has said no such thing, and Karen's version can't be trusted. The basement room has toilet facilities, it isn't so bad! I may have been a little cavalier in not letting the authorities, as you put it, know I had them with me, but that's all.'

Greg had to concede, within his own head, that she was right about Jake. He looked at Jim, to take up the questioning.

'Let's turn to another issue,' said Jim. 'Whose is the body we found in your garden?'

That did shock her. Her eyes widened and her fingers clutched at the edge of the table. She swallowed a couple of times before she managed to say, 'What? What body?'

'You tell me,' said Jim. 'Is there more than one?'

The solicitor was watching his client with some concern. 'Take a drink of water,' he said to her, then to the police officers, 'I think a few moments' break might be in order.'

Jim scowled at him, but as Greg rose from his seat, he followed suit.

Outside the interview room he turned to Greg. 'That was the only point we had her on the run,' he complained.

'You're right,' said Greg. 'I suppose a defence based on Jake's version of events being different from Karen's was predictable. I think, in court, Karen would be the more believable witness, so I'm not too worried about that. And the failure to let anyone know about the children plus keeping them under lock and key is just not defensible in reality, whatever she says now.

'But her reaction to the mention of the body was interesting, don't you think?'

'Yes, but I also think she'll go "no comment" on us now.' Jim was still irritated at having to pause his questions.

'You're probably right on that too,' said Greg. 'In which case, we'll need to wait for more forensic evidence to hit her with. There's no way that body found its way into the concrete column without leaving some traces somewhere.'

Both predictions proved to be accurate. When Jim and Greg reconvened at the end of the day with no further progress made, it was to consider tactics.

Greg looked at his watch. 'She's been in custody since the early hours of this morning,' he said. 'We have until tomorrow morning to charge her or apply for an extension.'

'On grounds that she's suspected of a murder?' asked Jim.

'Quite. Park her in the cells overnight and we'll see what science can come up with. Then we'll either charge her with false imprisonment or apply for an extension. For now, get yourself home, Jim, and I'll do the same.'

37

6 August 2020 – confidential location near Norwich

Buoyed up by Diana's delighted response to the news the children had been found safe, Jill had slept well and deeply. Now she and Jenny were sitting in her car outside the foster parents home near Norwich, waiting for the arrival of the designated social care worker from the council.

'What about the grandparents?' Jenny had just asked. 'I thought the mother's parents were still alive.'

'I spoke to them yesterday after Margaret Tayler let them know the children had been found and were well,' replied Jill. 'They said they were relieved about that, then said that, of course, they were too frail to take responsibility for two kids and they hoped we understood that.'

'Oh!' said Jenny, in a tone that spoke volumes. 'How old are they?'

'I don't know for sure,' said Jill. 'In their fifties or sixties I'd guess, and definitely not minded to put themselves out. I gather they've had little or no contact with the children since they were born, so it's probably not a great surprise.'

'And the father's parents?'

'Not known. It seems Kit Mirren was adopted as a baby, and lost contact with his adopted parents when he was in his teens. As far as we can tell from a quick and dirty search of records, they seem to have moved to Spain shortly after. His father's identity isn't recorded on his birth certificate and, according to the adoption records, his birth mother died of an overdose soon after he was adopted.'

'How on earth did you dig all that out so quickly?' asked Jenny.

'I did the digging around when we started the hunt for the kids,' explained Jill. 'I was trying to find out if there were any other family members they might have fled to.'

Jenny nodded her understanding. 'So the children will probably end up fostered or adopted,' she said.

'Seems so. Here she is,' said Jill, seeing a small Peugeot draw up in front of them. 'Let's get started.'

Jill went up to the woman climbing out of the car and held her hand out. 'DS Jill Hayes,' she said, 'and this is DC Jenny Warren. I suggest we keep everything as informal as possible and use Jill and Jenny.'

The social worker was a sensible-looking middle-aged lady in jeans and blue polo shirt, clutching a clipboard and tablet in one hand. 'And I'm Lily North,' she said. She leaned back against her car for a moment. 'Obviously I'm here as the children's appropriate adult,' she said, 'but I'm also going to take the opportunity to check with their foster mum how they're getting on and whether she needs any help.'

'Makes sense,' agreed Jill. 'I imagine a period of normality and calm would be recommended, so we don't want to be heavy-handed about this interview. We just need to clarify a couple of points from what the children told me in the hospital.'

'I understand that,' said Lily. 'But let's keep it short, if possible.'

Nodding agreement, Jill and Jenny followed her into the house, to be greeted by a lady in a voluminous kaftan and with vivid multi-coloured hair.

'This is Mrs Helga Ratcliffe,' said Lily. 'One of our best and most experienced foster mums. How are Karen and Jake?' she asked.

'Both doing surprisingly well, I'd say,' replied Helga. 'I'm waiting for reaction to set in. It's bound to happen sooner or later, but for the moment I think Karen, especially, is enjoying the change of scene and the fresh air in the garden. Jake was a little slower to get over his nervousness about catching Covid from us, but our old dog Maisie solved that problem. In fact, I think he's sharing her bed as we speak. Come through to the sitting room and I'll bring the children to you. You may have to have Maisie as well.'

'No problem,' said Jenny. 'My regular work partner is a springer spaniel, so I'll be delighted to have some assistance from Maisie.'

The sitting room was a comfortable and casual space, full of cosy sofas covered in throws against dog hair, piles of discarded toys and books. Jenny pushed a few books aside to make space on a battered coffee table for her recording equipment, then she and Jill sat down on one sofa while Lily chose a squishy armchair at right angles to them.

Helga reappeared with Karen, but no sign of Jake. 'He won't come without Maisie,' announced Karen.

'That's fine,' said Jenny. 'I'd like to meet Maisie anyway.'

After a short pause Jake appeared, hesitating in the doorway, and was firmly pushed aside by a large golden retriever which made a beeline for Jenny and started nosing her pockets.

'Nothing wrong with your scenting skills, old girl,' she laughed, and produced some gravy-bone biscuits from the pocket. 'Sit, Maisie,' she instructed, and the dog slapped its rump onto the floor.

Jake came forward. 'She'll shake paws too,' he told Jenny.

'Will she? That's advanced stuff,' said Jenny.

'I'll show you,' said Jake, and took a handful of the gravy-bones. 'Maisie! Shake!'

Karen sat herself down on the sofa opposite Jill and Jenny, while Jake sat on the floor with his arm round the dog.

'You know Lily, don't you,' said Jill. 'Today she's here to look out for you while we ask a few questions. Is that OK?'

'Yes,' said Karen. 'I want to answer your questions. You need to know what happened.'

'Where's Aunty Jo?' interrupted Jake. Karen sighed heavily and started to put him straight, but Jill interrupted.

'Aunty Jo is fine,' she said to Jake. 'She's safe with us and she's answering some questions too.' Karen got the message and smiled a little. Jenny nodded to indicate that the recorder was running.

'We're going to record this, just in case we forget anything you tell us,' said Jill. 'Is that OK, Karen?'

'Yes,' she said.

'OK. Just for the tape, we have here Jill Hayes, Jenny Warren, Lily North, Karen Mirren and Jake Mirren.'

'And Maisie,' added Jake.

'And Maisie the dog,' agreed Jill. 'Karen, yesterday you told me how you and Jake got to Ormesby by bus, and bought some food from the garage, before getting into a boat on a trailer in a drive not far from the garage. What happened after that?'

'I told you yesterday,' objected Karen.

'Yes I know. Sorry, I know it's boring, but I just need to go over it again.'

'OK. We climbed into the boat, ate our supper, and Jake was playing pirates, twirling the steering wheel round. I had just told him to be a bit quieter, when a voice told us to get out of the boat or she'd call for the police. I think she was a bit surprised to see we were only children,' said Karen, 'and after she looked us over, she told us to go into the house.'

'Who was that?' asked Jill.

'It was Aunty Jo. At least, that's what she told us to call her,' said Karen.

'And that was the lady at the house when we found you yesterday?'

'Yes, said Karen. 'That was Aunty Jo.'

'What happened next?'

'She told us to sit down in her sitting room, and then she asked if we were hungry.'

'No,' objected Jake. 'She asked if we were hungry first.'

'No she didn't,' contradicted Karen. 'Anyway, it doesn't matter. She brought us some egg butties, and crisps and a drink each.'

'What happened after that?' asked Jill.

'The next thing I remember properly, we were in the cellar, on the bed. I woke up and Jake was next to me.'

'Do you remember going down the stairs to the cellar?' asked Jenny.

'No. Not really. At least...' Karen screwed up her face with the effort to remember. 'I might remember being very sleepy and Aunty Jo saying we needed to go to bed, and her taking my arm ... but it's all muddled.'

'OK, that's fine,' said Jill. 'What happened next?'

'When I woke up properly, I started to look around and I went to the door, but I couldn't open it. Then Aunty Jo came in with some breakfast and told us she was going to look after us. I said, "What about our mum?" and she said...' Karen's eyes glistened with sudden tears. 'She said Mum was dead but we didn't need to worry because she would look after us. I guess that was true, because it was in the paper she showed us. The bit about Mum, I mean.'

'Yes, I'm afraid that was true,' said Jill.

'Then later,' went on Karen, 'she told us Dad was dead too and we were orphans and that we didn't have anyone but her.

'What's going to happen to us now?' she asked. 'Now we have no one. Even Tim has disappeared.'

Lily leaned forward. 'You are safe and you will be looked after, I promise you. I will personally see to it that you and Jake are found a new home together. It's a promise.'

Karen sniffed, and Jill pushed the box of tissues on the coffee table toward her, feeling that it would take very little for her to need the tissues herself.

'Is that the Tim who was a friend of your mother's? she asked.

'Yes,' said Karen.

'Well, I can tell you that he's going to be OK. He was in hospital for a bit, which is why you couldn't find him, but he's fine now.'

'Can we see him?' asked Jake.

'I'll talk to him about that,' said Lily.

'Tell me about your life in the cellar,' said Jill.

***

Comparing notes back in the car, Jill and Jenny tried to focus on the facts to suppress their horror at what might have been.

'Shorn of Jake's worries about Covid and his reliance on "Aunty Jo", the children's accounts are pretty consistent,' said Jenny.

'Let's summarise what they agree on,' said Jill. 'First, they agree that Aunty Jo gave them food and drink on the evening they arrived, and neither of them clearly remember going into the cellar. There must be a realistic supposition that she drugged or doped them. Make a note that we need to ask the forensic team if they found anything like that in the bungalow.

'Second, they agree that the door was kept locked, and that Karen asked on multiple occasions to be let out. That's false imprisonment.

'Third, they both say that on the one occasion Karen did get out, Aunty Jo pushed her back down the stairs quite violently. That's assault.'

'There's no suggestion she assaulted them in any other way,' said Jenny.

'Correct,' said Jill. 'But she did film them through that remote camera in the corner of the cellar, and there are images on her laptop which, while I suspect they weren't intended to be sexual, would qualify as Category C indecent images. That's another charge.'

'Then there's the body in the garden.'

'Yes,' said Jill, pulling her seat belt round and clipping it on. 'I don't think Aunty Jo will be out anytime soon.'

The rap of a knuckle on the side window made her look round. It was Lily.

'Did you get everything you want?' she asked.

'Yes. Thanks, Lily, for your help. Can I ask you something unofficially?' added Jill.

'Yes, of course, although I won't guarantee I'll answer unofficially,' said Lily with a smile.

'My partner, Diana Grain, taught Karen at school in Great Yarmouth,' said Jill. 'She suggested I ask you if you thought some remote teaching might bring a bit of normality back into the children's lives, in which case she'd be glad to help.'

'It's a thought,' said Lily. 'Although I don't think they should be exposed to any mass Zooms with other children just yet.'

'No, certainly not,' agreed Jill. 'Too much risk of the media gatecrashing, let alone other children being insensitive. No, what she had in mind was some one-to-one classes, or one-to-two if Jake wanted to join in.'

'I'll see how the children react and get back to you,' said Lily. 'Thanks for the offer.'

Hard on the back of another 'no comment' interview, Greg was pleased with Jill's summary.

'Good work,' he said. 'And a very thorough assessment of what we've got on Mrs Hamilton with regard to the children.' He checked his watch for the umpteenth time that morning. 'I think it's time we charged her with those offences, then we can keep her in custody until the forensic results come back on the body in the garden. Would you like to come with me this time?'

Jill nodded an eager thank you, and the two of them went back to the interview room.

'I hope you've come to release my client,' said Mr Streeter, rising to his feet to deliver what, Greg reflected, he must have known was a forlorn hope.

'On the contrary,' said Greg, after he had introduced Jill and sat down. 'We are here to charge your client with some serious offences.

'Joanne Hamilton, you are charged with the unlawful imprisonment of Karen and Jake Mirren from Friday, 27th of March 2020 to Wednesday, 5th of August 2020. You are further charged with assault on Karen Mirren, and with the making and possession of Category C indecent images of both children. You do not have to say anything—'

Joanne Hamilton's jaw had dropped, and she interrupted to ask, 'What indecent images? You can't accuse me of that! I never touched either child. I wouldn't. And what assault?'

'Both children agree that you pushed Karen Mirren down the stairs. That is assault,' said Greg. 'And indecent images of both children were found on your laptop. That is an offence in itself. You will appear before magistrates in the morning and your case will be remitted to the Crown Court.' In a patient voice he completed the interrupted caution and checked she understood.

'Other charges may follow,' he added. 'DS Hayes, will you see Mrs Hamilton back to the custody suite, please.'

Back in his office, Greg had barely sat down to complete the paperwork when the phone rang.

'It's me,' announced Ned unnecessarily, given his number on the display. 'I have some results back on the DNA samples. Can I come and see you?'

'Of course,' said Greg. 'But can't you tell me on the phone?'

'I'm just upstairs, and I think this is something you need to see,' said Ned. He rang off precipitously and the sound of footsteps galloping down the corridor soon followed.

'What's the excitement?' asked Greg as Ned entered the office.

'This,' said Ned, slapping a couple of charts on the desk. 'These are the results of the DNA tests on the body found in the garden, as compared with DNA taken from Joanne Hamilton. They prove that the body is Joanne Hamilton's mother.'

'They what!' exclaimed Greg. 'How confident are you of the match?'

'Over ninety-nine per cent confident. The body in the garden ornament was the mother of the woman we have in custody. Moreover, Dr Paisley has been consulting with your old friends in Bradford, George and Mildred, and sent them some photos of various key bones – I believe, the pubic symphysis, and of knee and hip joints amongst others.'

'And what do they say?' he asked.

'The body was, they estimate, around sixty to seventy years old when death occurred, and they also agree that death occurred around two years ago.'

'Hang on,' said Greg, doing the maths. 'If Joanne Hamilton's mother was, say, seventy years old in 2018, how did she manage to have a daughter who appears to be sixty-plus years old now? Sorry, I know that doesn't make sense. I'm thinking aloud. If the woman in the cells is the daughter of the body in the garden, then the body must be Joanne Hamilton, and the woman we have in custody is her daughter.'

'That's where I got to,' said Ned. 'Which means that she's been masquerading as her mother for a couple of years, claiming her pension, living in her home and using her bank accounts.'

Greg picked up his phone. 'Jim, you need to hear this,' he said. 'Get yourself along to my office.'

When Jim had joined them, Ned and Greg outlined the position between them, voices chiming in point and counterpoint. Jim took a few moments to assimilate the data, then his eyes gleamed.

'That's a good few charges to add,' he said, rubbing his hands together. 'Not to say a motive for murder. How on earth did she think she'd get away with it?'

'She has for over two years,' Greg pointed out. 'I suppose there was a family likeness which she exaggerated by dressing in her mother's clothes and maybe dying her hair. And the subterfuge would be helped by the fact everyone agrees her mother was a recluse. She'd just keep up the pretence with little or no interaction with neighbours. Easy!'

38

---

6 August 2020 – afternoon

Enjoying a hasty lunch at his desk, Greg seized the moment to make a quick call to Chris.

'There's been a development,' he said. 'It means I'm probably going to be late home again.'

'That makes two of us,' was the reply. She sounded tired and dispirited.

'What's wrong?' he asked.

'That family I mentioned. The woman I thought would give evidence to prosecute her husband... I was too optimistic. She's gone back to him again.'

'Oh, Chris. So sorry. That's a bummer.'

'Certainly is,' she said. 'She's *certain he's sorry this time – sure he means it.* There's no chance. This leopard has the same spots running right through, like a stick of rock. I just don't see why she can't see it!'

'Not that she can't, but that she doesn't want to,' suggested Greg.

'I suppose so, but I'm really worried that I'll be picking up a body next time. His violence is escalating. I don't know what else I can do, Greg. I've tried supporting her; I've tried scaring the bejaysus out of *him*; I've tried finding her and the kid a place in a shelter; I've tried introducing her to other women who've gone through something similar and got out. I've run out of options.'

'You've done everything you can,' said Greg. 'In the end, you can't make decisions for someone like that. For anyone, if it comes to that. It's hard, but sometimes all we can do is pick up the pieces after we've tried everything else. You've done everything right,' he repeated.

'No, there must be something I haven't tried yet. I'm going to have a chat with the woman who runs the battered wives shelter. She has a lot of experience. She might have a suggestion.'

'That sounds a good idea,' said Greg. 'But if she says the same as me, that sometimes you can try everything and nothing works, then you have to take a step back and look after yourself. Or let me look after you,' he added. 'I'm not doing a very good job of that at the moment, but we *will* take some time for ourselves soon, I promise.'

'You said you had a development too,' said Chris. 'Good or bad?'

'Don't know yet. Interesting, definitely. It turns out the woman we have in the cells seems to have murdered herself.'

'That *is* different,' said Chris.

'Strictly speaking, we've found a body in her garden that turns out to be the person we thought we'd arrested, and even more interestingly, is the mother of the person we *have* arrested.'

'Now I'm totally confused,' said Chris, but she sounded more cheerful. 'See you later.'

Greg and Jim convened just outside the interview room, with Jill observing from the suite next door.

'Ready?' asked Greg.

'Ready.' They opened the door and joined the elderly-looking woman and her brief at the table.

'DCI Geldard and DI Henning have entered the room,' said Greg. 'I would remind you, Ms Hamilton, that you are still under caution. I've asked you before about the body found in the concrete pillar in your garden.'

'And my client has exercised her right to remain silent,' Mr Streeter commented. 'I can't see that anything has changed.'

'What has changed, is that we now have an analysis of the DNA samples taken from the remains. In light of what that tells us about the identification of the body, I wonder if you would like to amend anything in your previous statements, Ms Hamilton?'

'How can my client comment when neither she nor I yet know what that evidence is?' protested Mr Streeter.

'Oh, I think your client is well aware of what the evidence will have told us,' said Greg. 'Isn't that so, Ms Hamilton? Or do you have another name? Other than your maiden name that is?' Mr Streeter looked up sharply, but Joanne continued to look at the floor.

'Still playing the game? It won't wash you know,' said Greg. 'Jim, read out the summary of the report, would you?'

'In summary,' read Jim, 'the DNA analysis shows that Sample A was taken from the biological mother of Sample B, with a 99.7 % probability.'

'Sample A, as I'm sure you realise, was taken from the remains. Sample B was taken from you. The body in the garden is your mother, and the rightful owner of the property in Ormesby. You are her daughter, and have been masquerading as your own mother, claiming her pension and making use of her property. Any comment?' asked Greg.

As the silence continued, Mr Streeter said, 'I would like a copy of that report and time for a private discussion with my client.'

'Of course,' said Greg. 'But first, I need to make one thing clear. Joanne Hamilton, you are further charged with the murder of your mother, also known as Joanne Hamilton, and with prevention of the lawful and decent burial of a body. Charges relating to theft and fraud—'

Joanne interrupted. 'Stop, wait. I didn't murder her. I didn't murder my mother.'

Mr Streeter attempted to interrupt in his turn. 'I recommend you remain silent until—'

'It was an accident,' said Joanne. 'I didn't mean it.'

Greg and Jim exchanged looks as the room fell silent. Next door, Jill punched the air with a whoop. 'You're saying your mother's death was an accident?' said Greg.

'I really think—' said Mr Streeter with an air of desperation.

'Yes, it was an accident.'

'Perhaps you'd like to tell me what happened,' said Greg, his voice deliberately quiet and low-key.

Joanne took a shuddering breath. For a moment Greg and Jim thought she'd taken her solicitor's advice and gone silent again. But she started to speak, and what she had to say made it difficult for Greg to suppress an audible gasp.

'She killed my son. She killed Frankie. I came home from work and found him dead. I lost it and I pushed her, but I didn't mean to kill her.'

So many questions filled Greg's head he didn't know which to ask first. 'Tell me about Frankie,' he said.

Next door Jill was leafing through her notes, a memory triggered. *Yes, I'm right. The name I saw inside some of the children's books in the basement was Francis Chalmers.* She scribbled a note for Greg, but held on to it, correctly judging that this was not a good moment to interrupt proceedings.

'Frankie was my son,' said Joanne. 'He was a good boy, a quiet boy. He liked reading and animals. We came to my mother when my partner walked out. I had no money and nowhere else to go. Worst decision of my life,' she said bitterly. 'I'd have been better to work on the streets and keep Frankie safe. As it was...' She paused to scrub at the tears on her face with her hands. Jim pushed a box of tissues across the table, but she ignored them. She sniffed and wiped her nose and eyes on her sleeve.

'What happened to Frankie?' asked Greg.

'I told you, I came home from work and found him dead. She said she'd given him crab for his lunch, and it had made him ill. I thought, after, it must have been that allergic thing. Shock. If she hadn't given him crab, or if she'd called for an ambulance quickly, if she'd done *anything* to help him, it might have been all right. But she did nothing. She killed my son. I saw red. I remember shouting and pushing her, and her falling backward onto the stairs. Then she was dead.'

There was a long pause. Then she went on. 'I buried Frankie in the garden, but I wasn't having that evil old witch anywhere near my boy. So, I put her in the freezer. Later, months later, I cemented her into that column.'

Greg looked up at the two-way mirror, behind which he knew Jill was sitting, and gave a slight nod.

In the soundproofed observation suite, Jill picked up a phone and rang Ned. 'We need a new search of the grounds,' she said. 'We've information that there's another body buried in the garden.'

Greg continued his questions. 'What should we call you, Joanne?' he asked. 'What's your real name?'

'Joanne Kate Hamilton,' she said. 'Joanne after my mother. Kate after my grandma. I've used Joanne Chalmers. I never married Frankie's father, but I wanted the same name as my son.'

'Where is Frankie buried?' asked Greg.

'I don't want you disturbing him. That's sick. Leave him in peace, for God's sake. Leave him alone.' She was becoming increasingly distressed and started to bang on the table. Mr Streeter opened his mouth to object, but Greg was there before him.

'Jim, get the duty doctor down here. Interview suspended at 16.50,' he said. 'Mr Streeter, when the doctor has seen your client, she'll be returned to custody. I don't envisage continuing this interview until the morning. You'll have plenty of opportunity to take instruction before then.'

Next door, Jill picked up the phone to Ned again. 'No further information on the location,' she said, 'just that it's in the garden.'

When Greg and Jim came in, she said, 'I've alerted Ned.'

'Good,' said Greg. 'I was sure you'd pick up the cue.'

'He'll need dogs and radar,' said Jim.

'It's not a huge garden,' objected Greg, but Jill chipped in.

'Ned said there was what he called GPR available in Cambridge, and he's already given them a ring.'

'Ground-penetrating radar,' translated Jim. 'It'll save a lot of time and manpower if it's available.'

The phone rang on the desk and Greg picked it up. 'We were just talking about that,' he said. Then he put the phone down. 'Ned says it'll be here in ninety minutes. It's worth the wait to avoid digging up the whole area unnecessarily.'

39

---

6 August 2020 – evening, near Elveden War Memorial

Nick pulled up in the southbound lay-by near the war memorial and looked at his watch. Then he sighed irritably and checked he had everything he needed: petrol, empty wine bottles – nicked from his party-mad neighbour's wheelie bin – a lighter with matches for backup, fabric nicked from his wife's sewing basket – he was oblivious to the fact she'd been saving the scraps for her lockdown quilting project and would definitely miss them – and the digital gadget from the dark web which had been so effective at starting the Leyton Estate Range Rover. What he hadn't got was his driver. After repeated attempts on WhatsApp, by text and by phone, he was forced to the conclusion that Jacko had blocked him.

'Cheeky sod,' he muttered again in recollection, and took a swig from his Thermos of tea. Still, at least he'd managed to borrow his brother's tow truck even though Ade had flatly refused to get involved this time. And not using his own vehicle meant he could leave it parked in a prominent position by his favourite pub, where Mick O'Hanlon would swear blind he'd spent the evening.

Nick was feeling a bit jittery and would have loved something stronger than tea. Maybe it was having to act alone that was getting to him, but being tipsy in charge of an arson attack was not a good idea, let alone driving his target away afterward. Whatever else went up in smoke this evening, he was determined it wouldn't be him or his future.

A large articulated lorry pulled into the lay-by in front of him. He got the message, from the way it swerved into place, that the driver thought he was taking up too much of the available parking with little excuse. *No matter. I won't be here much longer.* He looked at his watch again, then at the map lying on the passenger seat beside him. It wasn't far for him to backtrack toward Elveden and the large estate farm he'd originally scouted all those weeks ago.

The plan was to hide the tow truck down the back road between the A11 and the A134, then approach the back of the farmyard across the fields, much as he had on the last two occasions. Then he'd start the distraction, drive the Range Rover away while everyone was looking at the fire, and round the long way back to the tow truck. Easy.

He had miscalculated on two counts. First, all Norfolk farmers were now alerted to the presence of an arsonist in their midst, and the larger estates could afford high-tech precautions. Second, there had been no rain for some weeks, and everywhere was tinder dry.

He parked the borrowed tow truck in a field entrance at quarter to ten, exactly as planned, and slung the heavy rucksack laden with bottles and matches over his shoulder. Then he hesitated. It was a long walk to the farmyard, and he wasn't keen on carrying that weight very far. On the spur of the moment he jettisoned the bottles and set off across the field carrying just the petrol can, the matches in his pocket. The field had been harvested since he last checked it out, and he was walking over stubble. While it made for easier going, he did feel rather exposed to view and was relieved to arrive at the other side without being spotted. Two more fields, as he remembered, then he'd be close to the farmyard.

He paused just before the fence and spinney that divided the yard and farm buildings from the last field. This one had been harvested too, but the straw was lying in rows awaiting baling. He loosened the top on the petrol can, checked his matches were to hand, then surveyed the potential targets before him. The farm vehicles, including the Range Rover, had previously been parked in the open-fronted garage nearest the road. He saw no reason to think anything would be different today. The rudimentary plan was to fire the buildings furthest from the road, hide at the back of the garage block, then drive the Range Rover away while the farm staff were busy dealing with the blaze.

The plan unravelled immediately he crossed the boundary fence. What he hadn't realised was that, between his last visit and this, the estate had fitted a security beam round the perimeter. As he crossed the line, his body broke the beam and the ensuing siren was probably clearly audible in Cambridge, some twenty miles away. So startled he dropped his petrol can,

Nick froze, then picked it up and ran for cover in the shadow of the nearest barn. Some five or six farmworkers cascaded out of an accommodation block tucked away on the far side of the yard, and ran toward the grain stores. As they fanned out, Nick scuttled for the garage block, but a shout that went up behind him proved he'd been spotted.

On the spur of the moment, he tore the top off the petrol can and swung it round in a semi-circle, then dropped it and lit a match in shaking hands.

The petrol vapour went up with a *whump*, and flames shot up between Nick and the pursuing farmworkers, then across the yard, following the trail of petrol he had, unknowingly, laid behind him as he ran. He didn't waste time on the Range Rover but just legged it out of the yard and down the road.

A modicum of sense slowed his mad gallop as soon as there was some distance between him and the flames. He realised he had a long walk back to the tow truck, and also that his face, arms and the front of his legs were scorched. A flashing, jangling fire engine went past him as he approached the junction with the main road, then two more. That was when he realised that the farmyard wasn't the only blaze.

40

---

6 August 2020 – late evening near the Bure

By six in the evening, it had become apparent that the GPR wasn't arriving anytime soon. Roadworks on the A11, compounded by an accident and rush hour traffic meant a significant holdup. On the basis that the body of Frankie Chalmers had apparently been in the garden for over two years and wasn't going anywhere, plus the advice from both the duty doctor and Mr Streeter that Ms Hamilton was in no fit state to be questioned further that day, Greg concluded with a certain relief that the exhumation and subsequent renewal of questioning could be postponed until the following day. He headed for home and Chris with even more enthusiasm than usual, driven both by concern for her and a strong desire for a quiet evening with the woman he loved, and a good, long, sleep.

It was unfortunate, therefore, that they had scarcely greeted each other and sat down with a glass of wine apiece, Bobby on Chris's lap and Tally on Greg's shoulder, when Greg's phone rang. Tally was offended at the interruption and gave his ear an extra hard nibble.

'Ow!' exclaimed Greg as he looked at his phone, and his heart sank.

'Work,' said Chris. It wasn't a question.

Greg listened for a moment then asked, 'Have you alerted Jim and Jill?' The answer was obviously yes, and he rang off, pushing his, luckily scarcely touched, glass of wine to one side.

'The arsonist,' he said briefly. 'Near Elveden. Sounds like the same MO, only this time he's managed to set light to Thetford Forest. Every fire engine from here to Cambridge has been despatched.'

Chris was already on her feet, turning the salmon they'd been about to eat with salad into doorstep sandwiches, the kettle on for a flask of coffee.

'I don't suppose you'll have time to eat, so take this with you,' she said. Greg was pulling his shoes back on and hunting for his car keys.

'In the fruit bowl,' said Chris, the voice of long experience.

'I'm sorry about this,' said Greg.

'I'm just sorry I'm not coming with you,' said Chris. 'Never mind. At least we both know what we signed up for. We can take some time off together when this is over.'

Greg kissed her, thinking, not for the first time, how very lucky he was. Then he was on his way south. He rang Jim as he joined the A11 at Thickthorn. He was passed on the roundabout by an ambulance and a fire engine, both with lights flashing and sirens blaring.

'Where are you, Jim?' he asked.

'Right behind you,' came the answer, and lights flashed on the car in Greg's rear-view mirror.

'Jill?'

'Ahead of us, I think. Blues and twos?' asked Jim hopefully.

'Oh I think so, don't you?' said Greg. 'Jim, can you send someone into Norwich to check out Nick Waters's gaff? Find him, if they can. I don't think they will, as I suspect he's our arsonist, but it might be useful to establish precisely where he isn't, if you know what I mean. And if they can find him, at least we can rule him out. But, Jim, make sure they have some backup. He mixes with a nasty lot.'

'Got it,' said Jim. 'I think Steve's available.'

'And, while I think about it, get Bill started on scanning ANPR for any plates on our watch list,' added Greg. 'I'll speak to Jill and Ned about crime scene management, and I believe the local Thetford team are already on the scene. Thanks, Jim.'

The next call was to Ned. 'ETA?' he asked.

'I'm in touch with the fire commander,' Ned replied. 'No point busting a gut to get there before they'll allow us onto the ground. He says the farmyard blaze was put out quickly, thanks to the efficiency of the farm team, and they're just finishing damping down. Thetford have a cordon round the property, and they say we can probably get onto site around 01.00. The fire in the forest is another matter. Seems the accelerant was spread around quite a bit and set light to straw in an adjacent field, which in turn ignited the trees. Everything's tinder dry, so they've got quite a job on their hands. Said we're about to see how effective the Forestry Commission fire breaks actually are!'

Greg could see the glow in the sky long before he reached Thetford; an unpleasant reminder of the explosions and subsequent fire at the government laboratory a year or so ago that had resulted in numerous casualties. He fervently hoped that the casualty list, this time, would be much shorter.

When he arrived at the estate farmyard, Jill was already on the scene, liaising with a uniformed sergeant to organise control of the considerable perimeter. Early representatives of the media were already in evidence, together with gawkers from the local population. Luckily they were few, as the location was some distance from the nearest village. One of them tugged Greg by the elbow as he made his way toward Jill.

'You police?' he asked.

'That's right,' said Greg. 'I'm a bit busy right now. If you have anything to say, can you speak to one of the uniformed officers?'

'This might be important,' the man insisted. 'I was driving home from my late shift and I saw someone walking away from the fire. He looked suspicious.'

Greg turned to look at the man. He didn't look like a fantasist, but you could never tell. 'When was this?' he asked.

'Just after the fire started. At least, I could see the blaze and I could hear fire engines on their way. One passed me soon after.'

'And why did you think he looked suspicious?'

'Because...' The man paused and scratched the back of his neck. 'I'm not sure,' he admitted. 'But he was walking away when anyone else would have been rushing toward it, and come to think of it, he must have come out of the farm drive. Otherwise, I'd have seen him sooner. He was a biggish bloke, in work clothes. You know, dark jacket and jeans.'

'Which way did he go?' asked Greg.

'That way.' The man pointed a grubby finger down the road toward the south and the A11.

'Thank you.' It was a wild hunch, but there was nothing Greg could usefully do here until Ned arrived, or so he justified it to himself. 'See that plain-clothes officer over there?' He pointed to Jill. 'Tell her what you've told me, and give her every last detail you can remember, including the best description of the man you can manage. And thank you.' He looked round and beckoned the Thetford sergeant over.

'We have a tip that I'm going to check out,' he said. 'Tell DS Hayes I'll be back shortly.' And he got back in his car to drive in the direction the witness had pointed.

He was stopped twice in the first few minutes. Initially by a squad car stopping all traffic to keep the area clear for the fire service. Second, by a fireman waving a torch and warning him, even after seeing his warrant card, that he proceeded further at his own risk.

'The fire's reached those trees,' he said, pointing to the dark rustling mass to their right. 'At the moment it's headed away from here, but if the wind shifts that could change in a moment.'

'Is that likely?' asked Greg.

The fireman hesitated. 'I think you'll be OK for a bit,' he said. 'But if you hear a siren or horns, get the hell out. And don't leave the road. A fire will travel a lot faster than you can run.'

Nodding agreement, Greg drove on, keeping a very wary eye on the trees and with his window down so he would definitely hear any warning sirens. The last end he sought was immolation in a pinewood.

Joining the A134, he had a choice of turning left, away from the fire, or right. Sighing, and holding a finger up to test the wind direction, he reluctantly decided on right, and was almost immediately rewarded by the sight of a vehicle parked by the side of the road, blocking a field entrance. It looked remarkably like a tow truck. Greg stopped his car and watched for a moment, but could see no movement. Driving forward slowly, he parked his car across the front of the tow truck, preventing it from moving off, and waited. Still no movement. Adjusting his stab vest, and checking he had his phone, radio and taser, he got out of the car and walked over to the truck's cab to peer in. Two things happened simultaneously. A siren went off in the distance, and a man erupted from the passenger side of the truck to run off into the field behind them.

41

---

7 August 2020 – early morning

Greg hesitated for barely a microsecond before setting off after the runner. He fumbled for his radio as he ran and gasped into it.

'Geldard in hot pursuit of probable arsonist. Backup needed. Heading across fields from the B1106 toward the A11.'

He was already regretting the recent years of too little exercise as he watched the depressingly fit shape in front of him draw ahead across the stubble. He tried to put a spurt on and maintained it for perhaps fifty yards before realising he was falling back again. The siren had fallen silent but, to his right, Greg could see the red glow gaining ground and could hear the crackle of flames. He was about to give up and give his aching lungs a rest, not to mention his wobbling legs, when the figure in front of him crashed to the ground near the field edge. With a guttural roar that had more relief in it than triumph, Greg cancelled the idea of a rest and speeded up. He saw the man struggle to his knees, then fall back again, but by then he was on him.

Drawing his taser and trying not to collapse forward with his hands on his knees, he managed, 'You're nicked, sunshine,' which, he admitted to Chris afterwards, must have come from some long-forgotten and at the time disparaged TV crime series. It fell, in any event, a long way short of the formal warning, but at least had the merit of clarity.

The figure on the ground was lying on his face but made an effort to turn his head.

'Stay exactly where you are and put your hands behind your back,' bellowed Greg over what he realised was an increasing background noise from the fire.

The figure seemed to shrug his shoulders but complied, and Greg handcuffed him with a feeling of relief. Then looked about him.

He realised that the fire had advanced on two fronts, one behind him and the other to his right. In both cases the trees on the edge of the field were alight, and he could feel the heat on his exposed skin.

'Up you get, sunshine,' he said, still not sure why he was channelling *Life on Mars*, and tugged on the pinioned arms. The man on the ground groaned and rolled onto his side.

'Sorry, mate,' he said, 'but I think I've broken my ankle.'

Greg glanced round and back at his prisoner. 'You've got a choice,' he almost shouted, to make himself heard over the crackle of flames. 'Hop or burn. Which is it to be?' Then he bent down and hauled the man to his feet, or at least foot, while shouting into his radio. 'Assistance required and ambulance.' He looked round again to get his bearings and added, 'Head for the A11 War Memorial then roughly east from there. We'll try to meet you.' His message was obscured by the clanging bell of a fire tender passing on the main road, which he realised, to his relief, was only thirty or so yards away.

'Come on,' he said, putting an arm round his prisoner casualty. 'Roughly sixty hops and you're home and dry.' He looked into the man's face for the first time and recognised Nick Waters. 'Got you,' he added, in case the man had any doubts on the matter. 'And when we're clear of this,' – he nodded at the fast-approaching walls of fire – 'I'm arresting you for murder and arson.'

Their clumsy three-legged race against ignition resulted in at least two more falls before they reached the hedge that divided the field from the lay-by on the main Norwich road. Nick Waters screamed on each fall, and Greg was forced to the conclusion that his ankle was, at the least, badly sprained if not broken.

To his huge relief, just as he was contemplating the hedge-and-ditch boundary of the field and wondering how the devil to get over it, a squad car roared up the A11 on blues and twos, followed swiftly by an ambulance, ditto.

'Here!' he roared, with what breath he had left after the clumsy traverse of the stubble field. 'Here!' He waved his torch vigorously, and a welcome shout from the paramedics was the response. With two paramedics and a couple of uniformed police to help, Greg relinquished his role as criminal prop with enthusiasm and pulled his radio out.

'Jim. Jill,' he said with scant adherence to radio protocol. 'Geldard here. Have you got anyone over to the tow truck?'

'Just got here,' was Jim's reply. 'The fire commander wouldn't let us through straight away, but the wind's just changed again and he let me and one of the forensic team through, with strict instructions to do a quick and dirty lift of whatever we can find and get out again until later in the day. I've got Al Thorpe with me.'

'Anything of interest?' asked Greg. 'I've arrested Nick Waters on suspicion of arson, but I'm a bit short of proof at present.'

'We picked up a petrol can near the farmyard, which may or may not have his fingerprints on it. Just had a quick look in the back of the cab and there's an interesting collection of wine bottles and bits of fabric which look very like the makings of Molotov cocktails.'

'Very interesting,' said Greg. 'Do as the fire chief said and get out of there as quick as you can.' He would have said more, but was interrupted by one of the paramedics tapping him on the arm and signalling the need to get away from the flames. 'See you back at the farmyard,' said Greg and rang off, turning to the green-uniformed woman behind him. 'Tasha' was the name on her uniform jacket.

'Something I think you need to know,' said Tasha. 'Our casualty is claiming that you broke his ankle by hitting him with a baton.'

'He what?' asked Greg stupidly, then as his brain caught up with his ears he flushed with rage. 'Well, the dirty, ungrateful little...' Luckily, words failed him at that point. 'I should have left him to roast,' he growled. 'I didn't even have a baton with me. Just a taser, which I didn't use, as it happens. Wish I had!'

'Doesn't look like that sort of injury to me,' agreed Tasha. 'Looks like the sort of break you get when you trap your foot in a hole and fall over. But I'm not an expert. The doctors will obviously need a look. But I thought you should know.'

'Thank you,' said Greg. 'Which hospital are you taking him to?'

'West Suffolk in Bury St Edmunds,' she replied. 'We're being redirected there because of the disruption caused by the fire.' Greg looked round him at the two uniformed officers in attendance.

'You,' he said, pointing. 'I need this prisoner escorted. One of you travel in the ambulance and stay with him until relieved. The other drop me back at the farm then follow to the hospital.'

They nodded, and, 'Yes, sir,' said the elder of the two. He came up to Greg while the younger constable followed Tasha into the back of the ambulance. 'I heard what she said,' he remarked, nodding at Tasha. 'Forgive me asking, sir, but did you have your body cam on?'

'I... What? I ... yes, I did,' said Greg with a rush of relief. 'For a miracle! I put it on with the stab vest.'

'Then I suggest you keep it safe and hand it in soonest,' advised the senior constable. 'I've been on the receiving end of this sort of complaint. It's no fun.'

'So've I,' said Greg, recalling a certain incident during his time in the Met. 'But it's been a while. Thank you.'

42

7 August - Midday

It was much later than predicted before the forensic team were permitted full access to the farmyard and its surroundings. Jill watched them begin their painstaking fingertip search, then decided to sign off with Ned and head for the office. She'd phoned through the details of the tow truck to Bill and was keen to check in with Greg. However, by the time she arrived at the incident room, he was already closeted with Margaret.

'I suppose fire makes a change from water,' was Margaret's greeting, in reference to a couple of close shaves Greg had had with Norfolk's premier element. 'But what's this about a complaint?'

Greg sighed and picked up the very welcome mug of black coffee before making a response. 'It's not a complaint as yet, but it probably will be, the ungrateful little scrote. I wish I'd tasered him in the balls now,' he said. 'That'd have given him something to complain about! As it was, I probably saved his useless life. I wasn't going to leave him to burn. I was determined to get him to court.'

'Has it got legs?' asked Margaret, referring to the complaint, not the scrote.

'Don't think so,' said Greg round another slurp of coffee. 'As luck would have it, I had my body camera on. I've already had a look at it and sent you a copy. It's dark and there's a lot of movement, but it clearly shows Waters falling *before* I catch up with him. It also shows me threatening him with a taser, which I didn't have to use, then handcuffing him and hauling him to his feet.'

'So what do you think happened? How did he break his ankle?'

'He fell,' said Greg succinctly. 'He was running over a stubble field in the dark and he fell. It could as easily have been me. Lucky it wasn't, as I doubt the nasty little toerag would have come back for me. The paramedic said it looked like the sort of break you get if you put your foot in a hole and then fall. I haven't heard from Ned's team yet as they're busy with the farmyard and the truck, but I'm sure they'll be taking a look.'

'OK, we'll see what the doctor has to say,' said Margaret. 'If she agrees with the paramedic then I doubt this will go anywhere. What about the evidence against Waters?'

'Still coming in,' replied Greg. 'But we've got a probable witness placing him at the scene, walking away as the fire started. We'll be doing a photo lineup later to see if he picks Waters out. We've got a tow truck belonging to his brother that's covered with his fingerprints and stuffed full of what appear to be Molotov cocktails in the making.'

'Anything tying him directly to the farmyard?' asked Margaret.

'That's what we're waiting for. I've also got the team revisiting ANPR and other footage to see if we can place that truck at any of the other arson sites.'

'OK. That's the arson case. What about the Mirren children?'

'They're safe in a foster placement, as you know. I take it you're up to speed on the other developments there. Specifically, Ms Hamilton's claims about murder and mayhem?' When Margaret nodded he went on. 'We're using ground-penetrating radar to check for the body of her son, which Ms Hamilton claims she buried in the back garden after he was killed by her mother. The GPR team got held up yesterday, so they only headed over to Ormesby this morning. I'm waiting on a report from them.'

'When is Ms Hamilton due in court?'

'Monday, on the unlawful imprisonment charge. I was holding off on the murder charge while we investigate her story.'

'OK. That's good. Greg, get yourself home now. No—' She held up her hand as he started to object. 'I know there's a lot to do, but you need to be fresh to do it, otherwise you'll be making mistakes.'

'The whole team's tired,' objected Greg. 'I can't just swan off and leave them to it.'

'They didn't all spend the night dragging an injured arsonist across a ploughed field with a forest fire chasing you,' said Margaret. 'You're to go home now, and I don't want you back until tomorrow morning. That's an order. Jim Henning can take over for now, and if you take my advice, you'll send Jill

Hayes home as well. Then Jim and others in the team can take a break tomorrow. Rotate them on and off,' she advised.

Greg nodded his agreement. 'A stubble field,' he corrected. 'OK. Will do. Thanks,' he said. And took himself off to the incident room.

He found Jill on the phone to Bill, and a yawning Steve scrutinising video footage from the farm security cameras.

'OK, it's been an interesting night and a good result so far,' said Greg. 'But we've got a long haul before we can be sure we've got convictions in the bag. Jill, go home until tomorrow. Steve, sorry, I need you to stay at work today but you take tomorrow off. Jenny too. Jill will give you your instructions for the rest of the day. I'm just going to hand over to Jim, and I'll see you in the morning – those not on leave.'

He headed for Jim's cubbyhole en route to his car.

'I'm sorry, Jim,' he said. 'Margaret's ordered me home and she's not listening to argument.'

'Good,' said Jim. 'Quite right too. I'll keep an eye on things. Anything in particular you want me to do?'

'I think we can leave Ms Hamilton to stew until we have more data from Ormesby,' said Greg. 'In the meantime, I think the priority is putting together a detailed picture of what Nick Waters was up to last night: when, where and with what. I know I can leave that to you and Ned. If we could do a telephone handover in the morning, that would be great. And you have tomorrow off. I'll see you on Sunday.'

***

Over in Ormesby, the GPR team were not having a good day. On top of the traffic delays, they had struggled to get the kit up and working, and when it did deign to show some life, they had trouble with the calibration. Eventually they got started in the area of the back garden that Joanne Hamilton had indicated, and rapidly got a positive signal.

'Things are looking up,' muttered Brad the operator. He looked round at the two with spades and the accompanying camera man. 'I suggest you dig here, but go careful. It's not very far down. And I think a tent would be a good idea,' he added, glancing round at neighbours peering through the hedge.

A further delay ensued as a pale blue tent was erected over the site, and the constable on the gate began to be troubled by nosy parkers.

'We're just pursuing our enquiries,' he maintained stolidly to everyone who asked, but in a quieter moment got on his radio to Control. 'I think we need more feet on the ground,' he recommended. 'Interest is growing, and I guess the media will be here soon.' He didn't know it but at least one representative of the media had already been and gone. An Eastern Daily Press reporter lived in the village and had no objection to reporting something more exciting than planning disputes and village fetes.

Brad hung around to see how accurate his prediction had been, then wandered off as the spades, followed by trowels and brushes, rapidly exposed a small skeletal shape wrapped in fabric. The mouldering remains of a book lay by its chest.

Happy that he'd been right and knowing from experience that the next few hours would involve the boring, to him, slow processes of removal from the ground, Brad wandered off with his equipment, idly running it over the remainder of the garden to, as he said later, 'check that was the lot'.

In the side garden near the diesel tank that fuelled the central heating system, he paused and checked the readings. He checked the calibration. Twice. Then he went round to the blue tent and stuck his head in.

'We need another tent,' he announced.

His colleagues looked up from where they were painstakingly brushing soil from the wrapped skeleton before them. 'We're just waiting for the doc,' one of them replied, then took in what he'd said. 'You mean?'

'Yup,' said Brad. 'Found another.'

43

---

7 August 2020 –
afternoon

Jim hesitated with his thumb over Greg's contact details for some time, then put his phone down.

No. Whatever and whomever it is, the possible, or even probable, body has been in the ground for a long time. It won't make a lot of difference if Greg is told in the morning, rather than woken from whatever rest he is getting this afternoon.

He rang Ned and got a message saying that Ned too was now on leave until Monday, and giving an alternative number in case of emergency. Jim rang it and found himself talking to Ned's number two, Yvonne Berry: a slender woman of around fifty whom Jim didn't know very well, as she normally covered the lower profile cases. She didn't sound too put out at finding herself in the hot seat.

'Meet you there,' she said crisply. 'Be about forty-five minutes.'

'Thanks,' said Jim. 'I'll go straight there as soon as I've told the Chief Super and organised some extra help for crowd control. Once this gets out, we're going to be number two on the news schedules.'

'I take it you mean after the Covid death stats,' she said.

'Something like that,' agreed Jim.

He decided that this news justified a face-to-face with Margaret and poked his head round her door. She was packing her briefcase as he did so, and looked round, startled.

'Hi, Jim,' she said. 'I was just off. Anything I need to know?'

''Fraid so,' he said. He didn't mince his words. 'The GPR team have found a third body at the bungalow in Ormesby.'

'God's sake,' exclaimed Margaret, sitting down with a thump. 'Don't tell me she's a serial killer.'

'Too soon to say,' said Jim. 'But unless Ormesby is the site of a lost medieval battleground or a plague pit, it seems possible.'

'I hope to God they've finished looking,' replied Margaret. 'Heaven help us if they find any more!'

'I'm on my way there to check on exactly what is going on,' said Jim. 'But I think we'll need extra support for crowd control when this gets out. And if Forensics put up any more blue tents it's going to look like the day after Glastonbury. That's bound to attract attention.'

'OK,' said Margaret. 'I'll organise that for you.' She picked her phone up. 'Does Greg know?'

'Not yet,' replied Jim. 'I was going to leave him in peace until the morning.'

'Good call,' said Margaret. 'He'll be mad as hell when he finds out, but he needs the break. If he gets bent out of shape about it, put him on to me.'

***

By the time Jim reached ground zero in Ormesby, the third blue tent was up and the excavating team were at work therein. The pathologist had taken over in Tent 2, and a mortuary van was parked in the drive. Additional officers from Yarmouth had beaten Jim to it, and yards of tape were already in situ across the road, completely blocking it to through traffic. Indignant, but intrigued, residents were obliged to go the long way round to get to their own drives, and the resulting additional flow past the Spar shop in North Road was causing major traffic jams.

Jim waved to a familiar face on the traffic barrier. 'Sergeant Briscoe, good to see you again,' he said out of his car window.

The sergeant bent down to reply. 'Likewise,' he said. 'Even if you are causing trouble in my patch again, sir.'

'Sorry about that. How's Constable Drake?' said Jim cheerily, referring to the officer with an impressive turn of speed last seen chasing miscreants in Great Yarmouth.

'Over there,' said Sergeant Briscoe, pointing with one hand and raising the tape for Jim to drive under with the other. 'Bugger! Here come the first of the vultures,' he added, seeing a van marked '*Look East*', pull up in the road behind him.

'Carry on, Sergeant,' said Jim. 'And don't be too rude to our media colleagues.'

Once on the property, Jim decided his order of priorities had better be first the doc, second Ms Berry and then the over-active, over-achieving GPR team.

The pathologist, Dr Paisley, was just emerging from Tent 2 as he arrived at its entrance, pulling her gloves off and loosening her plastic coveralls at the neck as she did so.

'Phew,' she said. 'Next time you decide to uncover mass murder, can you try to do it in the winter? It's hot as hell in there.' She nodded over her shoulder. 'I imagine you want to know whether that's Ms Hamilton's son, as she claimed. Well, I can't confirm it definitively until we have a DNA analysis, but the remains *are* consistent with her claims. They are the bones of a young male, and they've probably been in the ground for around two years. There's been some dental work on the teeth, so dental records are a possibility. The mortuary team will take him back now, and I'll be off as well. The excavation in Tent 3 isn't ready for me yet.'

'Thank you, doctor,' said Jim. 'I'll keep you posted on their progress.' She nodded a thank you and farewell and headed for her car, ignoring the shouted questions from the end of the road. Jim went looking for Yvonne Berry.

He found her managing operations in the bungalow, issuing crisp instructions and advising her team of four. She turned as Jim approached.

'I've got two more in Tent 3 with the GPR team,' she said. 'But I wanted to consult you about something.'

'The extent of our operations in here?' Jim had been anticipating the question.

'Yes. The radar hasn't turned up anything else in the garden, but I think they should check in here and in the garage. It should at least pick up any dodgy-looking voids.'

'Agreed,' said Jim, making a mental note he'd better warn Margaret in case there were budgetary implications.

'Also,' went on Yvonne, 'I think we should carry out a Level 4 search.'

'Meaning?' asked Jim.

'Levels 1–3 are our normal searches. You know, Level 1 – eyes only – followed by minimal disturbance at Level 2 – things we can find without moving much – then the more intrusive level, where we empty drawers, turn mattresses over, etc. We'd normally stop there, but with three bodies found on this property already, I'd like you to authorise what I'd call a Level 4, which is still more invasive, and might result in some damage to property – walls and floors and so on.'

'Are you comfortable Ned would be recommending this?' asked Jim. Seeing her bristle slightly he added in a hurry, 'You're not the only one deputising here, you know.'

She smiled a little stiffly. 'I take your point. And you could argue that nothing's going to run away in twenty-four hours. Perhaps I am letting my enthusiasm run away with me a bit,' she allowed. 'How about I get a team organised and equipped for the morning, then we can call it off if your boss and mine don't agree? In the meantime,' she added, 'we could get the radar in.'

'Agreed,' said Jim with a feeling of relief just as his phone rang with the ringtone he had allocated to Margaret. 'It's ... I need to take this,' he said, suddenly realising that advertising the fact he'd given the Chief Super the quacking duck ringtone might not be a good idea. He moved outside to answer.

'Any news?' asked Margaret. 'I've got the Press Office on my back. Apparently, it's a slow news day!'

He walked into Tent 3 with the phone still pressed to his ear. The team with the spades, trowels and brushes had just exposed the crown of a skull. He stepped outside again.

'I can confirm the second body is of a young boy, according to Dr Paisley, and there *is* a third body. The top of a human skull has just been exposed. But we don't have any official reports yet. The info about the boy is just what Dr Paisley told me.'

'Understood,' said Margaret. 'I'll discuss it with the press officer and the top of the office, but it's likely we'll limit a statement to saying that two more bodies have been located at the property and our investigations are continuing. Keep me informed, Jim.' And she rang off.

***

How Greg got home from Wymondham in one piece he'd never know. Around the Thickthorn roundabout he felt his head starting to nod and opened all the car windows to deliver a gust of fresh air. Unfortunately, the air thus delivered was warm, and therefore not as refreshing as it might have been. He managed to keep his eyes open until the 50 mph section between Blofield and North Burlingham, when boredom and exhaustion combined to send him to sleep. He was saved by his car, as the lane keeper stopped him from swerving across the centre line and the cruise control braked when he got too close to the car in front, setting off an alarm as it did so. He woke with a jerk and seized his steering wheel in a vice-like grip as his heart thundered in his ears. With sincere gratitude to BMW for their technology, he drove the rest of the way home with exaggerated care and pulled up by his cottage with inordinate relief.

To his disappointment, Chris's car was missing. He dragged himself out of his car, feeling somewhere close to a hundred years old, and got his key in the door at the second attempt. Bobby and Tally got very brief greetings before he collected a bottle of spring water from the fridge and headed up the stairs. He sat on the edge of the bed to take his shoes off, took a swig from the bottle and thought a brief lie-down was merited before he got into the whole undressing and showering process. That was the last thing he knew for some hours.

When Greg woke it was to a still house, a cat curled up beside him, and a general sensation that Tally had, somehow, taken a dump in his mouth. Sleeping in his clothes hadn't been a good idea either. 'Alexa, what time is it?' he asked his latest gadget.

'Good morning, Greg,' the flashing pod in the corner responded. 'It is 3.20am.'

Muttering, he stripped off, stepped under a warm shower with eyes closed, and stepped out again with them still closed. Wrapped in his bath towel and back on the bed – a procedure to which Chris would *definitely* have objected – he went back to sleep. This time on his side, with his mouth closed.

His second wakening was just after 6am, and this time he felt much more refreshed. Running his tongue round his teeth, he felt that a thorough tooth clean was still called for, and a second shower wouldn't go amiss either. Finding all his clothes of yesterday strewn on the floor between the bedroom and the bathroom, he was, on the whole, glad that Chris hadn't come home to find all the mess. When he checked his phone, he found the battery now almost flat thanks to his having gone to bed without charging it, but also found a message from Chris to say she'd pulled an all-nighter, he wasn't to worry, kiss-kiss emojis and she'd see him soon.

'Alexa, play Radio 4,' he ordered as he was getting shaved, and nearly cut himself as the newsreader announced: *Police are still investigating in the east Norfolk village where two imprisoned children were found. Local sources claim that further bodies have been discovered. Over to our crime reporter...*

He turned it off and reached for his phone.

44

Saturday 8 August 2020

Greg took a moment to check for any new messages from Chris – nothing – then hurled cat and parrot food at the appropriate recipients before dashing for the door.

His hands-free was getting a workout before he made the turning into the road to Fleggburgh. He was horribly tempted to ring Jim for a handover, but in view of the early hour, opted for Control.

'Geldard here,' he said. 'Please put me through to whoever can give me an update on the Ormesby developments.'

'The incident room is staffed,' said the politically correct disembodied voice. 'Putting you through.'

Greg didn't know whether to be pleased or disappointed that the next voice he heard was Jill's. 'You were quick off the mark,' he said.

'Heard the news early this morning,' said Jill.

'Ditto. I'm on my way to Ormesby. What can you tell me?'

'On the bodies, not very much. Word is that the one we were expecting to find *is* that of a young boy, pretty much as described by Joanne Hamilton. The doc says we have samples that will probably yield DNA and dental records so an ID should be straightforward.'

'And the second?' asked Greg. 'I suppose I should say the third, if we're counting the one in the concrete pillar! Where was it found?'

'In the garden at the side, not far from the fuel tank. It's skeletal only, been in the ground, the doc estimates, for eight to ten years.'

'Gender? Age? Anything to ID it, sorry, them, or any distinguishing features?' asked Greg, hoping for a hip replacement with a chassis number, or similar.

'Male, estimate fifty-plus, apparently some osteoarthritis, but nothing else significant. The doc's consulted the Bradford experts...' Greg suppressed a hollow groan. 'Apparently they've offered to come over if needed, but they're busy with some plague pit remains from Gloucestershire at the moment. Doc said to wait until we see if DNA might help first. She said she was thinking of our budget.'

'And my sanity,' muttered Greg.

'Sorry, Boss, didn't catch that,' said Jill. 'What was it you said?'

'Doesn't matter,' said Greg. 'I'll have a look round in Ormesby then head into the office. What about our friendly neighbourhood arsonist?'

'Also due to see the magistrates on Monday, unless something changes. The fire service report came in last night, after they were happy Thetford Forest was out of danger. The main point for us is that the accelerant used was petrol, both in and around the farmyard.

'Key points from the forensic team are...' she paused, and Greg could visualise her checking the report on her screen.

'One, the petrol can found just inside the entrance to the farmyard had Waters's fingerprints on it.

'Two, ditto the wine bottles in the tow truck, which the DVLA say is registered to his brother, and which, incidentally, appears to be uninsured and lacking an MOT.'

'Any evidence Waters was driving it?' interrupted Greg.

'Yes, sorry, I meant to say, the steering wheel, dashboard, driver door, etc, etc, all have Waters's fingerprints on them. Better still, the report from the hospital helps put you in the clear, Boss, and supports him being at the fire. Their orthopaedic specialist says the ankle break is consistent with putting a foot in a hole while running, and they've also treated him for second-degree burns on his shins and the front of his thighs, which suggest he was a bit too close when he set light to the petrol.'

'Bit careless all round, wasn't he?' remarked Greg. 'Most people have the sense to wear gloves these days!'

'I guess overconfidence might account for that,' replied Jill. 'Maybe he assumed the fire would be such a distraction we'd never catch up with him.'

'OK. We should interview him when I get in. I'd like you in with me, Jill. Can you also chase up Bill to see if he's found anything to link that tow truck to the other arson attacks, because, so far, we should have him on toast for Thetford but we're going to struggle to tie him to the others.'

He arrived in Ormesby at the exact same moment that Ned's deputy got out of her car. He strained to remember her name as he walked toward her. *Something Berry*, he thought, and a first name came to him in the nick of time.

'Morning, Yvette,' he said.

'Yvonne,' she corrected.

'Sorry, Yvonne. I gather you were on duty yesterday as well.'

'Yes, and there's something I want to ask you,' she said. 'In light of what was found yesterday, I want to carry out a Level 4 search, but I need your authority to do that.'

Greg thought quickly. 'Is the GPR survey complete?'

'Yes.'

'Anything?' asked Greg.

'No more bodies,' Yvonne was quick to reassure him, 'but there were a few voids I'd like to check out. One under the basement and a couple in the garage floor.'

'OK, go for it,' he said. 'I agree that the circumstances justify turning this place over.'

Yvonne nodded and turned to walk over to the van parked behind her car. Greg headed for the blue tent in the side garden but was stopped by a familiar uniformed officer.

'Morning, sir,' she said.

'Constable Drake, isn't it?' he said. 'Good to see you again.'

'Yes, sir,' she replied. 'Might I ask you something, sir?'

'Of course,' he said automatically, although slightly on edge to get to work.

'Why do the forensic lot carry out their searches in levels?' she asked. 'Why don't they just go in and do one thorough search?'

'It's a good question, Constable,' he replied. 'And one you're probably best asking Ms Berry, but I believe it's because if they barged in and grabbed everything all in one go, they'd risk destroying evidence they hadn't had a good look at. For example, they might trample on fingerprints, footprints or even blood stains, while they were searching through drawers and cupboards. That's probably not a very good example,' he admitted, 'but the principle holds good. Are you interested in their work?'

'I am, yes,' she said. 'I have a degree in chemistry, and I've been thinking that forensic science might be an interesting career move.'

'You should definitely talk to Ms Berry then. Or Ned. Although we'd be sorry to lose you from the force.' He gave her a friendly wave and headed for the tent again, only to be stopped a second time by the sight of the GPR man packing away his kit.

He introduced himself. 'Hi! I'm DCI Geldard. I'm not sure whether to thank you or curse you for your thoroughness!'

'Brad Nesbitt.' The man introduced himself in return as he wound cable round a reel.

'How confident are you that you've found everything?' asked Greg.

Brad perched himself on the garden wall and looked around him. 'Very confident there's nothing else within the range of the radar,' he replied. 'Which on a dry, sandy substrate, like the soils around here, is substantial. There are a few voids I know the forensic team plan to check out, but I think they're unlikely to contain human remains.'

'Thank you. That's a relief,' said Greg, and took himself off to the blue tent covering grave number three. He found Yvonne Berry satisfying herself that her team had missed nothing.

'Just doing a final check in here before starting in the garage,' she said, looking up.

'OK. I knew there wouldn't be much to see by now,' said Greg. 'But I wanted a clear picture of where he was found and how he was lying.' He looked at the now empty grave and added, 'Either he was short, or was curled up. That space doesn't look long enough.'

'He was around five foot nine according to the doc, and was lying in a foetal position on his right side,' replied Yvonne.

'And I gather there were no conveniently identifiable materials. Hip replacement? Wallet? Passport?'

'Unfortunately, no,' said Yvonne. 'He was wrapped in what looked like a remnant of carpet, and that's all.'

'Back to some more old-fashioned detection then, missing person files and the like,' mused Greg. 'Fine. I'll leave you to it. I'm sure you don't want me getting under your feet. Obviously you'll let me know if you find anything significant? Those voids, for example?'

'Yes, of course,' she said. 'Thank you, sir.'

'Greg,' he said automatically. 'Call me Greg. Thank you for what?'

'For trusting me to get on with the job,' she said.

He headed for his car, checking his phone for any message from Chris. *Still nothing.* He felt a vague concern that she was having a very long day, or night, and sent her a text to let her know where he was. Then he checked the time, to make sure it wasn't still too early to contact someone theoretically having a rest day, and rang Jim.

'Gather you had an interesting afternoon,' he started.

'Ah, yes. I wondered whether to ring you, but Margaret was keen I left you in peace,' said Jim, cheerfully dumping all the responsibility for his decision to leave Greg in the dark for twenty-four hours on the shoulders he felt could best bear the weight.

'OK I get it,' said Greg. 'I'd say don't ever do that again, but I'm sure you would. I'm heading into the office shortly to interview Waters, but first I'd like your take on body number three. What are your thoughts?' As he spoke he was manoeuvring his car under the crime scene tape, waving to Constable Drake and then negotiating the row of cars reversing out of the village hall car park on the opposite side of the road.

'Watch where you're going, ladies,' he muttered as a smart Volvo came hurtling backward into the road. A lady in Lycra waved cheerfully and barrelled off up the hill toward the coast road.

'What?' asked Jim.

'Sorry. I seem to have hit the road just as the morning Pilates enthusiasts head off for coffee and cake,' said Greg rather unfairly. 'Either that, or this village has an unusual dress code. Not to say a curious predilection for enormous, luminous elastic bands. Ignore me. I'd still like your thoughts on the latest crime scene,' he added.

'I got there just as they began to uncover the skull,' said Jim. 'And I stayed until the whole skeleton was visible. He was curled up on his side, with most of the bones below the neck covered in the remains of an old carpet. I'd say the head had been around two feet below the surface. The body was on a bit of a slant, so the lowest part of the grave was maybe four to five feet deep.'

'That's a lot of digging,' remarked Greg.

'On the other hand, the skull wasn't very far down in the context of a garden. Someone digging a hole for a plant, or a trench for vegetables, might've had a bit of a shock.'

'Unless that someone was the property owner and they knew what was there. What was on the top?' asked Greg.

'Lawn.'

'So, less likely to be dug over. In terms of timing and everything else, it does seem that either Ms Hamilton or her mother is our number one person of interest. I wonder where the father is now?'

'Or Frankie's dad,' said Jim. 'At the lower end of the doc's age estimate, it could just be Ms Hamilton's ex-partner. And she already has form for killing a relative then concealing the body.'

***

Back at Wymondham and still no messages from Chris, Greg had to push his growing disquiet away and concentrate on what Margaret was saying.

'I take it that will be your first priority?' she finished. Greg was uneasily aware that he had no idea what she'd just said.

'Waters...' she amplified as his stare remained blank. 'Are you sure you've had enough time off?' she added, slightly irritably. Clearly *her* long hours were starting to tell as well.

'Yes, of course, Boss,' he said. 'Waters. I agree. I just need to check whether Bill has finished going through the ANPR records relating to the earlier arson attacks, to see if we can tie him to those as well. Then I'll be talking to him.'

'Make sure you have at least two witnesses,' recommended Margaret. 'Given his tendency to fling wild accusations around.'

'Absolutely,' agreed Greg. 'And I'll be dealing with that as well.'

The subject of the assault accusation was, indeed, the first subject broached as soon as the preliminary formalities were out of the way, and not by Greg.

'I wish to make a formal complaint,' said Mr Streeter. 'It is completely inappropriate that the officer who assaulted my client and inflicted grievous bodily harm should be interviewing him. It is intimidatory, and I must insist that you leave the room, DCI Geldard. If he is to be interviewed, it must be by other officers.'

Greg remained seated and leafed through the papers he'd just been handed by Jill, before looking up and nodding to her. She tapped a few keys on her laptop then turned it to face Mr Waters and his brief.

'For the benefit of the tape, DS Hayes is about to show Mr Waters a recording,' said Greg. Then as Mr Streeter opened his mouth again, Greg added in a hurry, 'If you'll just bear with me, DS Hayes is going to take you through the evidence relating to the alleged assault. If, after that, Mr Waters still wishes to pursue his complaint, I will leave the room.'

There was a pregnant pause, then after a glance at his client, Mr Streeter said, 'Please do show us what you have.'

Jill took over. 'This is the recording taken by DCI Geldard's body-worn camera on the night of the sixth to seventh of August. It is unedited, and we will let you have a copy at the end of this interview. Because it is unedited, it is very long. I propose to fast forward through the irrelevant sections to the material of particular interest, but if you wish me to slow it down or go over anything again, please do say. Is that clear?'

'Yes,' said the lawyer, as his client didn't seem inclined to comment. 'That is clear.'

'OK. The first section of particular interest is this.' The image on the screen blurred as she fast forwarded, then slowed to show a field lit only by the jerky light of a powerful torch, bobbing around somewhat as the holder ran over a stubble field, but mostly remaining focussed on the dark shape of a man running away. The torch was gaining on the fleeing runner only slowly, until the runner suddenly threw his arms up and fell. He seemed to try to get up, then remained on the ground.

'I'll repeat that section,' said Jill, and did so.

'I think we can agree that, from the evidence of this recording, Mr Waters fell over and remained on the ground some minutes before DCI Geldard caught up with him.'

'That's not proof he didn't hit me after that,' objected Nick Waters.

'I'm coming to that,' said Jill, and started the video footage again. 'For the benefit of the tape,' she said, 'the video is showing DCI Geldard approach Mr Waters while he is lying on the ground. The light of the torch clearly shows Mr Waters in a prone position and here,' – she froze the image for a moment – 'it can clearly be seen that DCI Geldard is threatening Mr Waters with a taser.'

She started the video again, and they all watched as Geldard arrested Nick Waters and hauled him to his feet. The images after that were of the torch beam showing their joint route across the field and the sounds were of two men, one of them limping badly, struggling on the rough terrain to get out of the way of the flames approaching through the woodland.

'The points this raises are as follows,' said Jill. 'First, as DCI Geldard was holding the torch in one hand and a taser in the other, how did he manage also to wield a baton? A baton, moreover, which at no point appears on the video and which, in fact, he had left in his car.

'Second, I trust we can agree that Mr Waters fell some two minutes before DCI Geldard caught up with him. The farm staff agree that the field in question harbours a badgers' sett and that holes frequently appear both at the field's edge and elsewhere. When we explored the site, after the fires were extinguished, we did indeed find a hole in the area indicated on the body camera footage.

'Third, the A & E doctor who treated Mr Waters at the Bury St Edmunds hospital, expressed the view that the ankle injury looked like a classic break caused by twisting the ankle in a fall. It did not exhibit the crushing injuries that you would expect to see in a blow.

'Fourth, the end of the video footage, which is rather better illuminated, owing to the headlights from the ambulance and the police car, clearly shows DCI Geldard handing Mr Waters over to the care of the paramedics. There is *at no point* any opportunity for DCI Geldard to administer the beating he is accused of between the end of the video footage and the handover to independent witnesses.

'In the light of all this,' concluded Jill, 'perhaps Mr Waters would like to reconsider his accusation.'

A silence fell. Greg and Jill sat back in their chairs and waited.

Mr Streeter looked at his client, who was himself looking at the floor. 'I would like a few moments with my client,' he said at last.

Waters stirred. 'No, it's OK,' he said. 'It was worth a try but it clearly isn't going to run. I withdraw my complaint.'

'To be clear, and for the tape,' said Jill, 'are you now admitting that DCI Geldard at no point struck you with a baton or injured you in any way?'

'Yes,' said Waters grudgingly. 'Although it did hurt like hell being dragged over that field.'

'Maybe next time,' said Jill swiftly as she felt her boss stir beside her, 'he could just leave you to the flames.'

Greg intervened. 'Now we've got that out of the way,' he said, 'I suggest we take a short break then reconvene to consider the more important questions relating to the fire that placed lives, property and a nationally significant woodland at risk. Interview suspended at 14.00. DCI Geldard and DS Hayes leaving the room.'

Outside the door, Jill and Greg high-fived. 'Well done, Jill,' he said. 'And thank you. Grab a drink and a bite, and we'll go back in half an hour.'

45

Saturday 8 August 2020 –
late afternoon

It took less than an hour to get Nick Waters to admit to setting the fire in the Elveden farmyard. The burn injuries to the fronts of his legs were a significant contributory factor to his capitulation, and the fingerprint evidence, combined with the farmyard CCTV, was more or less conclusive. But, try as they might, Greg and Jill couldn't get him to admit to any involvement of any kind in the earlier arson cases. As the second had involved a death and therefore a murder charge, this was perhaps not surprising.

'Trouble is,' said Greg to Jill and Steve in the observation room where they were reviewing their options, 'we have no real forensic evidence tying him to either the Downham Market or the Silfield attacks. He glared through the two-way mirror into the interview room next door, where Nick Waters was relaxing with his legs spread-eagled over half the room.

'Look at the sod,' he said. '*He* knows it too. His alibis for those nights are dodgy and we have his pickup in the vicinity, but, in both cases, only on major roads and hours before the incident. Defence will argue that a presence on one of the few major roads in this county is hardly evidence of criminal intent, and without anything tying him to the specific locations, we're stuffed.

'Given that we've got fingerprints from materials in Elveden, is it really impossible to pick up anything from the other two sites?'

'Ned's team have tried,' said Jill. 'But after the grain store explosion the fire was more intense, and they say that where they *do* have fingerprints, they're incomplete. Not good enough as evidence in court.'

'OK, what else have we got? The tow truck that belongs to his brother. Anything on its movements?'

'Bill says it shows up on ANPR in several places – enough to track its arrival at Elveden anyway,' said Steve. 'But that just confirms what we already know, since we have the truck itself.'

'We still need to talk to the brother,' said Greg. 'Ade Waters.'

'Norwich police are looking for him,' replied Steve. 'He's not showed up for work today and the garage he contracts for isn't best pleased. But Norwich say his wife's pointed them at one or two places where she thinks he might be. It seems she's not very pleased with him either, or her brother-in-law,' he added.

'Has Bill checked the records for movements of that tow truck near the other two incidents?' asked Greg.

'He's still working on that, but so far, nothing,' said Jill.

'In that case, it looks as though we'll have to settle for charging Waters with the Elveden arson and hope either ANPR or Forensics come up with something that ties him to the other two cases before he goes to court. Because if he's genuinely in the clear on those two, we still have an arsonist to find.'

While they all contemplated that depressing scenario, Greg picked up the other file on his desk. 'Meanwhile, we need to talk to Ms Hamilton about the third body. Steve, can you come with me? Jill, I'm going to ask you to follow up with Ade Waters and the wife. In fact, both wives, please.'

***

Back in Interview Room 1, Greg was beginning to think that he was seeing more of that room than he was of his fiancée. He kept checking his phone and messaging her, but there was nothing coming back, and he was starting to feel like a stalker. He kept telling himself she was just busy and she'd be in touch soon, recalling similar periods of work pressure earlier in his own career. Then he shook himself mentally, and sought to focus on the task in hand.

Ms Hamilton was in front of him again, but this time with a more senior duty solicitor. Greg recognised him as a burly ex-barrister who usually prowled the magistrates' courts to considerable effect.

The man introduced himself. 'Kenneth Wood. I'm taking over representing Ms Hamilton from Joseph Streeter. He's rather busy now with your other case.' He nodded knowingly at Greg. 'Ms Hamilton here is happy with the exchange.'

She did indeed look rather more confident in her new, more mature representative than she had in her younger, newly qualified legal support. Obviously Ms Hamilton prized experience over recent training.

Wary of future complications, Greg asked, 'Ms Hamilton, would you please confirm, for the tape, that you are content with this change in representation?'

'I am happy to be represented by Mr Wood,' she confirmed.

'Then let's to business,' said Greg. 'I imagine you will have gathered that we have been pursuing our investigations at your mother's house.'

She looked down at her hands, which were clenched together on the table in front of her. In the silence, Greg could hear sounds from the corridor behind them and the faint squeaking of Steve's chair as he shuffled to get comfortable.

As the silence continued, Mr Wood intervened. 'I think you will understand that Joanne is distressed by the prospect of her son's body being disinterred.'

'I asked you to leave him be,' said Joanne in a low voice.

'I'm afraid we couldn't do that,' said Greg, softening his tone a little. 'At the very least, and assuming you have told us the truth, he was buried illegally and you are guilty of preventing the lawful and decent burial of—'

'It was decent,' she interrupted angrily. 'I loved Frankie. It was a decent and loving burial and—'

'But not legal,' said Greg. 'And you must understand that we couldn't just take your word for it. We have to investigate the death of your mother and, sadly, Frankie's death, and burial is part of that investigation.' He looked at her for a long moment, then said, 'We did find Frankie, and his remains have been taken to the mortuary. I can assure you he was treated with care and respect throughout, and it will be possible for him to buried later in a cemetery, or whatever is your preference.'

'Thank you,' she whispered.

In a deliberately brisker tone, Greg then said, 'Although, his father might want a say in that decision. Tell me about Frankie's father.'

'Bob?' she said, looking up, startled. 'He's nothing to do with any of this. He hasn't been part of my life since he walked out on me and Frankie. If he hadn't,' she added bitterly, 'Frankie would still be alive, and we'd never have come to live with my mother. Never have come to Norfolk.'

'Where was it you lived with Bob Chalmers?' asked Greg. 'I think you said East London when we asked you before.'

'That's right,' she said. 'In Clapton. Before that in Crouch End for a short while, but we were in Clapton when he suddenly buggered off.'

'Where did he go?'

'I don't know. I don't think he wanted me to know in case I came after him for support, for Frankie.'

'You could have applied for child maintenance through the courts,' said Greg.

'What was the point?' she asked. 'I didn't know where he had gone. I didn't know where he was working or even if he *was* working. Mostly he did little jobs, like removals with his van, for cash in hand. They'd never have managed to get any money off him if they'd tried. I didn't need the hassle. It was tough enough as it was.'

'I take it you didn't let him know his son had died,' said Steve.

'How would I do that? I've just said, I didn't know where he was. How much clearer can I make it? I HAD NO CONTACT WITH HIM!'

Steve flushed a little and bent over his notebook.

'Well, we still need all the information you do have,' said Greg. 'His name is Bob, or Robert, Chalmers, is that right?'

'Yes,' she said sulkily.

'How old is he?'

'He'll be thirty-eight ... no, thirty-nine now,' she said.

Greg and Steve exchanged a glance. 'Describe him to me, as he was when you saw him last. We do need to see if we can find him,' Greg added. 'So anything you can remember would be helpful.'

'He's tall,' said Joanne. 'Just about six foot. It was one of the first things I noticed in his online profile. Dark hair, big nose. I don't know what else to say,' she said.

'Working as a van driver, you said.'

'Yes. But only freelance. I never knew him have a steady job.'

'Do you think he'll have stayed in London?' asked Steve.

'Oh yes,' she said. 'It's the only place he's ever lived. Probably north London for that matter. People never change sides of the river, have you noticed?'

Without needing to consult each other, it was obvious to both Greg and Steve that the third body could not be Bob Chalmers. Too old and too short.

'Tell me about your father,' said Greg, switching tack with an abruptness that left both interviewee and solicitor confused.

'I'm struggling to see the relevance of these questions,' said Mr Wood.

'Oh, I think they're highly relevant,' replied Greg. 'Ms Hamilton has been living in her mother's home for the last two years and has been claiming her mother's pension and allowances over that time. Quite apart from the problematic issue of how her mother came to be dead and concealed in a concrete pillar, that is undoubtedly fraud. What *is* puzzling me is how she got away with it, without her father intervening. Which is why I asked her to tell me about her father.'

'I haven't seen him for years,' said Joanne. 'Not since I left home. You must understand, we weren't the sort of family that got together at Christmas or exchanged birthday presents. I hadn't seen my mother for years when I made the mistake of taking Frankie to her home. I hadn't seen my father for even longer. Not since they divorced. He may be dead. To be honest, I don't care.'

'How old were you when you last saw him?' asked Greg. 'What sort of a man was he?'

'Fifteen. And he was a bully,' she said emphatically. 'My mother was cold, narcissistic and uncaring, and my father was a bully. Which I assume is why they divorced.'

'According to the marriage certificate we found, his name was, or is, Frederick James Hamilton.'

'That's right. Mum called him Fred, when she called him anything repeatable,' said Joanne.

'Was he a big man? Did he knock your mother around?'

'Not particularly, and yes, I think he did, although I never saw him do it. But she did have some odd bruises from time to time. He was a nasty piece of work. Always belittling you. Always putting you down.'

'Did you kill your father?' asked Greg.

She gaped at him for a moment, then gasped 'No! Of course I didn't! Where the hell did that come from?'

'You've admitted to killing your mother when she made you mad,' said Greg. 'Yes, I know you say it was an accident,' – he held up his hand to forestall her angry response – 'but, either way, she ended up dead and her body hidden in the garden. Now we've also found the body of a man, aged between fifty and seventy, roughly five foot nine inches tall. Seems reasonable to me to assume that it's the body of your father and that you killed him too.'

The silence that followed this statement was profound. Joanne gaped; Mr Wood gaped for at least a moment. Greg and Steve waited.

'You found another body ... in the garden? Near Frankie? Oh, tell me it wasn't near Frankie. Especially if you think it was my dad. Tell me he wasn't near my boy. My Frankie.' She was growing more hysterical with each question. Ken Wood tried to intervene, to recommend silence and a moment to discuss things with him, but she wasn't listening.

'He was not near Frankie,' said Greg loudly and clearly. A silence fell, broken only by Joanne's heaving breaths, and into it Greg spoke slowly and plainly. 'The latest body was not near Frankie.' She collapsed into sobs, but more quietly, and Greg started to say, 'Interview suspended—' when she raised her head from her hands and spoke again.

'It wasn't me. If you've found my father's body, then it must have been my mother. It must have been her.'

***

Back in Greg's office, he and Steve looked at each other.

'She didn't know where the body was buried,' said Steve. 'She didn't even know there was another body.'

'I agree. Either that, or she's the greatest actress since Judi Dench.

'First thing we need to do is nail the identification of those bones. If there's no DNA then we'll need to rely on dental records, since as far as I know the forensic anthropologists and the doc haven't found any significant changes other than a bit of arthritis. In the meantime, run a check on any record you can find that relates to the man. What was his name again?'

'According to the paperwork we found, Boss, the marriage certificate in fact, Joanne Hamilton senior married Frederick James Hamilton on the sixth of June 1969 at the Cambridge Registry Office. The bride's parents were present. Both since deceased. We found their death certificates in the same file, but no death certificate for Frederick Hamilton. In fact, nothing else relating to Hamilton at all. No bank records, passport, driving licence, nothing.'

'Then we start looking from scratch. Find out if he did have a licence, where he banked, and when any of those organisations last had any contact with him. Friends, relatives, you know the routine.'

'Yes, Boss.'

46

Saturday 8 August 2020 - in Attleborough

Bill was more than a little tired of working from home. He'd done a third Covid test that morning, and for a moment thought he was clear to go back to work, but a faint line had appeared in the wrong window and he'd thrown it into the bin, accompanied by a very rude word.

Still, perhaps the faintness of the line means I'm almost clear. I feel fine after all, apart from a general sense of frowstiness created by too much fast food, too little exercise and very little fresh air.

He looked out of the window of his tiny first-floor flat at the garden which belonged to his neighbour downstairs, and sighed for lack of outdoor space. Then he made yet another cup of tea and went back to his laptop. He was beginning to hate that screen too. Quite apart from square eyes, he felt he had spent hours staring at images and spreadsheets and contributed next to nothing to the investigation. He itched to be back at work properly and preferably actively.

He was checking through his notes from the day before, absently scratching through his beard as he did so, when he had an idea.

He'd checked on the movements of Nick Waters's pickup until he was sick of the sight of the registration plate. He felt he could track its every movement, on the major roads at least, for weeks, and all he'd achieve was to confirm what they already knew: that Waters was near both the previous arson sites at the right times, but couldn't be tied specifically to either. He'd also located the tow truck, currently sitting in the forensic garage in Wymondham, on the roads leading to Elveden. But that was hardly surprising since that was where they'd found it. It didn't seem to be linked to the Downham Market fire, and while he *had* seen evidence it was on the A11 prior to the Silfield fire, it was hours before.

Flicking through his notes brought to his notice the *what3words* reference they had shared with Suffolk police to no avail.

I wonder? he thought, and taking a slurp of tea he turned back to his screen. *Might be worth a quick look.*

He started to check ANPR records for that night, down the A11 between Silfield and the location near Felixstowe specified in the *what3words* code. It took some time, but eventually...

'Bingo,' he whispered to himself, finding two references either side of the Fiveways roundabout. Then he checked the times. *Odd! Even with bad traffic that took him a long time. He must have stopped.*

It was the work of moments to look up contact numbers for the various food outlets on the big roundabout, and he hit lucky with his educated guess as to which the driver of the tow truck might have used. McDonald's not only had some very effective CCTV coverage of their car park and approaches, but they also saved footage in the cloud for at least a month.

'Brilliant!' he said. 'Can I see footage for the early hours of the first of August between...' He went back to his screen to check the two times he'd identified, and passed them on.

'How do I know this request is kosher?' asked the voice at the other end of the line, rather suspiciously. 'We want to help the police, of course we do, but how do I know you *are* the police?'

'No problem,' said Bill. 'I'll get Control in Wymondham to send you an official request. If you still have any concerns, you can look up their phone number and ring them yourself to check. Is that OK?'

'I think that would be better, yes,' said the voice, and rang off.

Having alerted Control to the need for the official request, and Jill to the fact that he'd asked for one, Bill went to forage in his galley kitchen for something to eat. Surveying the depleted supplies in his small fridge-freezer, he made a mental note that a new online shopping order was required, and settled for beans on toast. By the time he'd eaten his lunch, his phone was pinging with incoming messages.

'This what you're looking for?' asked McDonald's, with an accompanying three images. Two were of a tow truck bearing a Range Rover and towing a Kawasaki Mule on a trailer. One was of a man in the tow truck, paying for his McDonald's meal at the drive-thru window.

Bill forwarded the lot to Jill with a muttered 'Eureka!' to himself, then settled to checking for the tow truck further south and east. It quickly became apparent that, later in the morning, the vehicle was heading north again; but as far as he could tell, it didn't seem to stop until it reached Norwich. Bill picked up the phone to Jill.

'You thinking what I'm thinking?' she asked without any preamble.

'That he made that *what3words* rendezvous near Felixstowe?' said Bill.

'Absolutely. Either way, we have him clearly linked to the vehicles missing from the burned-out store at Silfield. Well done, Bill. Very well done.'

When Jill passed the message on to Greg, he reiterated the compliment. 'That's very well done of Bill,' he said. 'Let's have a chat with Ade Waters. If I judge him right, he'll probably fold a lot easier than his brother. And worst case, we can play one off against the other.'

'He's not here yet, Boss,' she said. 'Norwich police only collared him this morning. I rang, and they've still got him, mainly because they couldn't spare anyone to bring him over here. Shorthanded,' she said in mitigation.

'OK. In that case, we'll talk to him tomorrow when Jim's back. For now, get yourself home, Jill. I'll head off as well, as soon as I've rung Bill.'

Congratulating a delighted Bill, while important, took only a moment, leaving Greg free to worry about the continuing silence from Chris.

After two more text messages and a phone call that went to answerphone, he gave in to his fears and rang Suffolk police, hoping he wasn't going to be paying for his interference for the next ten years, then hoping that he would.

The first reaction from the Suffolk exchange was to offer to take his number and, 'DI Mathews will ring you when she's free.' Just before they rang off, he interrupted and used his rank to get a little further up the food chain.

After a lot of hanging on and various irritating pieces of on-hold music – *why on earth whale song?* Greg wondered – he eventually found himself talking to DI Richards.

'Hi,' said the voice. 'I'm afraid I'm not part of DI Mathews team, but I'm all you've got at present. What with Covid infections and contact pings, there's hardly any of us working today, and those that are, are mainly working from home.'

Reflecting that that wasn't a piece of intelligence he'd want shared too widely if he was part of the Suffolk management team, Greg explained that he'd been trying to contact Chris, but had no luck, '...and there's a message I really need to get to her,' he said.

'All I know is that she's out on an operation and not readily contactable,' said Richards. 'If you give me your message, I'll try and get it passed on.'

'No, that's fine,' said Greg. 'I'll keep trying, thank you.' A thought struck him just as he was about to ring off, and he added, 'Are you the DI Richards we contacted a couple of weeks ago, about a possible rendezvous near Felixstowe involving stolen vehicles?'

'That's right.' The voice was instantly guarded. 'We were shorthanded then too.'

'Yes.' Greg waved the objection away, even though his interlocutor couldn't see him. 'It's just that we've new evidence that the stolen vehicles were indeed taken in that direction in the early hours of the first of August on the back of a tow truck. Obviously it's too late to intercept,' he said, unable to resist rubbing it in just a little, 'but it might be worth asking Felixstowe Port Authority to take a good look round for the specific vehicles – a Range Rover and a Kawasaki Mule. You have the registrations from the previous alert, although I appreciate they've probably been removed or changed by now. I can resend all the info, including the VIN numbers, if that would help.'

'Yes, thank you,' said Richards. 'I'll see what we can find at Felixstowe.'

47

Sunday 9 August 2020

No contact Saturday evening. No contact Sunday morning. Now Greg was seriously worried, and leaving messages just wasn't cutting it. Which was why his first port of call Sunday morning was Margaret's office. If his rank didn't have enough pull, maybe hers did. And Greg was, by now, beyond embarrassing himself.

So I might look an idiot. Whatever! I'd rather be an idiot and know Chris is OK, than live with this gnawing anxiety any longer.

It hadn't helped that his subconscious had seized the opportunity to spend the night serving up unpleasant memories of what had happened to their colleague Sarah when she'd been taken hostage. It was, therefore, with considerable disappointment that Greg found Margaret's office to be empty.

He smacked himself in the head with frustration.

Of course, it is Sunday! Why on earth would she be in?

He turned to head back toward his office, not sure where to turn next, when a woman passing by said over her shoulder, 'She'll be in later.'

'What? Who? The Chief Super?' he asked.

She turned. 'Yes,' she said. 'She's coming in later this morning. I'd come back later,' and disappeared round the corner.

'Later,' Greg repeated to himself, and went back to the incident room to catch up with Jim.

He found Jill taking photos and papers off the board at one end of the room. He was just in time to see Nick and Ade Waters dropped into a file.

'I thought I could start clearing this lot up,' she said.

'Yes, I think so,' agreed Greg. 'Where's ... oh, here he is,' he said as Jim backed through the door carrying three coffees clutched precariously in his hands. He managed to get them down on the nearest desk without disaster, and reached in his pocket.

'Don't tell me you've got three bacon rolls as well,' said Greg, picking up one of the coffees.

'You wish,' said Jim. 'Not on a Sunday apparently, at least not in this new Covid world. This is the best I could do.' And he produced three KitKats.

'Thanks,' said Jill. 'By the way, Bill's coming in today. He says he tested clear this morning, so he'll be here in an hour or so.'

'Good,' said Greg, pushing thoughts of Chris to the back of his mind. 'OK, priorities for today... Jill, chase up where we've got to on identifying body number three, and I'll catch up with you later. Jim, you and I are having a little chat with Ade Waters, and then probably another with his brother.'

'Have we got something new?' asked Jim eagerly, round a mouthful of chocolate wafer.

'Ah, yes, you won't know yet. Bill came up trumps. Come in here and I'll bring you up to date.'

'So,' said Greg after filling Jim in with the latest news, 'I'm hoping that leaning on Ade will deliver us Nick as well. I don't think Ade's as strong a personality. Ready? And are you OK to play bad cop?'

'Let's go,' said Jim, crumpling his now empty paper cup in his hand and throwing it in the bin.

The duty solicitor sitting with Ade Waters was yet another strange face to Greg, apparently hauled in from his usual beat at Great Yarmouth magistrates' court. Clearly that service too was suffering from a shortage of personnel. His mind still turning to Chris every few minutes, he missed the name but thought it didn't really matter – it would be on the tape. As agreed, Jim kicked off.

'So, Mr Waters,' he said, flicking through paperwork in front of him. 'You're about to be charged with murder.'

'What?' Ade was horrified. His already pasty face went, if anything, a shade whiter and he shot to his feet.

'Sit down,' said Jim, and waited in silence until he complied. 'Haven't you been told?' asked Jim.

Greg intervened. 'I don't think Mr Waters has seen the latest evidence,' he remarked quietly.

'Well we'd better remedy that,' said Jim. 'Here you are, Mr Waters, or may I call you Ade?'

He pulled an A4 photo out of the pile and turned it to face Waters. It showed a tow truck carrying a Range Rover, and was dated 1 August 2020. Jim pointed to the registration plate clearly visible in the photo.

'This is your tow truck, isn't it?' he said. Ade was still speechless. 'You can see the number quite clearly,' said Jim. 'You can also see the Range Rover on the back, the one stolen from Leyton Farm Estate near Silfield on the evening of the thirty-first of July. The evening when the estate yard was set on fire and the grain store exploded, killing the grain store manager. Hence the murder charge. I must press you for an answer, Mr Waters,' he said. 'For the tape, you understand.'

'Not me. It wasn't me,' said Ade. Then gathering confidence he said, 'Someone else must have been driving the truck.'

'Oh, really?' said Jim. 'And who might that have been? You didn't report it stolen, so presumably that someone was driving it with your consent?' After a pause he added, 'Don't struggle to rack your poor brains for an answer. You see, we know who was driving the truck.' He pushed a second photo in front of Ade Waters. 'You see here,' he said, pointing. 'This is you, isn't it, paying for your McDonald's meal, in that same truck, on that same occasion? Look, this one's time and date stamped too. I hope you enjoyed that burger,' he added, 'because you're going to pay dear for the decision to stop there on your way to Felixstowe.'

Ade looked as though he was about to be sick on the table but swallowed hard. 'It wasn't me,' he managed.

'Oh, come on,' said Jim. 'Look, we've got your truck, we've got your truck carrying the stolen vehicles. We've got you *in* the truck. What more do we need?

'Adrian Waters, I'm charging you—'

'No, stop!' said Ade, overruling the attempted intervention from his solicitor. 'OK, I'll admit, I drove the vehicles down to Suffolk, but I don't know anything about Felixstowe and I wasn't at that farm you said. I didn't set fire to it. I didn't. I wasn't there, and you can't pin that on me. You can't.'

'You think not?' said Jim, pressing home his advantage. 'You had the stolen vehicles on your truck! You were photographed taking them toward Felixstowe.'

'It wasn't me,' burst out Ade again. 'It wasn't me!'

'I think what my colleague is struggling with,' intervened Greg, 'is how did the vehicles get from the Leyton Estate farmyard to your truck if you didn't drive them? And who else could have lit the fire that covered their movement. You see what I'm getting at? If it wasn't you, who was it?'

'You're wasting your time, Boss,' said Jim. 'Look, we've got him cold on transporting that car to Suffolk, no doubt about it. We can run with this.'

'Wait,' shouted Ade. 'Just wait. Let me think!'

'What about?' demanded Jim. 'Either you tell us who it was, if it wasn't you, which I doubt. Or we charge you anyway.'

'It was Nick,' burst out Ade. 'It was Nick, OK? I knew he was going to create a distraction, but I didn't know it was going to be a fire. I didn't know anyone was going to die. I don't think he planned that either. He's not like that. That was an accident.'

'You're stating, for the record, that the man who lit the fires at Leyton Farm Estate and stole the Range Rover and the Kawasaki Mule, which you delivered to Suffolk, that man was your brother Nick Waters?' asked Jim.

Ade was crying now, tears washing silently down his face. 'Yes. It was Nick,' he said. 'But he didn't mean to kill anyone, I'm sure of that.'

'We'll be back,' said Jim, rising to his feet. 'Interview suspended...'

Outside, Jim and Greg exchanged delighted, and relieved, looks. 'Let's see if we can get a complementary confession from the other Mr Waters,' said Greg. His phone buzzed as he entered Interview Room 2, but he ignored it.

'Mr Nick Waters,' he said, taking his seat at the table. 'You understand you're still under caution?'

'And?' asked Nick.

'We've been chatting to your brother Ade,' went on Greg. 'He's been very interesting, hasn't he, DI Henning?'

'Very interesting,' said Jim. 'Positively inflammatory, I think you'd say.'

Nick looked wary, but his solicitor, the rather tired-looking Mr Streeter, looked merely weary. Greg wondered how many hours *he'd* been working.

'I think you'd better explain to Nick just how interesting his brother has been,' said Greg.

'My pleasure,' said Jim. 'The starting point was that tow truck you took to Elveden, Mr Waters. That was your first mistake, reusing a truck you'd already used at a previous fire. Even worse, that it belongs to your brother, because obviously we started looking at him, and his truck, rather carefully. Anything to say yet, Mr Waters?'

'You haven't asked a question yet,' remarked Mr Streeter.

'No more I haven't,' agreed Jim. 'Here's a question then. Given that we have photos of your brother driving that specific tow truck, on the first of August, all the way to Suffolk, and pictures, moreover, of the Range Rover stolen from Leyton Farm Estate that night sitting, large as life, on the back of that truck, how do you think the car got from the farmyard to the truck? And who set light to the yard?'

There was a long pause. Then, 'No comment,' said Nick.

'Oh really?' said Jim. 'Your brother was a lot more forthcoming. He says—'

The door opened and Bill came in.

'Not now, Bill,' said Jim and Greg, almost in chorus, both equally irritated at the ill-timed interruption.

'Sorry to interrupt,' said Bill, 'but there's an important message for you, Boss.'

'It can wait,' said Greg shortly. To his surprise, Bill stood his ground.

'No it won't, sorry, Boss,' he said. 'You must come now.'

DCI Geldard leaving the room,' said Greg, and marched over to the door, towing Bill after him.

'It better be good, Bill,' he said as soon as they got outside.

'It's not good, it's bad, Boss,' said Bill. 'The Chief Super wants you. There's news about Chris and it's not good. She said I wasn't to come back without you.' He was talking to empty air. Greg had gone.

48

Sunday 9 August 2020 – disaster looms

Greg made it up to Margaret's office at the speed of light, and burst in with the on-duty secretary twittering in his wake.

'Greg, good,' said Margaret, turning from her telephone. 'Sit down.'

'Just tell me! Please,' he added, remembering his manners.

'Sit!' she commanded as though addressing a recalcitrant terrier, and his knees folded beneath him.

'It's not good but it's not the worst,' she said. 'We believe Chris is alive, but she's in some danger. I've just had Suffolk police on the phone. Apparently, they tried to contact you but couldn't get through. They rang me on the assumption I'd know where you were.'

'Yes?' said Greg impatiently. 'Chris! What's the problem?'

'You know she's been working with a dysfunctional family?' said Margaret, employing an impressive grasp of understatement. 'I understand from Suffolk that she's been trying to support the wife to escape an abusive relationship. It seems she—'

'Yes, but where is she now?' interrupted Greg, driven to the brink of insanity by Margaret's circuitous tale-telling.

'Taken hostage,' replied Margaret, concluding that she'd better cut to the chase. 'She responded to a phone call from the wife and, as I was saying, it seems she was at the family home when the husband came back. He's refusing to let anyone leave the house – neither his wife and daughter nor Chris.'

'Threats?' asked Greg. 'He must be armed in some way, or Chris would eat him for breakfast.'

'Someone set off a rape alarm, and Chris radioed for backup saying she was being threatened. After that, nothing. Suffolk responded, but so far have been unable to gain access to the house. The husband has sent them video footage from his phone, of him holding a knife to his daughter's throat. A negotiator is there and—'

'Where?' asked Greg again.

Margaret handed over a slip of paper with an address and postcode. 'There,' she said. 'I'd advise you not to go if I thought...' Her office door banged on the wall and its hinges rattled. She was addressing empty air. '...you'd listen,' she concluded. She sighed and put her head in her hands, then picked up the phone again.

'Jim, come up here,' she said. 'I need a word.'

***

Greg looked at the crumpled scrap of paper clutched in his hand as he sat in his car. The address was for a village called Cavendish, on the Suffolk–Essex border. He had a vague recollection he might have driven through it, when visiting antique shops in the nearby Long Melford. His hands on the steering wheel were shaking, and he had to take a couple of long breaths to steady himself before he could put the postcode into his satnav. The black side of his imagination kept trying to push images of disaster in front of his eyes: Chris lying dead; planning a funeral rather than a wedding; Chris tackling some great bully and being kicked or stabbed; a life without the woman who had become so thoroughly part of his very existence that any future without her was just impossible. He thrust all the pictures and the thoughts away, with an almost physical effort. Time for all that if she was, indeed, dead.

She's done daft things in the past, and survived, he told himself, recalling explosions, near drownings and other high-risk episodes in Chris's turbulent career. She'd come swanning out of this one too, with a creative insult for her attacker and ridicule for the dire imaginings of her lover.

He followed his satnav blindly onto the A11 and south. Around Thetford he realised the fuel tank was almost empty and, simultaneously, that all he'd eaten that day was Jim's KitKat. He pulled into a service area to refuel and collect some sandwiches from the out-of-town Sainsbury's. He ate an egg and cress sitting in the car park and, his uneasy conscience making itself felt, he rang Jim.

'Thank God,' said Jim. 'Where are you? Are you OK? No scrub that, of course you aren't OK. Margaret told me,' he admitted.

'Jim, I'm sorry, I should have spoken to you before I left,' said Greg. 'I've dumped you in the hot seat, I'm afraid.'

'No problem,' said Jim. 'I wound up the interviews with the Waters brothers. It didn't take long for them to cave. I told Nick that his brother had coughed. Then I told Ade that *his* brother was leaving him to carry the can. After that, Ade came up with all sorts of details he'd kept quiet about earlier, and when I presented those to Nick, he caved in as well. So we've got two admissions in the bag. But you don't want to hear all this...'

'Yes I do,' replied Greg. 'It's one less thing to worry about. Good job, Jim. What's Margaret told you about Chris?'

'Just that she's been taken hostage in a domestic,' said Jim. 'And that you're on your way there. Anything I can do?'

'Yes, there is, as a matter of fact,' said Greg. 'I just shot off without any preparation or thought. I've been doing some thinking since, on the drive down here. Can you find out for me who the SIO is in Cavendish, and warm them up for my arrival? I suspect they'll want me there like a hole in the head, but, with a bit of luck, they'll extend me some respect as a fellow officer. Assure them I'm just there for Chris and I'll do my best not to get in their way.'

'Will do,' said Jim. 'Where are you now?'

'Thetford. It's nearly an hour yet to Cavendish. I stopped for fuel and something to eat.'

'Good. Sounds like common sense is kicking in.'

'Except it's not common sense, it's good sense...'

'And good sense isn't common,' finished Jim, 'to quote Chris.'

'What would I do without her?' asked Greg. 'These things can go so badly wrong...'

'And it could all be over by the time you get there,' said Jim. 'Don't give up yet. This is Chris we're talking about remember, and she's a force of nature. She'll probably come out with the scrote hog-tied and vowing to give up alcohol, sex, and rock and roll.' He hoped he was right.

'I hope you're right,' said Greg and drove off onto the A134 heading for Bury St Edmunds and Sudbury.

When he eventually arrived in Cavendish, it was to find the main access to the village heavily controlled by uniformed police. He pulled over and checked his phone. There was a text message from Jim.

SIO is Chief Inspector Pritty. She's expecting you. Don't make the obvious joke!

Leaving his car by the side of the road, Greg approached the nearest police officer and introduced himself.

'I believe Chief Inspector Pritty is expecting me,' he said.

'I'll check, sir,' said the officer and turned away to use his radio. Greg didn't catch any of the muttered conversation, but thankfully he soon turned back. 'Yes, she's expecting you,' he said. 'She says you can join her in front of the property, or go to the centre we've opened in the village hall.'

'I'll join her,' said Greg, determined to get as close to Chris as he could. 'Which way?'

The police officer pointed down the road to a turning signposted 'Memorial Hall'. 'It's down there,' he said. 'You can take your car as far as the hall. Leave it in the car park, and someone will direct you from there.'

He hardly needed directions. With tape and police everywhere, including an armed contingent, he soon found his way to a largish detached property round a corner at the end of the close. He was stopped twice. Once by a constable who consulted on his radio, and a second time by a sergeant checking his warrant card and remarking approvingly on the fact that he had taken the precaution of donning his stab vest.

'Although, you won't be getting near,' he added. 'At least, not until he's arrested. I'm sure you understand, sir.'

'I understand,' said Greg, but without making any other commitment. *If they think I'm likely to hang back with Chris at risk, they have another think coming.*

Chief Inspector Pritty was a young woman with long hair tightly controlled in a bun at the back of her head. She was sitting in a squad car in front of the target house, a phone in her hand, and leaned over to push the passenger door open, inviting Greg to join her.

'Sorry to meet under these circumstances,' she said. 'I don't have any news yet.'

'What exactly do you know?' asked Greg.

'Only that DI Mathews reported her intention to pay the wife, Mrs Bradbourn, a visit while her husband was away at a meeting. She had been working with Mrs Bradbourn for some time, hoping to get her to give evidence against her husband, but she kept changing her mind.'

'Oh, that one,' said Greg silently to himself.

'She was still trying. She called in at the family home on Saturday morning, then went off to arrange a place at a refuge. Went back Saturday late afternoon, we believe to collect Mrs Bradbourn and her daughter, but by then the husband had returned unexpectedly from his meeting. Nonetheless, DI Mathews entered the property.' Disapproval was evident in Chief Inspector Pritty's tone, and Greg recognised the feeling. Clearly Chris had, as usual, rushed in where angels might fear to tread.

'Neighbours report raised voices on Saturday evening,' she went on. 'Chris raised the alarm on her radio around 1am. After that, nothing. We tried to gain entry to the house shortly after, but were refused access and Mr Bradbourn threatened to kill his wife and child. We got the video footage shortly after that. Since then we've been trying to talk him down and negotiate our way in, but so far without success.'

'What's the plan now?' asked Greg.

'I've got an armed team deploying at the back of the property, and you've probably seen some others round here. If we can't talk him out, and he's judged a credible threat to his family or indeed DI Mathews, they have orders to take him down. But for the moment it's a watching brief.'

'Any indication of whether Chris is alive or dead?' asked Greg as calmly as he could.

Pritty gave him a sharp look. 'No,' she said. 'But we've no reason to believe she's dead, or even harmed.'

'She's either injured or in some way neutralised,' said Greg with certainty. 'Or believe me, she'd be making her presence felt.'

'I agree,' said Pritty with sufficient feeling that Greg knew she'd met Chris. 'Let's hope she's been locked up or tied up somewhere. His reasons for threatening his family don't apply to DI Mathews, but he wouldn't want her on the loose either.'

Greg tried to suppress his hollow feeling that if Bradbourn knew of Chris's attempt to get the wife to leave, that might constitute a pretty good motive, and returned his gaze to the eminently middle-class house in its tidy garden.

'I know domestic abuse can happen anywhere,' he said. 'But it still comes as a surprise, somehow, when it's in a small affluent village rather than a scruffy town backstreet.'

'When you meet Mr Bradbourn, you'll be surprised again,' said Pritty. 'He looks like the original geek, and as though butter wouldn't melt in his mouth. But he's apparently controlling and vindictive, with a nasty temper. Hang on...' She interrupted herself. 'Something's kicking off.'

She shot out of the car in response to a signal from the armed-team commander, pausing only to wave Greg back as he instinctively started to follow her. When she was looking the other way, he sidled closer until he could hear what was being said.

'Mikes are picking up an altercation,' the team commander said, somewhat unnecessarily, given that they could hear the shouts without amplification. 'More threats. Do we have the go-ahead to take him down?'

'I'll try ringing first,' said Pritty. She lifted her phone and pressed a saved number, but after some moments when the shouting continued, merging with loud sobs, she shook her head. 'He's not answering,' she said. At that moment screams, as well as sobbing, became audible from the house, and she nodded to the team commander. 'Do it,' she said.

He issued two crisp orders on his radio. The two armed officers Greg could see in the front garden raised their weapons. He assumed those on the other side of the house were doing the same. There was a long pause. A shot rang out from the back of the house and a muffled shout of 'Man down!' merged with more screaming. The armed police commander issued more crisp instructions and the team ran into the house. Pritty caught Greg by the arm as he went to follow them.

'You know better than that. Sir,' she said. 'Wait for the all-clear and then you follow me. Not before.'

He nodded, unable, for the moment, to speak but recognising her priorities. In other circumstances, he would be saying the same. Even so, the next few minutes were the hardest of his life.

Pritty's radio crackled and a voice said, 'Ambulances needed. Officer down.'

Pritty made the call, then turned to Greg. 'They'll be here in moments,' she said. 'They've been standing by.' Sure enough, two ambulances were visible at the end of the road almost before he could blink, and paramedics were running toward them even as the armed-team commander gave the all-clear. Pritty headed for the front door, followed by four paramedics and Greg. They were met on the step by the commander.

'Front room,' he said to the paramedics. 'And the perp's in the kitchen.' He caught Greg by the arm. 'Let them do their job,' he said. 'She's alive. The perp's down, as well.'

The paramedics split into twos, one pair heading for the front room and the other for the back of the house. As Greg hesitated, two officers came past, one shepherding a sobbing woman in her mid-thirties, the other carrying a small girl who was clinging to him with all her strength. Once they were out of the way, Greg turned into the front room.

One of the medics was kneeling next to Chris lying crumpled on the floor. There was blood coming from her head and she appeared to be unconscious. The second was attaching monitor leads to her chest. Greg was struck by the strong, metallic smell of the blood, and wondered just how much she'd lost.

'We'll be taking her to Addenbrooke's,' the first man said to Pritty and Greg. 'She has a head injury I don't like the look of, and I think she has internal injuries too.'

'I'll come with her,' said Greg, and would have dropped to his knees beside Chris but he was held back by Pritty.

'Let them look after her,' she recommended. 'You go and get anything you need from your car, then get in the ambulance. I'll detail someone to follow in your car.'

49

Monday 10 August 2020

Jim woke up on Monday morning to an early email from Margaret.

Greg is on indefinite leave while Chris is in Addenbrooke's. Court appearances booked for both current cases this morning. Are you OK to deal?

Jim vaguely remembered from one Latin class – just about the only thing he remembered from Latin in fact – that there was a particular way of asking a question that assumed the answer yes. This was one of them.

Yes, he emailed back, and rushed to his car. If both cases were due in the magistrates' court this morning, he needed some urgent conversations with the CPS about charges, especially for Joanne Hamilton.

Frank Parker was equally rushed off his feet, and demanded Jim appear in his room before the latter had even had a cup of coffee. He sat opposite the CPS prosecutor and glared enviously at the steaming mug before Frank.

'Let's take the Hamilton case first,' said Frank. 'Any update on how she intends to plead?'

'Last thing I heard,' said Jim, 'she intended to plead guilty to false imprisonment, but not guilty to murdering her mother, and she was dithering about pleading not guilty to preventing a lawful and decent burial because she had an emotional objection to that description of what she did with her son's body. We're not in a position to lay any charges yet relating to the third body, because we don't know who it is. I think sanity might prevail over the burial plea when Ken Woods has had another go at her.'

'I propose to adjust the murder charge to manslaughter,' said Frank. 'I've been talking to Ken, and he thinks she'll be willing to plead guilty to that. And I see no public good in trying her for the murder of her mother. Any objection?'

Jim thought quickly. 'No, it makes sense to me too,' he said. 'Unless, of course, we find evidence that she was responsible for body number three, in which case, all bets are off.'

'On that issue, we haven't revisited the possibility that she killed her son,' remarked Frank.

'True,' said Jim. 'We have absolutely no evidence that she did, but that's not evidence that she didn't. On the other hand, the doc says there is no indication of anything other than a natural death, and there are a lot of signs both that she grieved for her son and cherished his memory.

'Want to know what I think?' he asked rhetorically. 'I think it's likely her version of her mother's attitudes and behaviour is true, and that if we find body three is that of her father, then her mother is my suspect number one for having killed them both. I think Mrs Hamilton senior is our potential serial killer rather than her daughter.'

'I'm tempted to agree,' said Frank. 'But to play devil's advocate, the doc also said that it's next to impossible to pick up anaphylaxis on autopsy even when the body is fresh. After years...' He shrugged. 'However, I agree with you about the current lack of evidence. On the other hand, if we find the mother is suspect number one for body three, I shall want to reconsider the child's death.

'OK, now our problem case – the Waters brothers. I've just heard that Nick Waters is planning on pleading not guilty to the murder charge.'

'He what?' Jim was outraged. 'He put his hand up for it only yesterday.'

'Well, he's changed his mind again. Ade, however, is holding to a guilty plea, so it's not all loss.'

Jim breathed heavily for a moment. 'What's his thinking?' he asked.

'According to young Mr Streeter, he's decided that all we have tying him to Leyton Farm Estate is his brother's word, and that he can cast enough doubt on that to get a not guilty verdict. Personally, I think what he's really planning is to bully his brother into changing his statement, but I can't prove that. So, that case will go to trial, and we need to do our best to keep Ade Waters up to the mark.'

'Bail?' said Jim. 'What about that?'

'I'll ask for all defendants to be remanded in custody,' said Frank. 'I don't think there'll be much pushback on the Waters brothers, but we might get an argument about the Hamilton woman. With luck, her treatment of the Mirren children will swing things our way. I'd rather not have her on the loose until we've resolved the question of the other bodies.'

***

Over in Thorpe, Diana was shooing Jill out the door.

'See you later,' she said. 'I need to be getting on. I'm seeing the Mirren children this morning and I've stuff to do before I set off.'

'I thought you were going to see them via Zoom,' said Jill.

'That was the original plan, but social services and their foster mother decided that, if I was willing, a face-to-face class would be better for them. Part of reintroducing them to more normal life. Provided I did a Covid test first, that is! I did one this morning and it's negative so I'm good to go.'

'Where are you meeting them?' asked Jill, hovering by the back door.

'At the foster mother's home. You've been there, haven't you?'

'Yes. It's about thirty minutes' drive from here,' said Jill.

'That's what I thought. I'm setting off shortly. With luck' – she craned her head to check the sky – 'it'll be fine enough for me to do most of the class outside in the garden. There is a garden, I suppose?'

'Yes, there's a garden,' said Jill, and kissed Diana goodbye.

Diana was very pleasantly surprised by her greeting from Karen. After introductions to the foster mother and the social worker, who was just leaving, she had gone into the kitchen to be met by Karen running to her and throwing her arms around her.

'Miss Grain,' she said, her voice muffled by the embrace. 'It's so good to see you again. Can we read *The Lion, the Witch and the Wardrobe*? Mummy Helga has a copy and Jake has never heard it.'

Diana remembered that it had been the last book she'd read to Karen's class just before lockdown and could still picture the rapt face of Karen on the front row.

'We could do that,' she said. 'But you've heard it already, Karen.'

'I don't mind hearing it again,' said Karen. 'Really I don't.'

'Then, how about you do some sums first, and some history, and then I'll read to you both from the book. And when we've finished *that* book, I'll read to you from another book by the same writer. How does that sound?'

'Do I have to do the sums?' asked Karen, pulling a bit of a face.

'Yes, I'm afraid so,' said Diana, hardening her heart.

'But what will Jake do while I'm doing sums?'

'I'll find something for Jake to do, don't worry. And as soon as the sums are done, I'll tell you both a story about the Romans in this part of the world, then you can write some notes on Romans and Jake can draw us a picture of a Roman soldier.'

'But this is the school holidays!' Karen had one last shot at dodging the sums.

'Yes, and you missed a lot of the last term so you have a bit of catching up to do.' Diana was firm.

By the end of the morning, the hated sums completed successfully, the Roman legionary summarised in word and paint, the three of them settled down with C S Lewis's classic story. When it was time for lunch, neither Karen nor Jake wanted to stop.

'I'm afraid I have to go now,' said Diana.

'Can you come back tomorrow?' begged Karen. 'Please say you will. I want to know what happens next.'

'You know what happens next. You've heard it already,' said Diana.

'Jake hasn't,' said Karen.

'It depends on what Mummy Helga says,' replied Diana.

Mummy Helga, hovering with a plate of ham sandwiches, said, 'It's fine by me, if you can spare the time.'

Diana looked at the pleading faces. 'I suppose I can,' she said, pretending a reluctance she didn't feel.

Catching up with her at the doorway, Helga said, 'Thank you for coming. That's the most normal, most cheerful hour or two those children have had for a long time.'

'My pleasure,' said Diana.

'Karen seems very fond of you too,' added Helga. 'That's a bonus.'

***

The first thing Greg had done, on vacating the ambulance at Addenbrooke's, was to ring Chris's mother.

'I'm sorry, I don't know any more than that,' he said, before repeating the hollow trope, 'but she's in the best possible place. I shall stay here with her, obviously, until I'm sure she's out of danger.'

'I'll be on my way as soon as I've organised my neighbours to look after my cats,' she said.

Greg realised, with horror, that he hadn't given Bobby and Tally a thought. Before going back into the ward, he raked his contacts for possibilities then rang Ben Asheton. To his amazement, given the shifts Ben had been working, the phone was answered.

'How's Chris?' he asked before Greg could say a word.

'She's unconscious at present, in Addenbrooke's,' replied Greg. 'They're checking her over as we speak. I was ringing because it looks like I'm going to be here for a bit...'

'And you'd like us to feed Tally and Bobby,' said Ben. 'No problem. Either Paula or I will do it, morning and evening. Will that do?'

'Yes, thanks,' said Greg. 'I'll text you the keysafe code. And I'll let you know how things are going here.'

'Yes, please,' said Ben. 'But at least you know—'

'She's in the best place. Yes,' said Greg.

Time passed very slowly in the relatives' room. He was joined briefly by the Suffolk police officer who'd brought Greg's car, but he didn't stay long before being called away. On the whole, Greg preferred being on his own rather than making forced conversation. He kept looking at his watch, but the numbers seemed to revolve more slowly than ever before. He fetched and half drank several plastic cups of awful coffee, then abandoned them each in turn.

At last he saw a man in blue scrubs approaching at a fast walk. He sat down with Greg. 'Are you DI Mathews's next of kin?' he asked.

'I'm her fiancé,' said Greg. 'Her mother is on her way from Norfolk, but probably won't be here for at least another half hour.'

'Ah. You're not technically her next of kin then. And I don't want to wait for her mother. We need to operate immediately, as she has some internal bleeding, and we need to remove her spleen.

'I consent, if that helps,' said Greg. 'Just, please do whatever you can...'

'We will, no fear of that. She's got the top team,' said the doctor. 'But we won't wait any longer. We need to get on.'

He turned to leave, but turned back when Greg asked, 'What about her head wound?'

'She has concussion,' said the doctor, 'but not, as far as we can see, a skull fracture although there was some scalp laceration. She'll need a CT scan, but removing her spleen is the first priority.'

Chief Inspector Pritty arrived before Chris's mother.

'Any news?' she asked Greg.

'Being operated on to remove her spleen, then she'll get a CT scan to check for brain injury. We'll presumably know more after that. Have you found out what happened?'

'The wife's version is that her husband arrived home unexpectedly early from his meeting in Oxford. Personally, I doubt there ever was a meeting, what with most events taking place on Zoom or Teams these days. I think it was always a trap. But she believed the meeting story and told Chris her husband was going to be away. Chris was helping her pack for her getaway to the battered wives shelter and had carried a bag downstairs for her.

'Mrs Bradbourn looked up to see her husband come in through the door from the garage and screamed. Chris tried to calm things down, and got all parties sitting down round the kitchen table for a while. Unfortunately, it didn't last. Apparently, Mrs Bradbourn said something that triggered her husband again. He stormed off in a rage, then came back swinging a cricket bat that had been left in the garage. Chris was hit on the head and fell to the floor, whereupon Mr Bradbourn kicked her in the side before grabbing a knife from the knife block and his daughter from her mother's arms. As far as I can make out, talking to both the mother and daughter, Chris didn't regain consciousness after that.'

'Presumably it was the kick that ruptured her spleen,' said Greg as calmly as he was capable, which wasn't very. He realised his hands were clenching and relaxing, as though he were preparing to rip someone's head off. 'Have you charged him?'

'So far, we've charged him with attempted murder,' said Pritty.

A clatter in the corridor and the door flying open announced the arrival of Chris's mother. 'Where is she?' she demanded.

Greg got up quickly. 'In theatre,' he said, 'having her spleen removed. They'll be back to talk to us as soon as they've finished and she's had a CT scan of her head.' His phone buzzed at that moment and he looked at the caller ID. 'It's your DI Richards,' he said to Pritty. 'I suppose he's calling about Chris too.'

'He shouldn't be,' said Pritty. 'I told them all to leave you in peace and I'd bring them up to speed as soon as I knew anything. Do you want me to deal with him?' She held out her hand for the phone.

'No, it's OK,' said Greg. 'It's not as though I can do anything else at the minute.' He answered the call with a brisk 'Geldard' then listened. 'That, at least, is good news,' he said eventually. 'Can you pass the details on to DI Henning, please?' Then rang off.

'Anything I need to know about?' asked Pritty.

'It's to do with that tip-off we gave you in July,' said Greg, past caring about diplomacy. 'The one about the rendezvous we thought was connected to stolen cars. Felixstowe have carried out a search, and they've found two vehicles involved in one of our arson cases, in storage awaiting export. One of them, a Range Rover, has fingerprints inside that are a match to our suspect for the arson. So we can nail *him* at least.' He wondered about pointing out that if they'd responded to the tip they'd have got the transporters in the supply chain as well, but couldn't be bothered. A glance at Pritty's face suggested she'd made the connection for herself, but at that point the returning doctor diverted everyone's attention.

'She's come through the operation well,' he reported. 'The CT scan is indicating a small bleed on the brain and the neurology team are reviewing the options.'

'Can we see her?' asked Greg.

'In a short while, yes,' said the doctor. 'But don't expect too much. She's in an induced coma.'

50

---

10 August 2020 – leads and dead ends

Bill and Steve were doing a lot of sighing and nearly as much head-scratching. Both had a strong preference for being out and about rather than stuck in front of a screen. After his period in isolation, Bill's preference was almost pathological, but Jim had insisted that the initial database search for the ID of body number three had to be done by them.

'It's not fair to expect the girls to do all the boring stuff,' he'd said, thus revealing that, at heart, he shared their preference.

'Point is,' muttered Bill to Steve, 'Jill doesn't find it boring. She gets fascinated by it.'

'Tough,' said Steve. 'Just get stuck in, will you?'

It didn't take them too long to trace the name on the marriage certificate through government databases such as the DVLA and the Department for Work and Pensions, although they failed to find any death certificate. They soon established that he'd had a driving licence, but it had lapsed when he passed seventy. He was in receipt of a pension, and that was being paid into a NatWest account. There they hit the usual problem with banking privacy protocols and progress was blocked, they hoped temporarily, while their request was considered 'at a higher level'. Still, at least the pensions data gave them an address and the information that his pension had been paid regularly and was *still* being paid.

His name, date of birth and the postcode related to his pension enabled access to his NHS number, but they were unable to get any details of treatments or medical history. Again, personal data protocols stymied progress. They took their problem to Jim.

'In short,' summarised Bill, 'we have no evidence that the body isn't him, but also no evidence that it is. I think we should investigate that address. It's not far. It's in one of the backstreets near the magistrates' court in Great Yarmouth.'

'What about the bank?' asked Jim.

Bill shrugged. 'No doubt they'll get back to us in their own good time.'

'No phone numbers?'

'No,' said Bill. 'Not that we've been able to find.'

Jim grinned, fully understanding Bill's enthusiasm for a field trip. Any field trip! 'You could ask the locals to pop round,' he suggested, meaning the Great Yarmouth team. Then he took pity on Bill's expression of disappointment. 'OK,' he said. 'Check it out. If he's there, that's one possibility off our list.'

In less than half an hour, given the, still unusually quiet, roads, Bill and Steve were turning off the main road by the Bure, past the magistrates' court and down a side street running parallel to the river. There was absolutely nowhere to park. Both sides of the narrow road were already packed with cars.

'Ye gods!' said Steve. 'Is this people working from home, or people attending the court?'

'Probably both,' said Bill, driving along slowly while he searched for a specific house number. 'There it is,' he said, pulling up in the road and thus blocking it completely in both directions.

They both surveyed the small, mid-terrace house. Like the neighbour to the right, the tiny front garden of No 14 was untended and rife with both weeds and litter. The house to the left, in contrast, had neat shrubs, a hanging basket full of brightly coloured begonias, and a row of tubs, ditto. Its windows were polished to a diamond shine and its paintwork immaculate.

They both got out of their car, leaving it blocking the road, hazard lights flashing, and with identical gestures pulled their jackets straight before marching up the short, cracked concrete path to the dilapidated front door of their destination. They knocked politely, then loudly, then thunderously, with an equal lack of response each time. Steve had peered in through the grimy window and announced, 'Nothing here,' and they were about to make their way round to the back of the house when the smart door to their left opened to reveal a young woman with a baby on her shoulder.

'There's no one there,' she informed them, with an irritation that was probably explained by the wakeful baby. 'It's empty. It's been empty for as long as we've lived here.'

'How long is that?' asked Bill, holding out his warrant card. 'DC Bill Street, and this is DC Steve Hall,' he said, gesturing behind him.

'Coming up to eighteen months,' said the woman. 'We moved in before this one was born.' She patted the baby on its back.

'And there's been no one there in all that time?' asked Steve.

'No one we've ever seen. We did ask the council about it once, because it's so shabby it's making our house look bad, but they said it was an owner-occupied property and the council tax was paid, so unless we had a serious complaint like vermin or it was taken over by squatters, there was nothing they could do. We didn't get any support from the other neighbours,' she added. 'But that's probably because their house doesn't look very different. I don't think they care much.'

'Can I have your name, please?' said Steve, taking out his notebook.

'Pamela French,' she said.

'And a phone number.'

She propped the baby over her shoulder with one hand and fumbled in her pocket with the other, to produce a mobile phone. 'Here you are,' she said. And held it out with the number visible.

Steve wrote it down and said, 'Thank you. We may need to contact you again.'

'Has something happened?' asked Mrs French.

'That's what we're checking,' said Bill, and they went back to their car.

'Let's look round the back,' he said to Steve. 'But it might be a good idea to move the car to the end of the road so we're not causing such a blockage.' A large BMW was currently reversing, badly, back down the blocked road toward the courthouse.

Parking the car at the end of the track that led behind all the back gardens was the work of a moment, and the two of them made their way along, counting the houses to be sure they picked the right one. Most of the spaces behind the houses were more yard than garden, and quite a few contained a swing or a small football net. The one behind No 14 looked very like its front garden, with the addition of extra rubbish that appeared to have been thrown over from the scruffy neighbour. Mrs French's garden, by contrast, contained a vividly flowering hydrangea and a tiny neat lawn.

The gate onto the track was hanging on one hinge and took little effort to lift and open. Judging by the piles of small shiny capsules amongst the rubbish, some of the local youth had been using the backyard to enjoy their illegal use of laughing gas. It, therefore, came as no surprise to the two policemen to find the back door ajar.

'I'm surprised Mrs French wasn't complaining about the drug use,' remarked Steve.

'She may not have realised, if they had enough sense to keep the noise down,' said Bill. 'Or she may just have not wanted to get involved. Probably the latter. Come on, at least this means we can take a look inside.'

The first thing that hit them as they pushed the door open was the smell, and both men exchanged a look, fearing the worst.

Covering his face with one hand, Bill went into the kitchen. 'If Mr Hamilton's lying dead in here, he's not body number four,' he said. Steve didn't say anything, being preoccupied with keeping his breakfast down. 'But I'm surprised Mrs French hasn't been on to the council about this. Ah,' he said as he went through the half open door into the front room, disturbing a cloud of flies as he did so. 'Perhaps that's because it's recent.'

Steve stuck his head round to peer over Bill's shoulder, batting away a couple of flies.

'Could be worse,' Bill remarked. 'Although not much worse. Looks like a pile of burgers and fried chicken to me.'

With relief, Steve realised Bill was not using a simile. The smell-generating pile of maggots in the centre of the room was indeed enjoying what had once been a takeaway meal. Still holding his nose, Bill crossed the room to pick up a large pile of post from the floor.

'Bingo!' he muttered, brushing more flies away with distaste. 'Looks like we've got bank statements in amongst this lot.'

The upstairs rooms were similarly disgusting and empty, so they retreated to their car with the haul of post. A quick flick through the envelopes showed they had both bank and council tax statements, plus what were probably communications from a telephone company. They rang Jim.

'The neighbour reckons he's not been home for at least eighteen months, but judging by the envelopes, all his post is still coming here,' said Bill. 'There's evidence the house has been used, on and off, by the local youth, but no evidence of anything else that we can see with a swift look. I thought you might want Forensics in, so we've handled the post as little as possible – although I have to say the local louts have messed with most of it.'

'OK,' said Jim. 'I'll get Yarmouth to secure the house and Ned to send some of his chaps over. Bag the post and bring it into the office. We'll go through it in detail here.'

'How did the cases go in court this morning?' asked Bill.

'Ms Hamilton and both the Waterses have been committed for trial in the Crown Court. Joanne Hamilton took the good advice of her solicitor and pleaded guilty to all charges. Ade Waters did the same. Nick is playing silly buggers and went "not guilty" on the Leyton Estate murder, but we've had a development on that this afternoon.'

'What?' asked Steve and Bill simultaneously.

'Suffolk have found the Range Rover at Felixstowe, and it has Nick Waters's fingerprints inside.'

'Better late than never,' said Steve. 'Suffolk, I mean!'

'Will he change his plea?' asked Bill.

'Who knows, but we've got him cold now.' Jim's satisfaction rang down the line.

51

Tuesday 11 August 2020 – new directions

It had been a long night. Once they were allowed in ITU to see Chris, Greg and her mum had taken up the vigil either side of her bed. In some ways, Greg felt that the induced coma was a good thing, since he hasn't had to hide the horror he was sure was reflected on his face. The space seemed to be filled with clicking and flashing machines, alarms going off periodically, which only sometimes produced a response from the attentive nursing team. He wondered about those. *If they don't require a reaction, what is the point?*

In the middle of all this turmoil, Chris seemed very crumpled and small. Not at all like the outsize vibrant personality that usually filled a room to bursting.

He took her hand and clung to it throughout most of the nursing interventions, feeling that if he let go it would be like letting go of hope. And that he daren't do. Without the hope of Chris, he had nothing. As the darkness deepened beyond the hermetically sealed window, his optimism waned, and his mood darkened too. His mind, seemingly out of control, started to consider what he would do, how he would live with a gaping hole in his future. Watching him closely, Jane Mathews saw the mood change and intervened.

'You can just stop that right there,' she instructed in a voice and tone that was an irresistible reminder of Chris in full flow. Greg suddenly saw where Chris had got much of her steel and attitude from.

'I know what you're thinking, and it's rubbish. Don't catastrophise. It won't help. It's just the darkest-before-the-dawn effect. Think positive! Chris has come through the operation well. She doesn't need a spleen, so she won't miss it. She's being looked after in the best hospital in the United Kingdom, and they've even let us in! A few months ago and Covid rules would have kept us in the car park!'

Greg managed a small smile at the range of positives Jane had managed to drum up.

'You're right of course,' he said. 'Sorry. I'm not helping, am I?'

'You don't have to help me.' Jane shuffled in her seat, rearranging a capacious bag at her feet and trying to get comfortable. 'I'm here to help you. OK. I think we need to get organised for the long haul. You go to the loo, get yourself something to eat and drink, and take a walk round the car park. Don't come back until you've done all three. I'll stay here with Chris.'

'You'll need a break too,' objected Greg. 'And suppose something changes?'

'Nothing's going to change just yet. You've heard the experts. And I'll have a break after you. This way, I get to take my walk when it's daylight, and you have the fun of dodging the drunks in the dark.'

'Chris really is your daughter, isn't she?' said Greg as he gave in to superior powers and got up to go, with a final squeeze of Chris's hand.

'Well I should hope so,' said Jane tartly. 'Her father never doubted it!'

Outside, taking his walk in the fresh air as instructed, Greg breathed in the mix of field scents and diesel fumes with some scepticism as to their actual beneficial effects. But he did feel better, he had to admit. Whether that was the bracing effect of Jane's good sense, the exercise or the movement of a stiff breeze on his face, or all three, he was now willing to consider a more optimistic version of the future. Just before he went back up to ITU, he stood in the shelter of the portico and checked both emails and WhatsApp messages on his phone. As he did so, an ambulance clanged past, lights flashing to alert passing traffic at the junction beyond that a rapid exit onto the main road was required. He was heartened to find a host of goodwill messages for Chris from the whole team and the wider Norfolk police network. Word had travelled fast, and it felt like everyone she'd ever come into contact with was willing her to get better. Ben's message included an update on the welfare of Bobby and Tally, and the reassurance that he and his wife would continue to look after them for however long it took, followed by a hurried second thought to the effect that he was sure Chris would be better soon. Even his father had braved digital communication to send his best wishes. Greg wondered who had told him, and realised it was probably Jane. The last note he read was from Jim, including the information that Nick Waters had reconsidered his not guilty plea. Again. *Well at least that is one thing headed in the right direction.*

When he got back into the ITU, nothing had changed except that the dark in the window now had a streak of light.

'My turn,' said Jane, and gathered up her coat. 'I'll be back in an hour or so.'

Greg took Chris's hand again. 'Thank you,' he said.

***

It had been a disturbed night for Jill, and her partner Diana too. Not because of worry about Chris, although Jill was, naturally, concerned about her ex-colleague and friend. Rather, because Diana had been uncharacteristically restless.

Around six o'clock, Jill had given up and gone downstairs to make tea. When she brought a mug upstairs for Diana, she piled up her pillows to lean on and sat down.

'OK, what's bothering you?' she asked over the rim of her giant mug. 'You've been wriggling about all night like a tapeworm on speed.'

Diana pulled a face at the simile and took a sip of her tea. 'I've been thinking about the Mirren children,' she said. 'About the time I spent with them yesterday and what will happen to them next. Their foster mum, Helga, told me that the grandparents aren't interested.'

Jill nodded. 'I've only spoken to them briefly, when I told them the children had been found and were safe. But I've had a chat or two with their family liaison officer. She's been taken off their case now, but before that, she reported that they had no intention of having to take responsibility for the two children. They were estranged from their daughter, apparently have never met the children and don't want to. They said it would be 'needlessly upsetting for both them and the children' and it was 'better they are free to make a new life'. I think they meant the children, but I'm not sure,' she added drily.

'What will happen to them next?' asked Diana.

'You probably know as much as me,' said Jill. 'They'll stay with their foster family until a permanent solution can be found.'

'If one ever is,' said Diana gloomily. 'Maybe people won't want children they perceive to be damaged, and isn't it always harder to get older children adopted, let alone two together! Might they end up in council care for the rest of their childhood? And what about the court case? Will they have to give evidence?'

'They *will* probably have to give evidence,' said Jill. 'But the courts are good at adjusting circumstances for children these days. And if Joanne Hamilton stands by her guilty plea, then it will be minimal. As for council care, yes, I suppose that is a possibility, although I thought you said they seemed well settled with Helga.'

'Yes,' said Diana, twisting the edge of the duvet cover in her hands. 'But...'

'Yes, but what?' asked Jill.

'It seems such a waste! I don't know Jake very well, but he seems a pleasant boy with all the usual enthusiasms of a boy that age. Karen though, Karen is intelligent both intellectually and emotionally, mature for her years and a real hard worker. She could be, and do, anything, with the right support.

'How would you feel about *us* taking them on?' she asked in a rush.

Jill put her mug down on the bedside table. 'What exactly do you mean by "taking them on"?' she asked.

'I suppose I mean adopting them,' said Diana. 'We have talked about children before, and I know we always talked about a baby, not about adopting half-grown children, but this has just landed in our laps and it feels like fate.' She looked at Jill's face and added hurriedly, 'I've shocked you, I think. I'm not expecting a decision now, obviously not. But I wanted to know if it was technically possible. You know, would we be prevented because of your involvement in the case? And I wanted to at least start the conversation.'

Jill took a deep breath, let it go, then took another. 'You have surprised me,' she admitted. 'Although I don't know why I'm surprised. It's very you, this sort of generosity. It's why I love you.' She squeezed Diana's hand. 'I'll think about it,' she promised. And went downstairs with her head whirling.

***

When Jim got into work shortly after eight, he found Bill there before him.

'You're early,' he said.

'Just so glad to get out of the house,' said Bill. 'And it's a good time to focus on detail, with everywhere nice and quiet.

I've spent the last hour scanning in all the old letters from Mr Hamilton's address and sorting them into some sort of order.'

'Good job,' said Jim, sitting down beside him. 'Are they all safely back in the evidence store now?'

'Yes, Boss,' answered Bill. 'Look, these are the letters from the bank. They're mainly paper statements for the last three years. There's nothing earlier than 2018. Anyway, even these show that the pension was being paid in monthly, and that direct debits were taking care of utility bills and council tax, which explains why no one raised any concerns. There's a fair old balance on the account. I asked Ned, and they haven't found a will yet, so if the old chap is dead and there is no will, Joanne Hamilton may be entitled to inherit under the intestacy rules.'

'We haven't proved he's dead yet,' remarked Jim.

'Ah, well I've had an idea on that,' said Bill. 'We know the doc said body number three had some dental work in the past, but we've drawn a blank at the obvious local dentists. I did ask Ned if he'd found anything relating to a dental practice, and he says not.

'But now we've got some of the bank statements, can we chase NatWest for the earlier data? It occurred to me that if we found some payments to a dentist, that would tell us where to look for his records. It might be much quicker than chasing around every dentist in East Anglia.'

'Worth a try,' said Jim. 'Try NatWest as soon as there's someone in the office. Come to me if they need more authorisation.'

'Nearly forgot to ask...' said Bill. 'Have you heard anything from Greg, about Chris?'

'Not yet,' said Jim. 'I'll try ringing him later.'

***

The lead doctor didn't reach Chris on his morning round until after 11.00. He greeted Greg and Jane, consulted the notes at the end of the bed and had a quiet discussion with the sister at the end of the ward, before coming back to sit by Chris's bed.

'I'm pleased to say it's going well so far,' he said. 'This is what's going to happen next. We're going to do another CT scan of her head, and then the neurology consultant will check it. If he's happy, we'll start to bring her out of the induced coma, and then we'll be able to see if there's been any damage.'

'What's the prognosis?' asked Greg, clutching Chris's hand even harder.

'Impossible to say,' said the ITU doctor. 'There could be no damage at all, or there may be some impairment of function. We can't know until she's conscious and we can run, I'm afraid, yet another battery of tests. But it's so far, so good.'

He hesitated and Greg wondered what other devastating piece of news he had yet to impart.

'There is one other thing I think you need to know,' he said. 'As I expect you realise, we do a lot of tests as standard before we embark on a procedure. One of them was positive. Chris is pregnant.'

THE END...   FOR NOW!

Printed in Great Britain
by Amazon

60657652R00184